All my friends, family and readers.
Thank you for the chances you gave me.

FAT CHANCE

Nick Spalding

LAKE UNION
PUBLISHING

Text copyright © 2014 Nick Spalding

Published by Lake Union, Seattle

www.apub.com

Amazon, the Amazon logo, and Lake Union are trademarks of Amazon.com, Inc., or its affiliates.

ISBN-13: 9781477824566
ISBN-10: 1477824561

Cover design by bürosüd° München, www.buerosued.de

Library of Congress Control Number: 2014903955

Printed in the United States of America

ARTICLE ON STREAM FM'S WEBSITE
Posted January 3rd

Are you a couple?
Are you a FAT couple?
Would you like to win £50,000?

WE want to hear from YOU!

Stream FM is looking for six overweight couples between the ages of 25 and 65 to take part in our fabulous new competition:

'FAT CHANCE!'

Over a six-month period, we'll find out which couple can lose the most weight, and the winners will receive £50,000!

If you and your partner would like to enter, download the form and fill in your details, along with the reasons you think you should be part of the competition (in no more than a hundred words).

Deadline for entries is January 31st.

The competition will be launched on the
Elise & Will Breakfast Show at the beginning of March.

Good luck!

ZOE'S WEIGHT LOSS DIARY
Friday 3rd March
14 stone, 7 pounds

I've never been this nervous in my life, and all I'm doing is starting a diary.

The last time I wrote anything even remotely diary-like was for my English language A Level course—right before I got kicked out of college for poor attendance. That was seventeen years ago.

. . . it was *mostly* for poor attendance anyway.

There was the incident when Greg and I got caught 'enjoying each other's company' by the vice principal in the art department store room. That probably had a lot to do with it. I doubt the vision of me with my legs kicked in the air and Greg pumping me hard enough to knock several third-years' paintings off the wall did much for our prospects that year. It's a wonder we've both got jobs.

I've certainly never been asked to write about my private life in such detail before. The whole idea of putting it down on paper seems absolutely *horrific*.

The people at the radio station have told me to write whatever I want about my experiences. They've assured me that they'll edit and polish the diary entries before they post them online, in order to put me in the best possible light. I have a feeling that, no matter how much they cut or omit from my entries, my neuroses and bizarre personal habits will still be glaringly obvious.

And as for Greg, he takes to creative writing as well as an elephant would take to roller skating blind-folded. If he gets more than a hundred words written down without some kind of prolapse I'll be amazed.

Still, my best friend Elise thinks we're both smart enough to write these silly diaries—even with our combined lack of experience—so I guess I have to trust her judgement. 'You're both intelligent people, Zoe. You're my absolute favourite couple in the world and you'll be great for this,' she said to me in that oh-so-charming and persuasive manner she has. 'You could do it standing on your heads.'

Also, I don't have a self-censorship button and will indeed write what I like regardless of subject matter. I fear the editing staff at the radio station will be claiming a lot of overtime in the near future.

The first thing Elise suggested I talk about—to get the ball rolling, as it were—are the reasons we agreed to enter this competition.

I say 'we' like Greg had much of a say in the matter, but to be honest I've bullied my poor husband into doing it. I want . . . no, I *need* to change the way I live my life, and the way Greg lives his, for that matter, before the damage we've done to ourselves becomes completely irreversible. The weight gain we've both allowed in the last decade hasn't broken us, but there are some mighty big cracks showing. I'm as worried about his health as I'm sure he is about mine. He might not want to be a part of this competition, and I'll probably have to drag him kicking and screaming all the way through it, but I know he'll do it for me—and I know it's the right thing for *both* of us.

The closer I get to forty, the more I feel every one of the four stone I've piled on in the last decade. Enough, as they say, is well and truly *enough*.

So, how does this monumental decision to change really happen? How does Zoe Milton, a woman who's become more and more painfully self-conscious in recent years, agree to take part in a competition that will air all her dirty over-sized laundry in public for the next six months?

It starts late last year with a dress . . . and a great deal of mindless optimism.

⁂

It's a lovely evening dress from Marks & Spencer. One I've had my eye on for several weeks now. Sharon's Christmas bash in town is only three days away and I decide that I'll look bloody fantastic in this dark green silky number with the pretty pattern running down the straps.

What's more, the top half is designed with a definite corset-like effect that will hold a majority of Zoe Milton nicely in place while she dances her arse off to Girls Aloud at 3 a.m. This will prevent a repeat performance of what Greg likes to refer to as the 'titty flop trauma' of New Year's Eve 2010, when the flowery dress I'd bought from H&M decided to give up its futile resistance against my ample bosom—and gave way at two of the main seams. This provided my cousin Jeff with a clear view of my left tit as I swung past him during the chorus of 'Come On Eileen.'

Unsurprisingly, we haven't heard much from Jeff since.

This M&S green dress, however, looks like it can withstand all the abuse I can throw at it. Even as I admire it on the hanger, the emerald silk glittering under the bright arc sodium lights of the ladies' clothing section, I can tell it's going to be sturdy, steadfast and perfectly suited for the job.

There is just one *small* problem.

The dress is a size sixteen. I, sadly, am not. Not anymore. I sloped over the threshold into the dreaded world of the size eighteen lady about a year ago.

It's been a good few months since I last plucked up the courage to stand on the scales, but I'm pretty sure that the chances of me having lost any weight are next to none, given that I've done about as much exercise as half the cast of 'Supersize vs Superskinny' lately.

Inevitably, there are no bigger sizes of the dress available in the shop. A quick consultation with Google suggests that M&S don't actually make a size eighteen version of it *at all*. It's absolutely heartbreaking.

But I want this dress, dammit!

Just for once, I'd like to go out in something that makes me feel just a *little bit* sexy. A *little bit* confident. A *little bit* more like the girl I used to be before I wound up in this tired, unhappy body.

Sod it.

I'm trying the bloody thing on anyway. You never know.

Dress sizes are always different shop to shop, so I might get lucky and find out that M&S have decided to start taking pity on the fat people of England and are now being generous with their size charts.

With determination and hope I march off to the dressing rooms with the green evening gown billowing in my wake.

'Good morning madam,' the skinny blonde shop assistant greets me when I reach the changing rooms at the back of the store. 'How many items have you got today?'

'Just this dress,' I tell her, waving the object in question in her face.

'Okay, that's fine,' she replies in a disinterested tone, and hands me a plastic hook with the number one written on it. 'Feel free to use any of the cubicles.' She pauses and looks me up and down. I know what's coming next. 'The largest one is at the end of the aisle.'

There was a time I'd have been extremely insulted by this remark. That time was over two years ago, however. Now I have resigned myself to the fact that certain people think because I'm overweight, I can't possibly move through the world of the skinny person without knocking everything over and causing myself an injury.

This silly cow probably thinks that the second I step into one of the smaller cubicles, my enormous hips will become wedged in it, and I'll have to leave Marks & Spencer carrying the bloody thing on my back, looking like the world's biggest tortoise.

'Thanks,' I reply with a scowl. 'I'll try not to eat anything while I'm in there.'

This comment is greeted with a blank stare, so I just sigh and walk past her without another word.

I take one look at the largest cubicle at the end of the aisle and decide to resolutely ignore it for the rest of my life. Instead, I turn into one of the regular size stalls and pull the thick white curtain aside to enter, safe in the knowledge that I can fit inside it without needing a crowbar and a pound of butter—despite what the bony bitch outside might think.

Having said that, it is quite snug in here. Snug enough to make the removal of my jeans a bit of a trial, as I have to bend over to shrug them off. This causes my backside to hit, and then rebound off the wall, nearly sending me forehead first into the full-length mirror in front of me.

Taking a deep breath to curb the rising tide of anger and self-loathing I can feel making its way up from my nether regions, I remove my jacket and blouse slowly, placing them on the stool next to the jeans with a long sigh and some muted tutting noises.

I look at the green size sixteen evening dress now hanging from the hook on the wall and regard it as a prize fighter would his next opponent.

Inspecting it more closely, it's evident that this is a dress I will have to slip over my head. The tight corset style of the upper half dictates that stepping into it will be impossible.

I gather the bottom of the dress up in my arms and slip it over my head and shoulders, being careful not to wrinkle it too much.

I am delighted to find I can get the dress on without too much effort. I scarcely have to break a sweat, and spend only thirty seconds grunting and groaning before the hemline is below my knees.

Ha ha! Success is mine!

. . . Oh bugger, I haven't zipped the bloody thing up yet, have I?

It's all very well feeling triumphant that I've managed to get a size sixteen dress onto my size eighteen frame, but the victory is a hollow and shallow thing unless I can get that zipper all the way up.

Luckily, it zips to the side rather than the back, so at least I have a fighting chance.

I suck my chest in, mentally cross myself, and pull the zipper up.

It gets almost halfway before the laws of physics assert themselves, in no uncertain terms I might add, and refuse to let the sodding thing go any higher.

I could cry. Warm, satisfying victory has turned into the cold ashes of failure.

'Oh, you utter bastard,' I whisper under my breath.

At this point I should just give up the struggle, unzip the dress, remove it from my person, and rush home to eat the rest of the Ben & Jerry's Phish Food we didn't get through last night. This is my usual response to such disasters.

However, the anger and self-loathing that I've managed to keep a lid on since my brief conversation with Little Miss Bony-Arse outside is now taking steps to remove my rationality—and is apparently succeeding extremely well. I now decide to start wrenching the zipper in an upwards motion, in the vain hope that brute force will solve the problem.

If 'solving the problem' actually translates as 'yanking the zipper tab until it breaks off and leaves me trussed up like a Christmas turkey,' then I have been one hundred percent successful.

Incredulously, I hold the tiny broken piece of metal up in front of me. I then try to re-attach it to the rest of the zipper, hoping that I've suddenly developed superpowers that allow me to bond metal with metal through sheer force of will.

This is not the case, so I now find myself trapped inside a green dress that's squeezing my boobs so much I can nearly rest my chin on them. I'm also having to take short, shallow breaths that make me sound like a hyperventilating chipmunk.

Panic threatens to set in. Thankfully, the self-loathing has gone into hyper-drive now, which means any other emotions don't really get a look in.

I'm now left in something of a quandary.

As far as I can tell, I have three choices open to me.

I can call the shop girl to come and help me out of the dress—which is about as likely as Greg arranging a threesome with Bradley Cooper for my next birthday present.

I can try to pull the dress down as much as I can on my own, thus relieving the pressure on my ribcage, and allowing me to think about the situation a bit more clearly without the onset of suffocation.

Or, I can yank the dress *upwards* in a swift and decisive motion, in order to free myself as quickly and as effectively as possible from my material prison.

A less impulsive person would go with option two, but then again, a less impulsive woman wouldn't have tried to squeeze into a dress that's too small for her in the first place.

I take a deep breath, squeeze my eyes shut, grab the straps with both hands, and, with all the strength I can muster, I yank the dress upwards in what I think is the aforementioned swift and decisive manner.

Sadly, as I do this, the dress also twists round to the left and the tight corseting constricts around my ample upper body like one of those Chinese finger puzzles. Instead of flying off over my head, the dress becomes wedged at the shoulders, leaving me with my arms flailing above my head and my vision limited to a landscape of green material.

Compounding this terrible situation is the fact that I'm bound to be showing my enormous pink and black striped knickers to the world, thanks to the lower half of the dress bunching up and creating an unattractive pool of bulging material around my waist.

I'm in proper trouble now.

I've never been one to suffer from claustrophobia, but I now feel a new and acute appreciation for those who have the condition. I simply have no idea what to do.

I can't lower my arms thanks to the stiffness of the corseting, so I can't gain any leverage on the dress to pull it back down.

Panic really does set in now, and I start to fight against my impromptu straitjacket, wobbling my body back and forth in an attempt to shake myself free. I haven't writhed around with my hands in the air this much since I went to a rave back in the mid-nineties. If somebody sticks The Prodigy on over the M&S speaker system, I'll feel right at home.

Of course, in my mild panic, I've forgotten about the fact that I'm standing in a small cubicle containing a stool, which is currently adorned with my street clothes. I'm reminded of this fact when I painfully smack my knee into the stool as I whirl around on the spot for the third time, hoping that by building up some centrifugal force it might throw me clear of the dress.

'Oww! Fuck!' I wail in muffled frustration.

The usual human response to sharp pain is to back away from its cause as swiftly as possible. This makes me stumble into the heavy white curtain that shuts off the cubicle from the outside world. The curtain has seen how much fun the dress is having with me and wants in on the action. In my increasing distress, I twist around sharply as I hit the curtain—which neatly manages to wrap itself around my entire body, thus encasing me in *two* layers of material.

'Oh, for crying out loud!'

Now things have reached the level of farce usually reserved for amateur theatrics.

If I keep thrashing around as I have been, I'm likely to pull the curtain off its rail and go stumbling out into the shop looking like the most uncoordinated ghost in human history. Small children will run screaming from the bulky, swearing monstrosity. The shop staff will be on the phone to the Ghostbusters before I can say a damn thing in my defence.

Time for a cooler head to prevail.

I force myself to stand still and take a few deep breaths. If I can just calm down a bit, I'm sure I can work out a simple and easy way of extricating myself from this double-layered cloth prison with the minimum of further fuss and—

'Are you alright, madam?'

Oh for God's sake, it's Little Miss Bony-Arse.

I choose not to respond immediately, feeling that any explanation I try to give will be completely inadequate.

'Do you need some help?' the girl eventually says.

'No love, I'm absolutely fine,' I reply. The sarcasm manages to get past the curtain and the corset with no problem at all. 'I often like to wrap a curtain around my head in the middle of a shop. I find it *soothing*.'

'Really?'

Good grief.

'Yes. If you could go and brew me up a chai tea and pour it through the hole in the top, that'd be just super.'

'Ah . . . I think you should probably come out of there.'

'Do you think so?'

'Yes I do, really. The manager won't like it.'

'Ah well, we wouldn't want to annoy the manager, now, would we?'

'No. Mister Morris is very strict about this kind of thing.'

'You get a lot of fat women wrapping themselves up in curtains, do you?'

'No, but customers do act up from time to time.'

'I see. In that case, perhaps you could pull the thing off me?'

'Okay.'

The sales girl successfully manages to unwrap me from the curtain, leaving only the issue of the dress.

I can't see her face, but I know the expression she's making.

'Um . . . Do you need any help with the dress?' she asks tentatively.

'What? Are you saying I'm not wearing it right?'

'No, madam. It shouldn't be that high up.'

'*Really?* Because I was watching a programme about London Fashion Week recently and you wouldn't *believe* how many models were walking down the catwalk with their arms up like someone was pointing a gun at them, showing their Primark knickers to everyone.'

This is met with stony silence.

'Just pull the bloody thing off my head, will you?' I ask in a weary voice.

With Little Miss Bony-Arse helping out, it takes only two tugs to free me from my bondage. As the dress comes off I can feel it sliding painfully up against the rolls of fat on my arms and back. It reminds me, sickeningly, of how a sausage is made.

This is so embarrassing. I feel like I could throw up.

Then I remember that I'm now standing in my massive Primark knickers and bra in the middle of the changing room corridor, and my embarrassment levels rocket to hitherto unknown levels of stratospheric humiliation. This couldn't possibly get any worse.

'Er, can we use the changing rooms?' I hear a voice say from behind the bony shop girl.

I crane my head around to see no less than *four* women standing at the end of the corridor clutching a variety of garments. Two of them are thin and are therefore trying their best not to look at me with a combination of guilt and smug superiority. The third seems to be, like me, no stranger to the occasional late-night binge, and is looking at me with both pity and a certain degree of recognition. The fourth member of the party is a twelve-year-old girl, whom I've probably traumatised for the rest of her life. Not least because I'm about to swear at the top of my voice.

'Thanks a lot!' I wail at the shop girl. 'You could've warned me there were people waiting!'

She gives me the look of a kicked puppy.

I sigh, straighten my shoulders, and attempt to collect what is left of my dignity as I step back into the cubicle. The curtain is thrown across the rail with a growl.

On my own inside, anger gives way to misery. I slump onto the stool and feel the tears welling up. This isn't the first time I've felt like this recently, but at least on every other occasion I've been able to have a good weep in the privacy of my own home.

I have a little silent cry to myself on the stool for about a minute, before managing to pull myself together and get dressed.

I look in the full-length mirror once I'm back in my clothes and take in the hectic, blotchy red face staring back at me. I look an absolute state.

Great stuff.

Now I just have to get out of Marks & Spencer without another person seeing me—and hold myself together long enough to reach my front door.

With a leaden sigh, I pull the curtain back slowly and step out into the corridor. I walk down to the end and back out into the shop, where I see my friend the bony shop girl standing next to a rail of colourful t-shirts. She sees me coming and has the sheer audacity to give me a sympathetic look.

How bloody *dare* she.

It's one thing to look down your nose at me because I'm a fatty; it's entirely another to feel sorry for me.

I don't want you to feel sorry for me! I just want you to treat me like anybody else! Alright, I may need a bit more room than most people . . . and don't ask me to run the four hundred metres any time soon, but other than that I'm normal, so please give me a break, okay?

I want to say all of this to her narrow face, but being British, chubby, and horrifically embarrassed, I instead give her a little nod and a wet smile, before swiftly walking towards the exit.

By the time I do get home, I can barely lift my head, thanks to the curtain of self-loathing I've now wrapped myself in. It feels much heavier and more shameful than the shop curtain I was wrapped in less than an hour earlier. Unfortunately there are no skinny shop assistants around to help pull me out of this one, and

Greg is off out with his mates, so I'll get no husbandly support until he gets home. I therefore spend the next hour sitting disconsolately in front of a blank TV screen, before going to the fridge and eating the rest of the black forest gateaux.

This bleak frame of mind persisted right through the weekend and into Monday, so I was feeling very vulnerable when I met up with Elise at the Costa Coffee near the radio station for our regular mid-afternoon natter. Both being Stream FM employees, this daily time-out is much needed, and as far as I'm concerned, the only thing that keeps me sane. Working in local radio is rather like trying to herd cats, while someone pokes you in the eyeball every four seconds.

'I've got something I think you might be interested in,' Elise says as she takes a sip of her eggnog cappuccino.

'What's that?' I say, and grimace as I also take a swallow of my skinny latte.

'Please don't be offended,' she continues. This means she's about to say something related to my weight. People only ever start a sentence with 'please don't be offended' when they're about to tell me how fat they think I am. This usually pisses me off no end, but I'm pretty sure Elise doesn't have a nasty bone in her toned and tanned body, so I effect a pleasant smile that doesn't quite reach my eyes.

'Go on, Elise. Don't worry.'

'Okay. We're running a new competition early next year.'

. . . Oh, this is something to do with work. I've not read the signs right at all.

I feel strangely uneasy. When the most popular DJ at the station tells you to not be offended and then mentions a new project, it can only mean she's about to say something bad concerning your job.

'This is the first I've heard of it,' I say defensively. 'We can't turn around a good promo campaign in the marketing department if we're not given enough notice, you know.'

Elise shakes her head. 'No, no! It's nothing like that, Zoe! The higher-ups will sort all that stuff out in the New Year. I'm mentioning it to you now because you might be interested in taking part.'

'Taking part in what?'

'The competition.'

'What competition?'

Elise then spends five minutes laying out all the details of Fat Chance.

'You and Greg would be perfect for it,' she says when she's done. 'I'm sure if you put your name forward, you'd be in strong contention to be one of the six couples.'

'Elise . . . I work for the station. There's no way I could enter even if I wanted to.'

'Nope. You can! I asked Pete from legal about it. You're employed by Regency Marketing, right? Not Stream?'

'Yeah, but I still work in the same offices.'

'Doesn't matter. It's another company on a long-term contract. You can enter!'

'Well, I don't *want* to enter.' I take another sip of the disgusting skinny latte and try not to gag.

'Why not?' Elise's beautiful face scrunches up in a look of total incomprehension. Someone who spends as much time in the limelight as she does probably has no idea why I wouldn't want to be a part of a major event in the station's calendar.

'Because it'll be embarrassing,' I say in a low voice.

'Why?'

Because I'm fat, you gorgeous idiot.

'Because I'm . . . heavy, Elise.'

'Well, yes. That's the point though, isn't it?' The girl has always been blunt, I'll give her that. I first realised it two years ago on the day we met, when she told me my highlights made me look like a tart.

'I don't want to parade the fact that I'm overweight in front of thousands of people, though!' I point out to her.

'It's on the radio, Zoe.'

'You know what I mean. There'll be stuff on the website, at the road shows . . . it'll be horrible.'

Then Elise reminds me of the one thing that counterbalances my argument. 'It's for *fifty grand*, Zoe. Fifty bloody grand!'

I stir the hideous skinny latte with a spoon, staring down into its bland beige contents. 'That is a lot of money.'

'It is! And how many times have you said you need an incentive to lose weight?'

'Greg will never go for it.'

'He will if you make him. He dotes on you.' Elise flashes me one of her copyright dazzling DJ smiles. 'He'll do anything you tell him to . . . within reason.'

'You really think you could get us in?' I can't believe I'm even contemplating this, but fifty grand is an awful lot of money. I also don't want to find myself trapped in a dress again anytime soon. These two things are combining to make Elise's madcap idea seem almost sensible.

'Oh yes! Me, Will, and Danny will be making the final decision on who's picked. I've already spoken to them, and they think you'd make a great contestant as well.'

Well, that sews it up then. Will does whatever Elise tells him to, as he knows damn well that he's part of the most successful breakfast show in local radio history thanks to her, and Dan, the station controller, would cheerfully cut off one of his legs for a chance to have sex with her.

'I'll have to speak to Greg about it,' I say.

'Yeah, no problem.' Elise waves this off like it's inconsequential. She may think I have my husband wrapped around my little finger, but I'm not so sure. 'So you'll do it, then?' she asks expectantly.

'Er . . . if Greg's up for it, I suppose so.'

Elise gleefully claps her hands together. 'Brilliant!' Her excitement is palpable.

I, however, am not excited.

What I am is a combination of terrified and deeply apprehensive. This may be the stupidest thing I've ever done.

But . . . is that a faint glimmer of hope I sense under all that negativity?

Why yes, Zoe, I do believe it is.

This might just be the kick up the arse I need to finally drop some of this weight and start living life again.

If only I can convince my husband to do it with me.

GREG'S WEIGHT LOSS DIARY
Friday, March 7th
20 stone, 2 pounds

This is the single dumbest idea in history. I can't believe I'm sitting here at 7.30 on a Friday evening writing this.

I would get up and turn the laptop off, but Zoe is sitting on the couch watching 'EastEnders' and if I stop typing I'll never hear the end of it.

Why the hell does the radio station need us to keep a diary like this anyway? Can't they just interview us? Or send some menial dogsbody over here to write down everything we say? I spend enough of my day chained to a desk at work; I don't particularly want to spend my evenings chained to *another* one writing about how fat I am.

I know I'm fat.

I've been fat for years.

Twenty stone looks back at me every time I get on the scales (which isn't often).

I can hear how much I wheeze when I walk up the stairs, and the number of extra notches I've had to cut into my belt doesn't bear thinking about.

My size has stopped me enjoying the things I love like rugby and energetic sex.

I *wish* I was thinner . . . but if wishes were horses then beggars would ride them.

Until they were made into burgers.

Which I would then eat.

I don't feel the need to put all this down on paper, but Zoe and Elise say I *have to*, so here I am on a Friday night—when I could be down the pub—writing about how fat I am. How colossally, massively, *stupendously* fat I am.

Elise says these diaries are supposed to be the 'windows into our lives' during the course of the competition, so the audience will get to know us and understand what we're going to go through in the next six months.

This is a *complete* waste of time, as I can tell them what we're going to be going through in one word: *misery*.

Dieting is bloody miserable.

It's really no fun at all.

I know: I tried it once and really didn't get on with it.

There's only so many times you can eat salad and walk five miles on a treadmill before your will to live starts to dribble out of your ears.

But here I am . . . on a fucking diet.

I've agreed to do it for two reasons. One, fifty grand would pay off a big chunk of the mortgage and we could finally have that holiday in the Seychelles I've always wanted. And two, Zoe won't give me a blow job ever again if I don't do it.

'That's not bloody fair!' I moaned at her when she threatened this punishment the first time this ridiculous idea came up.

'I mean it, Greg. I want to do this. We both *need* to do this. If you're not going to go along with it, my mouth is staying closed for the foreseeable future.'

See?

It's just not bloody fair, is it?

Mind you, the blow job threat wasn't really necessary. Zoe knows there's nothing I wouldn't do for her. It's irritating in the extreme, but we've been married for so long now that there's no way I can hide it.

I love her to pieces and she uses that fact at every opportunity to manipulate me into doing things I would otherwise avoid like the plague.

For instance, there was the time she made me go with her to see 'Cats' in London.

What self-respecting straight man would go near a musical about bloody cats, were it not for the love of his other half? By the time the Magical Mister Mistoffelees started singing about how magical he was, I was ready to open a vein.

Then there was the holiday to Egypt.

I hate cruises, I don't like the heat, and history bores me, so you can imagine how delighted I was to spend a week on the Nile in forty degrees, looking at a never-ending series of beige ruins while my skin cooked slowly in the scorching sun.

Finally, I can't help but remember the salmon-pink jumper she made me buy in Burton's. I wore it to the Rugby Club annual ball, and didn't hear the end of it for months. My nickname became Fancy Doris.

It's the smile on Zoe's face, damn it. I just can't get enough of seeing the look of pure happiness. The one that makes her eyes twinkle.

When she's *really* happy, the smile gets even wider and her top lip curls up a bit, showing off her teeth. This may sound like I'm describing a horse about to get a sugar lump, but trust me, it's a lot more adorable to look at than it is to describe on the page. Even when you're being forced into a fucking pink jumper.

I'd put up with pretty much anything to see that smile.

Even being entered into a weight loss competition. A competition that will probably encourage the resurrection of 'Fancy Doris' as far as my rugby club mates are concerned.

I don't even *care* that I'm a bit chunkier than I used to be. Not that much, anyway.

Sure, the lads at work have started calling me Porkins in the past few months, and I haven't played rugby for years thanks to that wheezing when I walk up stairs, but I'm pretty happy with myself, all things considered. I certainly get to eat all the food I like, anyway.

I may get the piss taken out of me, and I might not be able to take part in much sport, but frankly I don't care as long as I can have Kung Po chilli chicken with rice, a Domino's Texas BBQ pizza, or a Big Mac whenever I like.

It's my body, after all; I'll do what I want with it!

But then Zoe comes home from work one day before Christmas and tells me all about this idiotic competition Elise has cooked up in that bleached blonde barnet of hers (yes, I know you'll read this, Elise. I just don't care) and now I'm not allowed to eat anything brown and fried any more.

For poor old Gregory Milton, the foreseeable future consists of heavy sweating, starving to death, and feeling astronomically miserable.

Right, that's it. I can't be arsed to write any more. What the hell else am I supposed to say anyway?

Apparently my rant above isn't good enough, according to my wife. She's just made that fact very clear to me in an hour-long screaming argument. My eardrums may never recover. Zoe's now taken herself off into the bedroom and is refusing to speak to me again until I write something a bit more constructive in this stupid diary.

'You're not happy being fat, you lying git!' she screeched at me. 'Stop talking bollocks and be honest!'

'People are going to read it,' I pointed out to her.

'That's the reason we're doing it!'

'But I don't *want to*.'

I hate squirming. It's something five-year-olds do.

Nevertheless, here I am—sitting at the dining room table, squirming like a worm in the clutches of a particularly psychotic child—under the baleful gaze of my irate wife.

'It's part of the deal, Greg,' she says. 'If we don't write these diaries, we don't get to stay in the competition.'

'S'not a problem with me,' I mumble.

'What?'

'Nothing.' Squirm. Squirm. 'What am I supposed to say, then?'

'They told you what to write about. Your emotions, Greg. How you feel. Stuff like that.'

'Right now I'm feeling extremely bullied.'

'About how it feels to be fat, I mean.'

I cross my arms. 'You mean how bad I'm supposed to feel about myself? Is that it?'

'Yes, Greg! We're both miserable. You know we are.'

'I'm not miserable. I'm perfectly okay, thanks.'

'Oh really?' Zoe's arms also fold across her chest and she shoots daggers at me. 'What about Roger's barbecue last week?'

'I don't want to talk about that.'

'No, you wouldn't, would you? You weren't happy about what happened there, though, were you?'

'There's no way I'm writing about it.'

'Yes, you are! That's the point of all this!' Zoe lets out a weary sigh and sits down next to me. 'Come on, Greg. Stop lying to yourself. You're no happier than I am. We've spent the past ten years eating far too much and moving about far too little.' She shakes her head. 'Too many takeaways in front of the telly. Too many hours spent sitting on the couch. It's just piled up and piled up, until we're at the point where I can't look at myself any more, and I'm pretty sure you can't either.' Her eyes go wide. 'I wheeze, Greg. A woman of my age should not bloody *wheeze!* We need to make a change in our lives, and if this competition is the only way to do it, then that's what we'll do.' She puts her hand on my shoulder and squeezes it. 'Something's got to change, baby. We're not getting any younger and we can't keep rolling around like a couple of Weebles.'

'Weebles?'

'Yes Greg. Weebles.' Zoe gets up again. 'I'm going to read in the bedroom. Sit here and write about what happened at Roger's . . . the same way I did with the incident at M&S.'

'I can't write as well as you can. You're a lot funnier than me.'

'Bullshit, Gregory Milton. You write for a living.'

'I'm a technical writer for an electronics company, woman, not a journalist.'

'Well, just treat this as a user manual for being fat.'

'Are you serious?'

'Yes! Get writing, Greg, and stop making excuses!'

And with that, Zoe turns around and marches out of the living room, leaving me sitting here at this computer, trying to avoid having to spill my guts, but knowing that if I don't I'll face a verbal crucifixion from my enraged spouse.

You wouldn't expect an invitation to a barbecue in the first week of March, would you? Especially not in the South of England.

It's no more than five degrees outside, and a raw, bitter wind blows across the whole country. Not exactly the ideal conditions for standing around outside eating a burnt beef burger.

'Don't worry!' Roger assures me in my office a week before the barbecue. 'I've hired these bloody great big heaters and we're having a gazebo put up. Seriously, I can guarantee it'll be like the Bahamas under there!' He gives me a friendly poke in the ribs with his elbow. 'Besides, you're a big lad. I'm sure you'll keep warm,' he finishes with a grin.

Why do people automatically think that because you're carrying extra weight you don't feel the cold? I'm not a fucking walrus. My blubber is not that beneficial when it comes to staving off cold temperatures.

'Okay Roger, we'll come along,' I tell him.

At least the food will be good. Roger has a two-thousand-pound barbecue he bought for less than half price when the local garden centre went out of business last October. I know he's been dying to use it ever since. His impatience is most probably the reason for the event's ridiculous timing.

It helps that his wife is a chef, which will at least lessen the chances of us coming away with food poisoning.

'Great!' Roger says, and turns to leave. Just as he reaches the door, he drops the bombshell on me. 'Oh, Eileen wants it to be a fancy dress party.'

'What?!' I say, failing to hide my horror at the prospect.

'Yeah. It'll be fun!'

'No it won't, Roger, it'll be *awful*.'

'Eileen wants it,' he says and picks at an imaginary piece of fluff on his jacket.

I've known Roger enough years to know that what Eileen wants, Eileen gets. He and I are very similar in that respect. 'Oh, fuck a badger, alright,' I say in disgust. 'I'll just do what I always do. Stick on my funeral suit and come as John Travolta in *Pulp Fiction*.'

'You can't do that.'

'Why not?'

'It's themed.'

'*Themed?*'

'Yes.' Roger looks like someone's wafted something unpleasant under his nose.

I know I look like someone's just shot my favourite childhood goldfish. 'What's the theme, Roger?'

'Children's television characters.'

'Seriously?'

'British ones only. From the 1970s and 80s.'

'You're kidding me?'

'Nope.'

'Bloody hell. Why doesn't she just stipulate it has to be programmes broadcast between 3 and 4 p.m. on independent local television in 1985 and have done with it?'

'I told her it might be a bit too specific.'

'You think so?'

Roger affects a conciliatory smile. 'The fun kicks off at eight, Greg. Looking forward to seeing you both!' And with that, he's out the door and gone before I can kick up any more fuss.

So now I have to come up with a costume for a British children's television show from the seventies or eighties.

'You could paint yourself blue and go as what's-his-name from "The Trap Door,"' Zoe says that evening while we're discussing the matter.

'What? Berk? Don't be ridiculous. Apart from anything else I'll freeze to death.'

'Grotbags?'

'Grotbags?'

'Yeah, you know. She used to turn up on that show with Rod Hull and Emu.'

'So you're suggesting that I cross-dress as a green witch, are you?'

'Why not?'

'You need to be quiet now, Zoe. Please.'

Zoe shrugs her shoulders and walks into the kitchen, leaving me with my conundrum.

It's alright for her—she decided on her costume in less than three seconds. Zoe is going as Velma from 'Scooby Doo.' Her costume has been in our loft ever since her mum's similarly awful fancy dress party five years ago. She concedes it might need letting out a bit thanks to her more recent weight gain, but Zoe's always been a dab hand with sewing so, bar an hour or two of cutting and stitching, she's pretty much sorted. While not technically British, the cartoon was on here for so many years, Zoe is confident she'll get away with it.

'What about Captain Pugwash?' she hollers at me from the kitchen over the sound of the microwave.

'Can you stop suggesting fat people, please?' I shout back.

'Sorry!'

Another couple of minutes roll by until inspiration strikes.

'Aha!' I say in triumph.

'Got something, have you?' Zoe asks from over her mug of steaming hot chocolate.

'I have indeed. Is my suit ironed?'

Zoe groans. 'You can't go as John Travolta again.'

'I'm not. I'm going as Mister Benn!'

'Mister Benn?'

'Yeah . . . you remember, don't you? Cartoon from the seventies. Bloke in a suit and bowler hat would go into a clothes shop, pop on a costume in the changing room out the back, and find himself on some adventure relating to the costume.'

'What, like if he dressed as a ninja, he'd wind up in Japan cutting people's heads off?'

'I don't think he ever did that. It was a kids' show. But yes, you get the point.'

'You haven't got a bowler hat.'

'They're bound to have one in that fancy dress shop in town, aren't they?'

'Probably.'

Probably turns out to be definitely. I manage to pick up a plastic bowler hat that just about fits on my head the next day on my way home from the office.

By seven that evening I'm standing in front of the mirror dressed in my black suit and tie, with the cheap hat on my head. I don't quite look *exactly* like the cartoon character, but this is a fancy dress party being held in someone's back garden, so I don't think anyone is expecting the costumes on offer to be hyper-accurate doppelgangers of the real thing.

This is just as well, as it is plain to see that the suit doesn't fit me anymore. I've had to strap on my biggest, thickest belt to stop the trousers from popping open at the clasp, and I can't lift my arms above a 45-degree angle. I tell myself that it is only for one night and that by the time nine o'clock rolls around everyone will be heavily intoxicated and therefore unlikely to care. I'll be able to take a majority of it off with no fuss.

'You look very dapper,' Zoe says, kindly.

'I look like an utter dickhead, love, but I wasn't expecting much else.'

Zoe gives me a withering look. 'Oh, cheer up. It might be fun.'

'I suppose so. Let's just hope Roger's heaters do their job okay. The forecast is for two degrees tomorrow night.'

'Good job my Thelma sweater is pretty thick, then.'

. . . and orange. Really, *really*, blindingly orange.

As we walk to the car the next evening, I can't help but feel that I'm being accompanied by a giant ambulatory tangerine. I have the tact to keep this to myself, though.

The drive over to Roger's is an uncomfortable one, what with the suit jacket being so tight that I can't lift my arms properly, and the tightened belt around my waist feels like its burrowing its way into my intestinal tract.

The car dashboard readout tells me it is in fact a balmy *zero* degrees outside already, and it's only 7.30. Those heaters had better be very, very big.

'Evening!' Roger exclaims joyfully as he throws the front door open.

I say Roger, but what I really mean is Roger dressed in an alarmingly bright Bananaman costume.

Roger Jarvis is six foot three inches tall, has been a prop forward for ten years on the rugby team, and is built like a particularly sturdy garden shed. But even he can't make a bright yellow and blue superhero costume look anything other than the gayest outfit on the face of the planet.

'Want a banana?' he asks and waves a bunch of Fyffe's in our faces. 'They give you superpowers!'

'No thanks, mate,' I tell him. 'Don't want to ruin our appetites.'

'Fair enough! Come in, both of you.'

Zoe enters first and I follow on behind, trying to protect my eyes from the glare radiating from Bananaman. What with Zoe's bright orange jumper, I'm starting to feel a seizure coming on.

'Hello!' Eileen waves at us from the lounge. She has donned a blonde mullet wig over her cropped red hair, and is wearing a bloody awful silver jacket, complete with lapels which are so large that they would be ideally suited for hang gliding. The jacket is paired with red chequered flares that defy belief, both in terms of garishness and flappiness around the ankles. The ensemble is topped off by the enormous Long Island Ice Tea she's waving around in one hand.

'What the hell have you done to yourself?' I blurt out, almost involuntarily.

'My costume, you mean?' she says and grins like a maniac.

'Yes!'

'I'm Cheggers!'

For a second, I don't quite get what she means. Is Cheggers a newly discovered disease of the mind that forces you to dress like an utter twat?

Zoe is quicker on the uptake. 'Cheggers! I used to love that show!'

Then it clicks into place. Cheggers . . . 'Cheggers Plays Pop.' The seminal children's quiz show from the 80s, hosted by short, chubby British institution Keith Chegwin.

'You're dressed as Keith Chegwin, aren't you?' I say in stunned disbelief.

'I am!'

My eyes narrow. 'Was this entire fancy dress party manufactured to give you an excuse to dress as Cheggers, Eileen? Be honest.'

'It was!' she cries, unashamedly.

'Brilliant!' Zoe crows and gives Eileen a hug.

'I love the Thelma costume, sweetheart,' Eileen tells my wife, before looking at me a bit cockeyed, clearly already under the influence of Long Island's finest alcoholic beverage. 'Not so sure about yours, Greg. Never really liked Thomas the Tank Engine.'

'What?'

'You're dressed as The Fat Controller, aren't you?'

'I'm Mister Benn!'

'Are you?'

'Yes!'

'Really?' Roger says from behind his mask of banana-flavoured justice. 'I thought you were The Fat Controller as well.'

My face goes red with embarrassment . . . just like The Fat Controller's. 'I'm dressed as Mister Benn,' I tell them through gritted teeth.

Both Roger and Eileen realise the implications of their mistake and employ that nervous laugh people fall back on as a get-out clause at times such as this.

'Great costume!' Roger exclaims.

'Absolutely!' Eileen agrees a little too quickly.

'Thanks very much,' I say with a fake smile plastered across my face.

Still, the social faux pas they've just committed can now be brushed under the carpet without another mention. We'll all just pretend they didn't mistake who I've come dressed as just because I'm a big fat bastard.

'Shall we go through to the garden?' Roger asks, inadvertently looking down at my gut. 'I bet you're both hungry.'

Oh, *of course* we're both hungry, Roger. We're big fat balloon people who can't walk past an edible substance without immediately grabbing it and stuffing it into our giant, slobbering maws.

This party is starting to go south *fast*.

What's really bloody annoying is that I *am* starving, having not eaten anything since lunch. But now that Roger and Eileen have neatly highlighted how blubbery Zoe and I are, we're going to have to eat like shrews so the rest of the partygoers don't look at us like we're the evening's entertainment.

I can just about stand looking idiotic in an uncomfortable and badly put together fancy dress costume, but if people are staring at me and my wife like we're a freak show who eat everything in sight, I might just have to kill myself.

The audience will just have to do without a performance from 'The Colossal Balloon Twins' this evening.

'Lead on,' I say to Roger with a poorly concealed sigh.

I was worried that it would be too cold under the gazebo as a result of the March weather. I needn't have worried.

Roger has bought not one, not two, but *eight* large outdoor heaters that he has placed around the edge of the party area. Each one produces a similar amount of heat to what you'd find on your average afternoon in the Serengeti. People are actually standing away from them, and some are even leaning out into the cold night air to get a bit of respite. The plastic patio chairs they've put out for guests to sit on are probably in danger of melting into puddles of white gunge.

Were this heat not enough, it's married with the inferno being put out by Roger's enormous barbecue sitting along the back wall of the house. Clearly, we'll all be lucky to get out of here without third-degree burns and kidney failure brought on by severe dehydration.

There's roughly twenty people under the gigantic white gazebo. Happily, Zoe and I know (or at least recognise) a good 80 percent of them. Most are from my work or the rugby club, and are the same motley collection of lunatics I've socialised with for the past decade.

'Fuck me! It's The Fat Controller!' I hear a voice cry from just beyond the ring of infernal patio heaters. The unmistakeable cockney accent belongs to Ali, my friend, fellow rugby enthusiast, and utter prick of the highest order.

He emerges from the frigid garden wearing the biggest turban I've ever seen in my life, a couple of gun bandoliers strapped across his otherwise naked chest, and a set of black balloon pants that terminate in combat boots. I don't remember this getup from any TV shows I watched when I was a kid. Ali is taller and broader than both me and Roger, so the ensemble is pretty terrifying.

'I'm not the sodding Fat Controller!' I snap at him as he walks towards me.

'Father Christmas at a job interview?' he retorts, sniggering.

'I'm Mister Benn!'

Ali peers at me, laughs, and takes a swig from the huge Tiger beer bottle in his hand.

'And what are you supposed to be?' I ask him, raising a suspicious eyebrow.

He looks disgusted. 'Don't any of you wankers watch movies? I'm a bloody thuggee!'

'A what?'

'A thuggee! From *Indiana Jones 2*, you know . . .'

'That's not a British children's TV character Ali,' I point out.

'Bollocks. It's from the eighties and kids watched it; that's good enough for me. Besides, I can double up as a genie.' He puts down his beer, crosses both arms, and stares us down. 'I will give you three wishes!' he says in the worst Arabic accent I've ever heard. 'Then I will eat a camel and put a jihad on your head.'

'Ali!' Zoe cries. 'Don't be so racist!'

'Racist? I'm a bloody Indian!'

'So?'

'I'm allowed! They're my people.'

'Ali, you were born in Chepstow,' I point out. 'Not to mention the fact your family is from Mumbai, which isn't in the Middle East.'

'Oh fuck off, we're all in it together, you imperialist bastard.'

'Can I have everyone's attention!' Roger shouts from over by the barbecue.

'Heads up! Bananaman's about to dole out some fruity justice,' Ali yells.

My friend might be right, but the import of Roger's words may be ruined by the pink pinny he's now sporting over his costume in order to protect it from the fat spitting aggressively from the cooking meat.

'The food's ready, everyone!' Roger announces proudly. 'The meat's in these trays here on the side of the barbie, and Eileen has laid out all the plates and other food in the dining room. Help yourselves!'

'Great stuff!' Ali exclaims and wanders over to the mountain of food Roger and Eileen have prepared.

In unspoken agreement, Zoe and I don't budge. We'll just let everyone else get the food before we venture over. As hungry as I am, I really don't want to feed the already engorged stereotype of the starving fatty being the first one to the buffet at every party.

'Shall we get a drink?' Zoe says, purposefully turning away from the food.

'Yeah, I think I need one,' I reply and we make our way over to the alcoholic's sanctuary laid out on the patio table at the back of the gazebo.

I take my time selecting my drink of choice, weighing up the different brands on offer. I'm driving tonight, so I can have a couple of beers maximum. I spot Ali's stash of Tiger bottles and grab one. If the bastard's going to insult me, he can pay for it with alcohol.

Zoe pours herself a Malibu and Coke and we stand there for a good ten minutes chatting about nothing in particular while everybody else gets food.

I'm not going to lie: this takes a superhuman amount of self-control on my part. My stomach is rumbling like crazy, and I can feel a faintly pulsating headache coming on due to my lack of sustenance.

I eventually concede defeat. 'Sod it, I'm getting some grub,' I tell Zoe, and march towards the dining room.

Inside, what was formerly a mountain of meat now resembles a slightly steep hill—a geological shift that Ali has been mainly responsible for, I don't doubt. Thankfully, there's more than enough left for us, and I select two particularly juicy-looking burgers.

Then add a couple more.

. . . along with two sausages, a pork chop and a chicken leg. I'm comfort eating, and couldn't give a shit.

'Add something green, Greg, for Christ's sakes,' Zoe admonishes as she scoops coleslaw onto her plate, next to the pork chop and burger she's selected for her meal.

'Alright,' I say and throw a handful of salad in the remaining space I have left. Its green healthiness offends me, though, so I smother it in ketchup and dressing before returning to the party.

There are a couple of plastic patio chairs still free, so we won't have to eat standing up and risk indigestion. Sadly, they are the two closest to one of the patio heaters and there's no room to put them anywhere else, so we're going to have to endure sub-Saharan heat blowing on the backs of our necks while we eat.

Furthermore, the nearest guests to us are a right couple of middle-class stiffs that Roger knows from his clay pigeon shooting club. His name is Anthony. I can't quite remember hers, but 'Pruneface' really leaps out at me as an appropriate substitute until I do.

'Gregory, isn't it?' Anthony says as I lower myself into the patio chair. I feel its plastic arms grasp my love handles in their firm embrace, and I know that I'm going to have to use a considerable amount of leverage to get back out of the thing again.

'Yeah, that's me,' I say. 'We met at Roger and Eileen's twentieth, didn't we?'

'That's right! Lovely bash that was.'

'Yep. You remember my wife Zoe?'

'I do indeed! Delighted to see you again, my dear. You look positively radiant tonight!' This makes Zoe giggle. She's always been a sucker for a bit of old-school charm.

We both wait for Anthony to introduce us to Pruneface, who is looking off into the middle distance while she munches demurely on a pickled onion.

The introduction never comes. 'Lovely grub!' Anthony remarks and bites into a sausage.

'Looks like it,' I agree and take a big bite out of my own pork-based product.

The next ten minutes go by in light conversation with Anthony, including an invite to his country manor and the next pheasant shoot in April—which I have no intention of attending.

Still, my belly is now full of meat and I'm enjoying the last of Ali's beer, so for the first time that evening I feel myself relaxing and actually having something vaguely approximating a good time.

That is, until I hear and feel the back legs of the patio chair I'm sitting on start to buckle.

It's only a slight feeling, but I can definitely hear a worrying scraping sound coming from below me as the chair legs move on the concrete flagstones under my feet.

'. . . and that's when I thought why not?' Anthony says. 'You only live once and there aren't many of them left, so I went for a look.'

I know he's talking about going to see some rare animal across the other side of the planet, but I couldn't tell you which one. All my thoughts are concentrated on the quiet sounds of distress emanating from below me.

I daren't shift in the chair too much. Any sudden movement may tip the balance in favour of disaster and I seriously don't think I could take the embarrassment.

Here I am, squeezed into a patio chair, wearing a suit that's too small for me, with a bowler hat perched on my head like a Christmas pudding. If the chair collapses from under me, I might as well charge Roger and the rest of the guests a fee for my entertaining clown act.

As Anthony waffles on about the rare Siberian Lynx, I sit still and tense, waiting for the inevitable.

However, another five minutes go by and, miraculously, there's no sign of the collapse occurring.

'Greg and I want to go to the Seychelles, don't we Greg?' Zoe says to Anthony.

'What? Oh, yes. One day, anyway,' I reply in a distracted fashion.

'Ah! Wonderful place. Went there myself twenty years ago, before it became all commercialised and horrific,' Anthony tells us.

I can actually listen to what he has to say now as the chair seems to have ceased its protest.

I breathe a sigh of deep relief and feel comfortable enough to pick up what's left of my pork chop and have a nibble.

As I munch contentedly on it, I think about the best way I can yank myself out of the chair and make a beeline for the dining room to grab another chop before they're all gone. The barbecue sauce covering them is particu—

Both of the patio chair's back legs give way in sudden, catastrophic fashion. This pitches me backwards at a terrifying rate of knots.

My plate of half-eaten food flies into the air as my arms pinwheel in an attempt to prevent the inevitable.

'Awwggle!' I screech. The cry of terror is somewhat muffled by the remnants of pork chop still in my mouth.

'Good grief!' cries Anthony.

'Bloody hell!' shouts Zoe.

Time seems to slow, as it does in all situations like this. The utter bastard wants you to live through every glorious detail of your downfall, and decides to temporarily break the immutable laws of physics so it can really stick the boot in.

I see Zoe's left arm fly out and grab my shoulder.

Bless her.

Her first reaction is to try and save me, but it will be for naught, I fear. I am over 20 stone, while she is only 14. The same laws of physics that time likes to flaunt are sadly unbreakable for us human beings.

This is proved conclusively when, instead of stopping my descent by grabbing hold of me, Zoe merely joins me in my backwards plummet towards disgrace and mild injury.

What Zoe's actions do accomplish is to halt our combined fall for a couple of seconds—more than long enough for the majority of the people at the barbecue to realise something is going on, look over in our direction, and get a good eyeful.

I continue to fall backwards, but now thanks to Zoe's intervention, I'm also swinging slightly to the left. This puts me in the path of the patio heater standing right behind me.

For her part, my wife achieves a more straightforward downward trajectory and is on course to make friends with the cold, wet grass of Roger and Eileen's landscaped garden in about half a second.

No such luck for yours truly.

No easy fall into soft grass for Greg Milton this evening.

My left shoulder and the back of my head hit the metal heater, producing a noise that can only be described on the page as *GLOING!*

Those irritating laws of physics come into play again at this point, as the full force of twenty-stone Greg Milton meets all five stone of portable patio heater, and sends it tilting backwards like a felled beech tree.

The heater smacks into one of the gazebo's legs, causing it snap in half and send one corner of the enormous party tent crashing in on itself.

People scream and start acting like extras in *The Poseidon Adventure*. Plates and tables are strewn across the patio as the victims try to flee the scene of destruction.

Hitting the patio heater once again changes my trajectory in favour of a grass-based landing, and I topple onto the ground, winding myself painfully as I finally make contact with the ground.

I find myself laid out on the grass right next to Zoe, watching the gazebo collapse from my prone position and trying to desperately force some air back into my lungs.

'Bloody hell, Greg!' I hear Roger shout as he leaps over to the broken corner of the gazebo, his Bananaman cape fluttering in the cool night air. He looks every inch the superhero . . . other than the pinny and the look of horror on his face.

'I'm sorry, Roger! I'm sorry, everyone!' I squeal breathlessly, and attempt to get up.

Then the final, crowning insult of the evening rears its ugly head. I can't get out of the broken patio chair. Its arms are still wedged firmly around my ample hips.

Do you know how hard it is to stand upright when there's a plastic chair stuck on your arse?

No. No, you don't.

Let's not pretend that anyone else in this planet's history has ever been at the centre of an incident as mortifying as this. I flail my arms and legs around in an attempt to extricate myself from the broken chair's seemingly vice-like grip around my love handles.

Now I look like an abandoned baby turtle.

'Zoe!' I wail. 'Give me a hand out of this thing!'

My wife disentangles herself from her own chair and stands up, surveying the scene. 'You'll have to roll over, Greg,' she tells me.

'What?'

'I can't pull the chair off without you rolling over.'

'Oh, for fuck's sake. Alright.'

I rock back and forth a couple of times before throwing myself over.

Now I'm stuck with my arse in the air, waving the patio chair around like I'm conducting some kind of mating ritual. I have no idea what creature I think I'm going to attract with this display, but I'm pretty sure it'd be gigantic, moronic, and possibly blind.

Zoe takes hold of the chair leg and pulls. This scrapes a square inch of skin off my left love handle, but does very little else.

'I can't do it, Greg. I'm not strong enough. I'll have to get some butter.'

Oh God, how can this get any worse?

'You twats need help?' I hear Ali say from behind me.

'No! We're fine!' I shout and wave him away.

'Don't be such a pillock, Milton. You're obviously not in a good way. Here, let me have a go, Zoe.'

I feel Ali's enormous hands grip the two broken chair legs and yank as hard as he can.

My hips buck and I almost feel myself leave the ground. 'Owww!' I scream in pain as more skin is flayed from my sides.

'Don't be such a baby,' Ali snaps and yanks again, making my hips buck upwards once more.

Now it just looks like he's raping me with a plastic chair.

I grab two handfuls of grass, clamping down to stop myself being lifted in the air again. This seems to do the trick as the chair's death grip is finally released on Ali's third yank.

'There you go!' Ali exclaims and offers me a hand. I take it and he pulls me to my feet.

I become horribly aware that everyone is looking at me. Even Roger, who is still holding up the fallen end of the gazebo, is staring through his superhero mask.

'Sorry, everyone,' I repeat, hands held up.

Eileen bustles over. 'Don't worry, Greg!' she says. 'Those chairs were cheap from B&Q. I'm surprised one of them hasn't collapsed under anyone else!'

Except it didn't, did it? It happened to *me*.

The fat one.

I'm no heavier than Ali, but because most of my weight is blubber and his is still muscle, everyone will think that the chair only broke because I'd squeezed my enormous bulk into it.

That's the way it goes. Fat people are always the heaviest ones in the room. Even when they aren't.

I turn to my wife. 'I think I hurt my shoulder, sweetheart. I'd like to go home.'

My shoulder is fine, but Zoe gets the point instantly. 'Okay, honey. That's fine.'

As Roger reassembles the gazebo as best he can, and puts everything back where it should be, my wife and I make our excuses to everyone. Most people look like they believe the bad shoulder story, but I'm sure they know the real reason we're leaving with such haste. The permanent red flush of embarrassment on my face is a dead giveaway.

'You sure know how to fuck up a party!' Ali comments as I grab our coats.

'Thanks, mate,' I say, not entirely keeping the hurt out of my voice.

'Ah, don't worry about it,' he adds. 'I got so drunk at a party once I threw up over the record player. People were ducking to avoid the sick as it spun off the turntable.'

'Lovely.'

'Bloody hilarious, it was.' Ali grins and slaps me on the back. 'I'll see you in the pub Sunday, you big dickhead.'

And with that, he turns and hurries back to the alcohol table, no doubt to take advantage of the fact that everyone else is distracted.

'So sorry to see you leave,' Eileen says by the front door, with a grimace.

'Yeah, hope that shoulder is alright,' Roger adds, having come away from his repairs to see us off.

'It'll be fine,' I tell them. 'Thank you for having us . . . and apologies once again.'

Roger waves his hand. 'Don't worry about it. It'll make a great story in the future!'

Oh yes. I can't wait to hear you telling everyone at work, Roger.

Zoe says her goodbyes as well, and we make our way back to the car in silence.

'I don't want to talk about it,' I say as she opens her mouth.

'Okay, baby,' Zoe replies and strokes my arm as I start the engine.

I feel such a combination of shame, regret, and humiliation as we drive home. It is a wonder I don't crash the car into the nearest wall.

So there you go.

That's why I've agreed to do this stupid competition.

I just can't keep living like this.

If doing what Zoe wants means I can go to a party without destroying half the furniture, then I'll be a happy man.

Besides, it might put *that* smile back on her face, and I haven't seen it in such a long time.

Nonetheless, I still have deep, *deep* reservations about the whole thing.

I guess only time will tell.

ZOE'S WEIGHT LOSS DIARY
Tuesday, April 8th
13 stone, 10 pounds (11 pounds lost)

I'm starting to think this was a really bad idea.

We've had a month to get used to being on our diets, and in the glare of the local media. If the rest of the competition goes the way these first few weeks have, I may need to check into the nearest psychiatric hospital imminently. I'm all for dropping five stone, but not at the expense of my mental health, thank you very much.

The actual diet bit of the competition is relatively straightforward. I was expecting to be under the constant watchful eye of some kind of horrendous personal trainer, but Stream want our weight loss programmes to be similar to the type an average audience member would be able to manage, which means going it alone to a large extent. Of course, we have the carrot of fifty grand dangled in front of us. I'm pretty sure most people would stick to a diet better if they had that kind of motivation. I'll trade an extended stomach for an extended house any day of the week.

I was slightly disconcerted by the amount of paperwork we had to sign at the start of the whole process. Lots of indemnities and contractual stuff I probably should have read more closely before putting down my signature. I have no doubt that at least some of it stipulated that Stream could not be held responsible if I starve myself to death or if blow an artery during exercise.

While the diet is straightforward and pretty much under my control, my new-found local celebrity is anything but.

The first time I saw my face on a billboard in town was so exquisitely dreadful that it almost reduced me to tears. I knew they'd be using our likenesses for advertising and promotion when I signed the contract to be part of the show, but I thought it would be largely confined to the website and some of the local papers. I clearly wasn't prepared for the scale of this enterprise. No event that I've been involved in at the station has been on this scale before, so I guess I lulled myself into a false sense of security. More fool me.

They've really gone to town on this bugger, though. It feels like they've thrown more cash at it than a Hollywood movie company would at a blockbuster.

Everywhere I look I seem to see billboards, advertising banners, flyers, posters, and cardboard standees—a majority of which feature my ugly mug.

I don't know if I'll be able to cope with this kind of local celebrity. I know damn well that Greg won't.

I know one other thing for certain. If I hated Mondays before Elise convinced me to take part in Fat Chance, I loathe them with a passion that's almost holy now.

Quick side note: Who thought the title *Fat Chance* would be a good idea? I'm willing to bet all the money in my bank account that it was a thin person. They probably thought it sounded extremely clever, without taking into account the fact that it sounds pretty fucking *unkind* to those of us taking part.

Anyway, Monday is 'check in' day at the radio station, where we all go on the Elise and Will morning show and chat about how our weight loss programmes are going. If it wasn't bad enough that I have to spill my guts in this diary all the time, I also have to stammer my way through a mini-interview with my so called best friend and her effeminate co-host at the start of each week.

And while Elise is a lovely person off air, once you stick a microphone in her hand she turns into the kind of door-stopping aggressive journalist that cheating politicians have come to know and fear.

A good case in point was yesterday's show.

It was our third appearance on the radio, and by now Greg and I are getting to know the rest of the couples engaged in this madness. Before every on-air conversation with Will and Elise, we get to sit in the green room together, drinking poor-quality instant coffee and trying to pretend we're not nervous.

Here's a rundown of our fellow contestants. I'll largely skip the physical descriptions as there's only so many adjectives I can use to describe someone who's overweight without descending into insult (and obligatory self-loathing).

Valerie and George look like they should be running a tea shop somewhere. A successful one, no doubt. Both in their early sixties, they look like the sort of kindly rotund grandparents we all wish we'd had when we were kids. George has the variety of bushy moustache that milk must stick to like a magnet every time he consumes it. Val wears a tiny pair of round spectacles that she hangs around her neck on a silver chain when she's not using them to peer into her copy of the latest Mills & Boon. You can just tell that these two homely, avuncular folk owe their weight gain to a lot of foodstuffs containing cream. I doubt they've ever looked a Big Mac in the eye, but are entirely at home around clotted cream and scones.

Angela and Dominica are a lesbian couple, who look completely bewildered most of the time. It's as if they were convinced they'd be firmly rejected for the show given their sexual orientation, were dumbfounded to discover that they weren't, and are actually now part of this madness. I love the pair of them, though. Even in the few brief conversations we've had, they seem like friendly, open people. Angela is a bit of an old hippy, quietly spoken and calm of manner, while Dominica is a loud, flamboyant Spaniard, who throws her arms around in an animated fashion even when she's talking about the most mundane of subjects. Neither wears dungarees, which is rather disappointing, but Angela does favour a headscarf most of the time, which conforms to at least some of the hideously outdated imagery of the average lesbian I carry round in my twentieth-century brain.

Then there is—and I kid you not when I say this—Frankie and Benny. I don't know whether Stream FM have got some kind of sponsorship campaign running with the well-known restaurant chain, but if they have, these two folk of Jamaican extraction would have to owe their place in the competition to it. I like Frankie; she's a friendly, happy sort with a big booming voice, and a laugh you can probably hear in Paris. Benny looks like he'd rather be anywhere else than right here, given the tormented expression on his face most of the time. I would be critical of his attitude, but then I can look round and see the exact same expression emanating from Gregory Milton's face next to me, so I'd better not judge the man too harshly. The cynic in me would think that these two had been included in Fat Chance just to fill out a quota of some kind, but I'm sure Elise wouldn't have anything to do with that kind of discrimination, so I guess Frankie and Benny are happily here on their own merits (unless I'm right about that sponsorship deal).

The biggest couple out of the six of us are Shane and Theresa. Theresa outweighs me by a good three stone and poor old Shane looks like the Grim Reaper is perched on his shoulder, waiting for him to make a sudden movement and over-exert his vital organs. The man must be over thirty stone. He makes my portly husband look positively anorexic. Shane's face has that unhealthy pallor of the morbidly obese and you can tell that just living day-to-day life is a struggle for him. Theresa isn't that far behind, either. I know damn well that she is who I'll become in the next few years if I don't do something about my life. I asked her how old she was last week and was distraught when she revealed that she was three years younger than me. The woman looks in her late forties, such is the strain being put on her body by all that extra fat. If anyone needs the impetus to lose weight that this stupid competition provides, it's these two.

At the bottom of the heap are Lea and Pete. I've barely managed to engage them in conversation so far, as when they're not outside chain-smoking cigarettes—having dumped their enormously fat three-year-old offspring named Ashton onto an unsuspecting production assistant—they're sitting on their iPhones in the corner, ignoring the rest of us. He's always playing Candy Crush and she's always leaving Facebook status updates about how wasted they got last weekend, or how wasted they're going to get *this* weekend. Pete has five teeth from what I can count (I can't look at his mouth for longer than a few moments without feeling nauseous) and Lea has a hairstyle that suggests some sort of horrific and violent encounter with a malfunctioning blender full of red food colouring. You can tell they've been hired for their shock value by Elise and her cronies. You can't do a reality show without at least a couple of people who look like they've barely made it through the early stages of human evolution.

. . . and there you have it. Along with Greg and me, these are your contestants, competitors, guinea pigs, and objects of mild public interest for the next few months. A broad cross-section of modern society, designed to appeal to as much of the listening demographic as is humanly possible. Stream FM is injecting an awful lot of cash into this project, so it's understandable that they'd want to get as big an audience as they can, but I can't help thinking that the obvious pigeonholing going on here creates an air of artificiality that—

What the *hell* am I saying? This entire process is *one thousand percent* artificial.

I need to remember that the people who will be benefitting most from this process are not any of us fatties, but the radio station executives who dreamt the whole thing up in the first place. The number of promotional deals the station has struck in the past few weeks with the local gym chain and health food stores is testament to the fact that Fat Chance is all about dragging in the profits for a bunch of rich, well-tailored people who I'll never meet. Oh sure, I get to use the gym facilities for free and get a decent percentage off all my health food purchases, but that's about as far as it goes. The real money is most definitely going elsewhere.

If successful, the competition will do no harm to Elise Bailey's career prospects. Already a rising star of local radio, if Fat Chance is popular, Elise will have the chance to go national—which has been her aim for the past three years. This doesn't bother me. The girl's been a good friend for many years, so if my debasement in front of the masses will help her out a bit, I won't complain an enormous amount.

Having said that, Elise did manage to push my buttons good and proper this morning, by bringing something up on the radio that I would have preferred to stay between us . . .

'Got a fag?'

'Excuse me?'

'Got a fag, love?'

Lea and her abnormal haircut are staring at me.

'No, I don't smoke, I'm afraid.'

I can almost see her synapses firing behind her eyes as she digests this information. 'Oh fuck,' she says and shuffles off. I can't be entirely sure, but I think she might be wearing slippers under that tracksuit.

Lottie, one of the plethora of production assistants that seem to be strewn randomly all over the Stream FM office, appears at the door to the green room. 'Okay, gang. We'll take you through to the studio now.'

'Here we go again, then,' Greg mutters next to me.

'It'll be fine, ' I try to convince him.

'As long as she doesn't ask me any questions about what my favourite takeaway food is again.'

'Yes. The drool on the microphone was a bit unpleasant,' I tease.

We get out of our seats and shuffle reluctantly through the office block with the rest of our fellow contestants. In my job with Regency I'm normally stuck in the back of the complex of buildings that make up the station, so I'd never actually ventured into the production area before Fat Chance started. It's a hive of young, desperate-looking individuals all running around with bits of paper in their hands, trying to look important. I also get the impression that there's very little real work going on, despite the level of frenetic activity.

Eventually we reach the actual studio, and are led into a sound booth opposite the one Elise and Will host the show from. Needless to say it's the largest booth in the studio. Shane's size alone would probably dictate its use, let alone the rest of us.

Lottie shuffles us into place. I notice she always keeps Lea and Pete away from the microphones as much as possible. I gather from Elise that the producers like to keep them away from the live broadcasts, given that the use of the word *cunt* is rather frowned upon during early-morning breakfast shows. My friend is terrified of people swearing on air anyway, so I'm sure she's more than happy to minimise the chances of letting Lea or Pete turn the air blue.

Lottie leaves us and shuts the soundproof door. This is when I begin to feel the claustrophobia set in. It's not so much the confined space, as it is the notion that we're like a herd of wild animals that have been penned up in a cage, awaiting the attention of a crowd of tourists.

'Woo! It's bloody hot in here,' Frankie says, and wafts her hand across her face.

'Of course it is, woman,' Benny replies. 'You get enough sweaty fat people in one place and what do you expect?'

I'm sure somebody once told Benny about the concept of tact when he was young. He just chose to ignore them.

'Morning, guys!' I hear Elise's happy disembodied voice coming at me from all angles. Peering through the glass dividing window, I can see her and Will across the way, prepping for the next section of the show.

We all mumble a half-hearted 'Good morning' back to her. There's something about being crowded into a small room with other people that stops you from being too demonstrative.

'We're just in a break,' she continues, 'but when we come back we'll get on with today's chat. How's everybody feeling?'

This is again greeted with mumbling, which Elise either doesn't register or chooses to ignore. 'Great! I've got a few questions lined up for some of you, but if I don't ask you one directly, feel free to chip in on somebody else's answer if you like.' Elise has said this every time we've stood in here, but so far, no one has felt much of a desire to break free of the pack and offer up information without it being forcibly teased out of them by the two DJs sitting in the booth beyond.

This has created a severe problem for me, as, without much input from the other couples, Elise keeps retreating to me for questions as I'm her friend, and someone with experience of working in local radio. So far I've easily done the most talking in the previous two weeks on the show—including having to recount a sanitised version of the M&S changing room farce.

'Can you at least *try* to leave me alone this week?' I said to Elise on the phone last night.

'I'll try my best, chick,' was her rather noncommittal answer.

The ad break has ended and we're about to kick off another update on how Fat Chance is going.

'Welcome back, everyone,' Elise says into her microphone in that smooth DJ voice she's spent years perfecting. 'It's 8.36 and you're listening to the Elise & Will Breakfast Show here on Stream FM. We're here once again with all six of the lovely couples who are involved in Fat Chance, the fantastic weight loss competition we're running here at Stream.'

'That's right, Elise,' Will takes over. 'And what a pleasure it is to have them back here once again. Can't believe it's only been a week since we saw them last, can you?'

'No, it only seems like yesterday since we spoke to them,' Elise replies cheerfully.

'Looking forward to hearing what updates they've got on their progress, though!' Will adds.

'Me too. Should be interesting to hear how the weight loss is going.'

'Exactly. Especially with only a week to go until the first weigh-in, eh?'

'That's right. Just seven days until we see which couple has lost the highest percentage of body fat since we started the competition in March!'

These are the kinds of conversations only DJs can have. What you or I may say in two words, these buggers can say in umpteen dozen sentences, with scarcely a pause for breath.

'I wonder which of our couples will be in the lead after the first few weeks,' Will says, feigning interest like a fucking champion.

'Well, why don't we go over to them and ask them what they think?' Elise suggests, as if the idea has just popped into her head, and as if this conversation hadn't been rehearsed three times before coming on air.

'Great idea!' Will exclaims, like his on-air partner has suggested a clever new way to cure cancer.

I really *hate* local radio.

And so our congenial hosts engage us in painfully stilted conversation.

Elise first tries Valerie and George, asking them who they think is doing the best so far. This is a fairly silly question, as neither has met the rest of us more than three times.

'I don't know,' Valerie says, eyeing the rest of the crowd. 'Maybe Angela and Dominica?'

'How about it, guys?' Will asks them. 'Is Valerie right?'

'Not really,' Angela hesitantly answers. 'I've lost nothing, and Dommy has put on a pound.'

'Angela!'

'Sorry, sweetheart.'

I see Elise grit her teeth and force a smile. 'How about Shane and Theresa? Who do you guys think is doing the best out of you two?'

Shane has missed the question completely as he's spent the last five minutes staring up at the microphone near his head, occasionally poking it to watch it spring around on its metal arm. This leaves Theresa to answer. 'I don't really know. We still look pretty bloody fat from what I can see, Elsie.'

My friend's eyes bulge a bit. 'It's Elise, actually,' she corrects. I have to stifle a laugh. I must remember to call her Elsie at every available opportunity.

'Oh, sorry,' Theresa says and pokes Shane in the side before he can bugger about with the low-hanging microphone again.

Will looks a bit desperate and tries another couple. Unfortunately he turns his attention on Lea and Pete, much to Elise's horror.

'Over to Lea and Pete then,' Will says, forcing a low, almost inaudible squeak from his co-host. 'Who do you think is doing well in the competition so far?'

'Dunno, mate,' Pete answers. 'We ain't met none of them much. Like that bird said, we're all still fat bastards, ain't we?'

'I lost an ounce,' Lea adds. 'Though our scales is shit ones from Asda, so they don't work right.'

Excellent.

At least two potential fines for swearing are now heading Stream FM's way from the regulators.

Will and Elise both look like a live electrical current has somehow been connected to their headphones. There's a brief pause while they come to terms with such flagrant use of bad language on air.

This interview is going absolutely *brilliantly* so far.

Then the inevitable happens.

Elise, looking for a way to salvage this situation, turns her gaze on me. I lock eyes with her and shake my head vigorously. I know what's about to happen. 'Don't you bloody dare,' I whisper under my breath.

'Over to Greg and Zoe now,' Elise says, an apologetic look on her face. 'Who do you guys think is doing the best so far?'

Greg looks at my red face and decides to jump in before I explode. 'I think Frankie's lost some weight,' he says.

'Aww, thank you honey!' the Jamaican lady replies with a smile.

'My pleasure,' my husband replies with a smile.

'Thanks, Greg. And over to Zoe,' Elise continues. 'We really enjoyed your story last week about the troubles you had in Marks & Spencer. Any other anecdotes you'd like to share? Maybe about any diets you've tried so far?' The look of desperation and pleading in Elise's eyes is unmistakable. If I don't provide her with some sort of worthwhile conversation, this entire segment will only be remembered for its use of bad language and boring responses from a bunch of uncomfortable fat people.

I know what Elise is after.

She wants me to talk about the cabbage soup diet.

For the past week I've been giving it a go, and made the stupid mistake of telling her about it on the phone.

I've been backed into a corner. I can either leave my friend swinging in the wind, or once again regale the world with a tale of my weight loss misfortune.

Sigh.

Sometimes being nice to your friends is a real pain in the arse.

The version of the story I'm about to tell the Stream FM listeners will be short and simple, and will leave out a majority of the gory details. But for the sake of accuracy—and because I have to fill the rest of this diary entry with something—I'm now going to recount the horror of my experience with the cabbage soup diet here in its entirety.

Now in my defence, I've never been one for going on a diet. I've simply never felt the need until the last few years. I've done little to no research into what kinds of diets exist—and whether they actually do you any good or not.

So hopefully I can be forgiven for thinking that the cabbage soup diet *sounded* like a good idea.

I'd Googled 'lose weight fast' and it came up as one of the first suggestions.

It sounded absolutely marvellous on paper—and extremely easy to plan for. Simply eat as much cabbage soup as you like, alongside a variety of other healthy meals, and drink only water and unsweetened fruit juice.

All I'd have to do is follow the regime of eating cabbage soup and other healthy food for a week, and *ten pounds* would come off my weight!

Ten frickin' pounds, people!

'If it's that easy, we'll win this competition for sure,' I said to Greg after having read the details out to him from the computer screen.

'If it's that easy, everyone would be doing it,' he replied cynically.

I ignored him.

If the cabbage soup diet didn't work, then why were there so many websites on the internet dedicated to it? It must be a good diet . . . otherwise no one would be talking about it, would they?

Would they?

With a hale and hopeful heart I set about on the cabbage soup diet on a Monday morning, looking forward to being three-quarters of a stone lighter by the following Sunday.

Day one is okay.

It's absolutely *fine*.

By the time nine o'clock in the evening rolls around I feel like I could eat a chair leg, but other than that, I feel good about myself and the diet.

During the day I've had three bowls of cabbage soup, drunk about five litres of pineapple juice, and eaten about twelve of my five a day in fruit. I've stuck to the diet plan religiously, and by the time I go to bed I really feel like I've accomplished something.

Okay, I need to get up to pee seven times during the night, but it's all going to be worth it in the end!

Day two allows me more cabbage soup (obviously) as well as all the vegetables I can eat—and some carbs in the form of one jacket potato with a little butter.

I skip breakfast, because the last thing I want to eat at seven in the morning is broccoli and cabbage.

By the time lunch arrives I'm so ravenous that I eat my portion of cabbage soup at work in three nanoseconds flat, washing it down with apple juice and a pint of water.

The jacket potato doesn't stand a fucking chance at tea time. I manage to make it through a bowl of cabbage soup as well.

I'm starting to dislike cabbage soup a great deal. Only forty-eight hours have past, but it feels I've already eaten more of the stuff than the population of war-torn Leningrad.

I only have to pee five times during the night, which I choose to see as a positive thing.

Day three dawns with me blowing the covers off the bed, thanks to the kind of flatulence that really shouldn't exist outside a badly drawn comic strip.

The buggers don't tell you this part on the websites, do they? There's not a mention of how all that cabbage makes you gassier than a hot air balloon.

Today I can eat only cabbage soup, along with fruit and vegetables, excluding potatoes and bananas. Oh joy.

I eat a tin of pineapple chunks for breakfast, half a bowl of cabbage soup for lunch, and a pile of steamed vegetables for dinner.

I hate vegetables.

Limp green little packets of blandness, with all the excitement of an 'Antiques Roadshow' marathon.

What I wouldn't give for some *meat*.

What I wouldn't give never to look a cabbage in the face again.

Unfortunately, I have already lost four pounds, so the diet is actually working—which means I'll have to stick to it.

Day four allows me the pleasure of eating up to eight bananas.

I've consumed all of these by the time lunch rolls around.

I've also farted so much in the office, it's a wonder no one's called the Health & Safety Executive to come down and take readings.

I have fucking cabbage fucking soup for lunch.

By three o'clock I'm feeling decidedly light-headed.

By six o'clock I feel like throwing up as I smell the cabbage soup heating in the microwave.

I force it down my gullet with all the pleasure of eating a bowl of fresh sick.

I fart my way to bed with arms and legs that feel like lead weights, and a tension headache forming across one eye.

How I've longed for day five to roll around. It means I get to eat some meat! Ten ounces of beef, along with up to six tomatoes.

Do you know how big a ten-ounce portion of beef is?

Not bloody much.

Not when you've had no meat for a week.

Still, I spend the entire day fantasising over the burger I'm allowed to eat for tea. And I'm going to fry the bastard thing as well. I don't care what anyone says.

The cabbage soup I have for lunch is so laced with cayenne pepper to give it some flavour (any flavour) that it makes my mouth burn for an hour afterwards.

The people at work now have to make a decision. Do they avoid my backside to keep away from the constant stream of flatulence erupting from it? Or do they avoid my frontside to dodge the nuclear bad breath emanating from my mouth?

The aroma of frying beef that evening is the best thing I've ever smelled in the world, ever. I eat the burger as slowly as possible, luxuriating in every bite, along with the six fried tomatoes I've put with it.

By the time I go to bed I've actually stopped farting, and I drop off with a smile on my face knowing that there's only two days of this hell left.

I've also dropped eight pounds!

Day six is Saturday and I don't have to go to work. This is just as well as I'm barely able to stand upright for most of the day. I feel weaker than a day-old kitten, and spend the entire morning sitting on the couch staring at the ceiling, lost in a daydream where I'm mercilessly torturing a cabbage farmer. His imaginary screams for mercy give me no end of pleasure.

I still have to eat his produce at lunchtime though.

I can't begin to describe my loathing for cabbage at this point. It's a stupid green plant that tastes of vomit, looks like a diseased brain, and smells like a sewage works. It doesn't matter what seasoning you put with it to make it taste better, it's still a bland, pointless vegetable that leaves you feeling dreadful.

In the afternoon I attempt to go out for a walk with Greg in the nearby woods. This goes relatively well until we reach a gentle incline. I barely make it halfway up before having to stop and go back to the car for a rest.

I feel like an eighty-five-year-old woman. I may have lost nine pounds at this point, but I've also aged fifty years—a rather extreme trade-off that I'm not happy with in the slightest.

Still, only one more day to go of this nightmare and then I can have Kentucky Fried Chicken.

Day seven, and I force Greg out of bed by creating a Dutch oven in the bedroom the likes of which no human being should ever be made to suffer. My poor bottom has been forced to endure so much activity this week I'm amazed it hasn't dropped off due to exhaustion.

Today I'm allowed eat some brown rice with my cabbage. Oh *whoop-de-do.*

Nobody likes brown rice. It's only ever eaten by people on diets and hippies who are too stoned to know any better.

Today I try sugar on top of the cabbage soup because, frankly, why the fuck not? Unbelievably, it doesn't taste any worse than usual. It's evident that my taste buds have shut down. To test this, I chew on a piece of kitchen roll. It tastes of cabbage soup.

My brain is so starved of proper nutrients that I forget my husband's name for two whole minutes. I'm convinced his name is Grant until he manages to convince me otherwise, using simple hand gestures and a flip chart.

At seven o'clock, after my last bowl of cabbage soup (of which I manage two spoonfuls) I fart my way up the stairs and weigh myself.

I have indeed lost ten pounds.

Sadly, I've also lost the feeling in my toes, the ability to taste food, my long-term memory, and all hope of seeing the sun again.

By Monday morning I've come to the stunning conclusion that the cabbage soup diet is a load of horseshit.

Most of my weight loss appears to have been in water, as I pile three pounds back on by the end of the day—which should be impossible, unless you eat the entire cream cake selection in your nearest branch of Asda.

So to sum up, if you want to give your colon a workout, enjoy feeling dizzy, and want to develop a pathological hatred of vegetables belonging to the Brassica family, then go right ahead and try the cabbage soup diet. If, on the other hand, you want to actually lose some bloody weight, try something different.

I give a highly truncated account of my week-long experiment to Elise and the radio listeners.

'Well, that does sound like something I'd have to think long and hard about having a go at! It might not be a diet for everyone!' Will says in that noncommittal, politically correct way that commercial radio DJs always adopt about *any* subject, for fear of offending the wrong person and harming advertising revenues.

'No it doesn't!' Elise agrees politely, in an equally irritating and bland manner. I've heard the girl call at least two people wankers so far this week in private, but you wouldn't think that anything so negative could possibly come from the mouth of that sweet, attractive blonde sitting across the way from me, her headphones cocked adorably to one side.

It's enough to make you sick.

'Is there anything else you'd like to say about the effects of being a larger lady Zoe?' Elise then asks me.

Hang on. I've done my bit. Why don't you ask somebody else this?

What angle is she going for here?

'How do you mean?' I respond, suspicious.

'Well, being large must have quite a negative impact on your life, yes?'

'How do you figure?'

'As a woman, I mean?'

Oh, you little bitch.

Now I know what she's getting at.

Tears of embarrassment and rage prick my eyes as I realise what game my supposed best friend is playing. I've been manipulated into joining this competition, just so she always has someone to come to on air for the juicy material.

And this is the *juiciest*.

Greg and I have been trying for a baby on and off for *years* now, with no success.

In the natural course of a relationship like ours, a baby should have appeared on the scene a long time ago. That's how it works, isn't it? You meet someone, you fall in love, you get married, you buy a house, you have a baby.

Greg and I have successfully negotiated the first four, but the bouncing bundle of joy has eluded us. I'd like to say it's something I don't worry about constantly, but I'd be lying through my teeth.

Whenever I think about our lack of children I flash back to a conversation we had in the early years of our relationship. Greg had taken me to Thorpe Park as a birthday treat. I would have preferred a day in a spa, but he'd already booked the trip to the theme park before I had a chance to argue, so I had to go along with it.

It actually turned out to be a lot of fun. We'd only been together for a year and we were still in the kind of happy, honeymoon period that usually doesn't end until one of you farts audibly in front of the other. In those salad days, it didn't matter where we were; it just mattered that we were together. Even if this did mean following my boyfriend onto a series of increasingly horrific roller coasters that did my stomach and my hairdo no good at all.

Speaking of stomachs, neither of us had one, so we had no problems getting into the seats on the hair-raising rides dotted across the park.

Towards the end of the day we sat down on a conveniently located bench in order to rest our weary legs. The bench was right by one of the concession stands, which was surrounded by a horde of buzzing children intent on getting as many sweets out of their parents as possible.

Greg wrinkled his nose and pointed over to them. 'Urgh. Can you imagine having to trawl around this place with one of those biting at your ankles all day?' he said.

'What? A kid, you mean?'

'Yeah.'

I looked across at one boy of about three, holding up a bright green lolly to his mother with a beatific grin on his face. 'Oh, I don't know. I think it would be kind of fun.'

Greg looked a bit surprised. 'Really?'

'Yeah. Why not? Kids are great. Especially cute ones like that boy with the lolly.'

Then it hits me . . .

Greg and I have never had 'that' talk. The one about having kids. Unbelievably, after a year, it's never come up before. We'd talked about ex-partners, hopes for the future in our jobs, what kind of house we want to live in, and where we want to go on holiday—but had never broached the topic of children.

'Um, do you want to have kids one day?' Greg asks tentatively.

My heart rate rockets. This is one of those conversations that can make or break a fledgling relationship. If Greg is dead set against children we could have a major problem. 'Yeah,' I tell him quietly. 'I would like them one day. You?'

He scratches his nose and looks away from me, towards where the little boy is now crying due to the fact he's dropped the luminous lolly. 'I've never really thought about it,' he says.

'Oh.' I pick at a thread coming out of the seam of my jeans.

Greg turns back to me. 'But you know what? If I ever did, I'd want them with you.'

'Would you?'

'Yeah. I reckon our kids would be gorgeous.'

Just like his smile.

'And smart!' I point out. 'They'd be really clever.'

He grins. 'And if it was a boy . . . he'd be hung like a donkey.'

'Of course!' I laugh and throw my arms around him.

Greg kisses me with a passion that makes me wish we were already on our way home. At that moment I feel a swell of contentment that warms my soul. I love this man more than words can say, and one day (when I'm past the age of thirty, obviously) I will happily bear his child.

At least that was the plan . . .

Then life got in the way. As did about a million calories.

By the time we started trying to get pregnant—several years after our theme park chat—I was overweight, unhealthy, and highly unlikely to conceive.

No-one ever, *ever* plans to get fat.

I am constantly irritated by people who think that fat folk are just lazy slobs who have let themselves get into the state they're in via their own shortcomings.

It isn't like one second you're thin . . . and then you're fat. It happens over months and years.

It happens because *life gets in the way*. Because at some point, unless you're blessed with a bank balance that ends in a lot of zeros, you stop looking at yourself in the mirror because you're too damn busy looking at the bills.

If you don't get fat, then maybe you smoke too much, or drink too much, or hit your kids, or gamble—or any one of a thousand other bad habits that human beings fall into when they're stressed to high heaven—thanks to the vagaries of day-to-day existence.

I'm not trying to make excuses for the fact I put on over five stone between the ages of eighteen and thirty-seven. All I'm trying to say is that *I didn't know it was happening until it was too late*. When I did eventually realise I didn't have the time or energy to do anything about it. There never was a baby past the age of thirty. Never was a small child to cart around the sweet shops of Thorpe Park on a sunny afternoon.

Instead all the sweets went in *my* mouth.

And now I'm thirty-seven and the likelihood I'll ever have a baby is fast diminishing. It would be even if I wasn't grossly overweight.

And who have I confided my fears, doubts, and worries about never getting pregnant to?

Elise Bailey.

'What are you asking me, Elise?' I say to her in the coldest voice possible.

Her face blanches. She knows what's going on in my head right now. I can see indecision cross her face.

Does she let me off the hook and lose the strong material? Or does she soldier on and keep pressing me?

'I'm just wondering if being so large has affected your life as a woman.' She gulps almost audibly. 'Some reports indicate it's harder to get pregnant when you're overweight. Have you encountered that issue by any chance?'

Unbelievable.

A friendship potentially thrown out of the window for the sake of entertaining the listeners.

'I suppose I have,' I say flatly. I can feel my face flushing redder and redder. 'I haven't been able to get pregnant.'

'Because you're overweight?'

That's what the doctors have been telling me for a long time, Elise. You know that, you utter cow.

'Yes. That's why.'

I fold my arms across my chest and stare down my ex-best friend through the thick studio glass, daring her to carry on this line of questioning. I'm *this close* to calling Elise some very unpleasant names, which would no doubt force the station to make an on-air apology for explicit language.

Elise has the good sense to realise this. 'Well, thanks for that Zoe. Hopefully this competition may help you with that problem over the coming months.'

'And that's about all we've got time for on Fat Chance today,' Will interjects, clearly sensing the need to swiftly wrap things up.

'You okay, sweetheart?' Greg says in a half-whisper, knowing full well what the answer will be.

'I want to go home. *Now*,' I reply, pushing my way past the other couples and out through the door to the sound booth.

With Greg in tow, I barge my way past Lottie and the rest of the production minions.

'Er, we need you to stay for the post-show briefing! There's a schedule for the next few weeks we need to give you!' Lottie shouts after us.

'Post the fucking thing!' I shout back over my shoulder.

I have no intention of sticking around to look at a room of sympathetic faces for the next half an hour, so I storm through the building with Greg in tow. Within seconds we're emerging into the morning sunlight through the main doors.

'Um, baby, where are you going?' Greg asks me.

'Home!'

'But this is where you work?'

Shit.

He's right.

I can't even leave this bloody radio station, as I now have to walk round to the back of the building and do a day's work.

No doubt everyone will have heard Elise's little question and answer session. The sympathetic faces will follow me around for the entire day.

I look up at the lovely spring sun and make a decision. 'I'm taking the day off,' I tell him with my hands on my hips. 'I'll blame it on stress.'

'Stress?'

'Yes Greg! *Stress*! Telling thousands of people on their morning fucking commute that I'm barren is *stressful*!'

'Fair enough. I'll get the car,' he replies as quickly as possible, and scuttles off to the car park, leaving me to seethe on my own for a moment.

Elise comes rushing out from the building, a combined look of guilt and fear on her face. 'I'm sorry, chick!'

'Why did you do that?' I shout at her.

'I'm sorry! The segment was going badly and I needed something to spice it up.'

'And my inability to have children was spicy enough, was it, you bitch?'

'Please Zoe, I'm so sorry. I shouldn't have done it.'

'No, you bloody shouldn't!'

'Let me make it up to you.'

'How are you going to do that?' I snap my fingers. 'I know, how about we go back on air now and we tell everyone about that drunken fuck you had with Will's supposedly gay roommate two years ago?'

Elise's head whips round to see if anyone caught that. 'God, Zoe, keep your voice down,' she whisper-shouts.

'Oh! Oh! You'd like me to keep my voice down, would you? I guess that means you don't want me to march back in there and tell all your listeners about how he tried to stick it in your arsehole, then?'

I shouldn't be, but I'm taking huge pleasure in the way Elise is cowering like a spanked puppy. 'Please Zoe, shut up!'

I take a deep breath. 'Not so much fun when it's your dirty laundry being aired in public, is it?'

Greg has pulled up in the car and is watching developments with a wince on his face.

Elise looks at me with doe eyes. 'Are you going to stay in the competition?'

The word 'no' forms on my lips, but then I swallow it down. Much as I'd like to have nothing more to do with Elise and this silly competition right now, I know that if I quit I'll regret it for the rest of my life. If I have to put up with a bit of embarrassment in order to lose weight, then so be it. I guess I'd just prefer to have a flaming red face thanks to severe public humiliation, rather than a flaming red face thanks to a severe heart attack.

I sigh. 'I've started it, so I'll finish it.' I stab a finger at Elise. 'But if you ever do anything like that again, I *will* let everyone know how painful it was for you to sit down for a week.'

Feeling a bit better about myself, I climb into the car.

'See you tomorrow?' Elise asks from the kerbside.

My eyes narrow. 'Drive,' I order my husband, who doesn't need telling twice.

So now I have to deal with the fact that my inability to get pregnant is in the public domain.

Whether I like it or not, it will become the defining aspect of my character to everyone who listens to the show. That's just how these things work.

Zoe Milton is now 'the one who can't have a baby.'

Elise may have deeply embarrassed me live on air today, but at least I know she won't be doing it again.

The aborted anal sex with a confused gay man isn't the only anecdote I've got squirreled away in my brain about Elise Bailey.

The next time she decides to dredge up my unwashed linen in public, I'll counter by telling everyone in earshot about how she suffers from occasional vaginal discharge.

That should do it.

GREG'S WEIGHT LOSS DIARY
Sunday, April 20th
18 stone, 13 pounds (1 stone, 3 pounds lost)

Oh God.

Oh dear sweet God in Heaven.

Every part of my body aches.

Even my eyeballs.

And hair.

Merely sitting in this chair and writing is a monumental effort. Each hand movement across the keyboard is agony, and every look up at the monitor sends a fresh wave of pain down my back.

If I close my eyes and concentrate very hard, I think there's an area just above my left elbow that isn't suffering. Mind you, this could be caused by the breakdown of my nervous system, following what can only be described as a week spent in the company of Lucifer.

Getting a personal trainer sounded like a good idea.

Even if I could only afford a week's worth, I could at least take a note of the exercise plan the trainer would have me on for seven days . . . and just repeat until thin.

'That's a great idea,' Zoe says to me over another one of her bowls of snot soup. I may not be all that keen on strenuous exercise, but given the choice between that and eating that green, foul-smelling shit, I'll take the press-ups any day.

'I'll go on Google and see if there are any local trainers in the area,' I tell her and turn away before I start to gag.

It turns out there are three personal fitness trainers close to home and affordable enough for my wallet. I try Darren Bouchard first, as he's the closest and has been a trainer for eight years.

Sadly, Darren (who sounds a wee bit too effeminate over the phone to be a personal trainer anyway) is so popular that he's booked up until the middle of summer. I give him my email for his mailing list and put the phone down.

Next up is Mike McPartlin. Mike is an ex-Olympic coach and sounds ideal.

He also speaks in a Scottish accent more impenetrable than the Amazon basin. Mike would love to train me, but he's currently suffering from a bad Achilles tendon injury and won't be back to fighting fit for at least another two months.

This leaves my third and final choice—and it's the worst of the three.

Alice Pithering.

Yep, that's right, her name is Alice Pithering.

According to the photos on her website, Alice is all of five foot two, as skinny as a rake, and blessed with a set of the bulgiest eyeballs I've ever seen in my life.

She's apparently ex-Army.

Salvation Army possibly, judging by her diminutive stature.

Her thin, reedy voice over the phone doesn't do much to dispel the impression that Alice is as fragile as a Ming vase.

'Yes, I have free slots coming up in the next couple of weeks, Greg,' she tells me. I'm not surprised in the slightest. It's a wonder this woman gets any work at all.

'That's great.'

I'm lying. It's not.

I was hoping she'd be booked up solid so I could just put the phone down and forget the entire thing.

'Are you sure you want the week-long intensive course?' she asks. 'It is quite difficult, and if you're not used to exercise it might be a better idea to go with something a bit less strenuous.'

Strenuous? I used to play rugby four times a month and train for it five days a week. I hardly think this little woman can tax me too much, even if it has been a little while since I was at my optimum.

My self-delusion at this point is so rock-solid you could climb up it and plant a flag. The last time I played rugby four times a week was actually a *decade* ago. My ego has conveniently forgotten about the intervening years, all the late-night kebabs and pints of beer, and complete lack of exercise, in an effort to sound like I'm capable of coping with bulgy-eyed Miss Pithering and her fitness regime.

'No, the week-long course will be fine,' I reply confidently— and stupidly.

'Okay then. We'll start Sunday if you like, in the city park, and we'll do two hours every day until Saturday.'

'That sounds perfect.'

With the course arranged I put the phone down on the reedy-voiced Alice and turn to my wife. 'All sorted,' I tell her. 'Should be a better way to lose a few pounds than eating that slop,' I add, unable to keep an unpleasant smug tone out of my voice.

Zoe arches one eyebrow. 'We'll see, dear. We'll just see.'

I don't like the way she peers at me over the bowl of snot. It's disconcerting. 'What do you mean by that?'

'I think you're underestimating how hard it's going to be.'

I wave a hand. 'Nah. It'll be okay. I'm used to aching a bit from exercise.'

'Okay, honey. I'm sure you know what you're doing,' she replies in that irritating sing-song way people adopt when they're obviously humouring you.

'The timing is good as well,' I point out. 'I'll get her to do our last session first thing Saturday morning, and I can go straight from training to the radio station for the weigh-in.'

The following Saturday marks the first of many regular weigh-in sessions live on air at Stream FM. Each couple will be weighed, and the twosome with the highest percentage of fat loss since the start of the competition will be rewarded with a bottle of low-calorie champagne (which looks like horse piss as far as I can tell) and two tickets to the fitness expo happening at Earl's Court next month.

A combination of Zoe's bizarre cabbage diet and my week-long intensive training should give us a good crack at winning, even if I don't want to drink horse piss and can think of nothing worse than attending a fitness expo in London.

So Sunday morning I walk over to the park in the spring sunshine, ready to see what Alice Pithering has in store for me.

To decide on an appropriate regime, she'd already asked me to email her my vital statistics, exercise and medical history, and what I hoped to achieve from our week-long session. She also had me pay her the three hundred quid for the course up front, which I was a bit dubious about doing, but that was the way she wanted it so I had no choice.

I'm certainly wearing the right clothes for someone about to embark on a glorious programme of uplifting exercise.

Brand-new running shoes adorn my feet, and my expensive Nike tracksuit has been brought out of mothballs. Well, the bottom half, anyway. I tried to squeeze the zip-up top on as well, but my tits just weren't having any of it. I've instead had to settle for my England rugby jersey, which still looks pretty sporty when you get right down to it.

Alice Pithering is waiting for me by the bench at the top of the hill in the middle of the park. She's decked out much as you'd expect for a personal trainer—in black spandex shorts and a purple spandex shirt. I note that the woman is as flat-chested as a twelve-year-old. I know I shouldn't be looking at such things in these circumstances, but spandex is a material designed to highlight every curve and bulge—or lack thereof.

If I tried to wear it I'd look like a badly made sausage.

'Good morning, Greg!' Alice says to me as I saunter up the hill to meet her.

'Morning,' I reply and stifle a yawn.

'Looks like we could do with waking you up a bit!' she exclaims and her eyes protrude even further.

They really are quite disconcerting. I want to cup my hands under her face to catch them every time she wobbles her head.

'Shall we start with some warm-up exercises?'

'Why not?' I tell her and smile as the sun bathes us both in its spring warmth.

Alice starts me off with some stretches to get the blood flowing. This all seems fine and I can feel a light sweat beginning to surface. By the time ten minutes have passed I feel ever so slightly out of breath, but otherwise content.

'Right, then!' Alice claps her hands together. 'I thought we'd begin with a jog round the park. How does that sound?'

'Great.'

'Excellent! I'll increase the pace as we go, so just try to keep up with me.'

And with that she's gone, bouncing along the path with her skinny heels kicking up gravel as she goes.

I set off in pursuit, and find it quite easy to keep up with her for the first three hundred yards or so. I'm comfortable, breathing evenly, and feeling good about myself.

Then Alice starts to jog a bit faster. I adjust my speed to compensate.

For another fifty yards I'm alright, but then my lungs start to protest.

As do my feet.

And my thighs.

And my ankles.

Have you ever owned a car for more than a few years? Perhaps quite an old one?

You know how they can run and run for ages with no problems, but once one thing goes wrong, *everything* starts to fall apart on the bugger?

My body is now going through much the same process, only in a mere matter of minutes.

'Just going to go a bit faster now, Greg,' Alice says . . . and bolts off like a scalded cat.

The woman obviously has no comprehension of the term 'gentle increment.' One minute she's jogging along next to me; the next she's doing her best impression of Usain Bolt with a firework up his arse.

In my defence I try my hardest to match her speed, for about twenty feet. Then my body essentially tells me to go fuck myself in no uncertain terms.

It does this by tangling my legs together.

This has never happened to me before.

In all my years on this planet I've always been able to work my legs in a proper, co-ordinated fashion. Not once have my lower limbs ever decided to clash at the knees and send me sprawling onto the ground, no matter how drunk/high/exhausted/all of the above I happen to have been at the time.

Today, though, it's like they have magnets strapped to them.

As Alice rockets away from me and I try my best to catch up, I feel my left ankle clip the right painfully. This makes me wince and start to stumble. My forward momentum keeps me upright just long enough for my knees to whack into one another and for my legs to go completely out from under me.

'Aliiiiice!' I cry forlornly with one hand outstretched as gravity does its job, sending me sprawling onto the gravel path.

Falling onto gravel while running in a park is more painful than falling off a chair at a barbecue. The embarrassment factor is less, though, given there aren't so many spectators around to witness it.

I haul myself into a sitting position and grab one scraped knee as Alice trots back to me.

I look up at her face, expecting her to commiserate with my misfortune. A few words of comfort from that reedy little voice will go down very well at this point.

'What are you doing?' she says in a perfunctory manner and puts her hands on her hips.

'I fell over,' I tell her and rub my knee by way of further explanation.

'What do you want, a medal?'

'I'm sorry?'

This is most unexpected. I would have thought old Bulgy-Eyes would have been full of sympathy, judging from her demeanour so far, but not so, it appears.

'I said, what do you want? A fucking medal?'

I look up at her, not quite knowing how to react.

She holds out an arm. 'Come on, Greg. Get up. We've still got the rest of the park to run round yet before we get going properly.'

She expects me to *carry on*?

'I don't think I can,' I say. 'I've hurt myself.'

'You scraped your knee, Greg. Just get up and shake it off.'

'It hurts.'

'Are you a poof?'

'Excuse me?'

'You heard. Are you a poof?'

'Er . . . no?'

'Well, get up and stop acting like one, then.' She shakes her hand at me. I take it, still somewhat shell-shocked by her aggressive use of such a politically incorrect term.

Alice's grip is like steel.

She hauls me to my feet with seemingly no effort whatsoever.

'Ready then?' she says.

'I suppose so,' I reply, ever so slightly afraid of what she might do if I say I'm not.

'Good! Let's go.'

Alice takes off again and I follow as best I can, trying to ignore my throbbing knee and aching joints.

I now find myself in something of a dilemma.

On the one hand I would like nothing more than to stop this charade and limp home for a cup of coffee and a bun. On the other hand, I have paid several hundred pounds up front for this training, and have the small matter of my gentleman's ego to consider.

It really isn't nice to be called a poof. Especially when it comes from a tiny blonde girl with bulgy eyes. I now have the desire to prove to Alice that I am not, in fact, a poof. Nor am I a fairy, a big girl's blouse, or a right wuss.

So for the next ten minutes of my life I stare at her narrow spandex-clad arse as I stumble my way around the rest of the park, huffing and puffing so loudly that the three little pigs would take cover in the nearest nuclear bunker if they were in earshot.

By the time we've done a complete circuit and ended up back at the bench on the hill I am absolutely broken. But I've also proven that I am not a poof, wuss, fairy, or blouse.

I collapse onto the grass and look up at the cloudless blue sky. I also try to keep the strange high-pitched whine out of my voice every time I breathe out.

'Right then!' Alice bellows at me. 'That was a good warm-up. Now we can get on with the exercise program.'

I laugh hoarsely. 'That's funny Alice. Very funny.'

She looks perplexed. 'What's funny?'

'The joke you just said about doing more exercise today.'

'I'm not joking.' The hands have gone back on the hips. The tone of voice has darkened. The bulgy eyes have become exponentially more bulginous.

I sit up and pull myself onto the bench. 'You . . . you can't be serious? I can't do any more today.'

Now Alice crosses her arms. 'Look Greg. You can have this two ways. You can either work with me, lose weight, and win that competition . . . or you can cry and squinny like a big fat baby and not win. The choice is yours.'

Great. She's moved on from comparing me to the homosexual members of our community and is now accusing me of being a squalling newborn. This is much worse.

'But I really don't think I can do any more,' I squinny.

'Of course you can. You're just not used to pushing yourself. It's what you're going to have to do if you want to shift all that whale blubber.'

Gays, babies, whales. Check. We've just about covered all the obvious comparison points now, other than maybe pigs.

'You really think I can do it?'

'Yes, of course I do. But only if you let me do my job and moti-vate you properly. It's the only way we get things done in the Army.'

Unbelievably, I find myself coming to my shaky feet and looking Alice square in the bulgy eyes. 'Okay, let's do it,' I tell her.

'You're sure?'

'Yeah!' I try to remember all those war films I'd seen. 'Er . . . sir, *yes sir!*'

Alice claps her hands together. 'Excellent!' She smiles.

I smile too.

The smile drops off her face.

I'm suddenly terrified.

'Drop and do twenty push-ups right now,' she orders in a low, rather menacing tone.

'What?'

'Are you fucking deaf, you big pig? I said drop and do twenty push-ups, you loathsome sack of shit!' Alice imperiously points one finger at the ground in front of her.

'Okay,' I reply in a thin, reedy voice.

'What did you say, dickhead?'

'I said okay?'

'Say it like you mean it, Milton!'

'OKAY!'

'GOOD! GET DOWN ON YOUR KNEES, BOY!'

I do as I'm told, prostrating myself in front of this lunatic with her bulbous eyes.

'And ONE!' she screeches, the sound of her high-pitched bark echoing across the park like a sonic boom. Such is the power of her voice my limbs immediately respond long before my brain has chance to tell them what to do. I've done one press-up before I'm fully aware of what's going on.

'And TWO!' Alice shouts.

A couple of children fall off the swings over in the play area.

'And THREE!'

Two dozen car alarms go off in the car park to our left.

'And FOUR!'

Several birds fall from the sky twitching.

'And FIVE!'

I feel my bladder loosen—though I can't be sure if this is down to it resonating with Alice's commands, or just because my vital organs are starting to malfunction due to extreme fatigue.

'And SIX! . . . I said SIX! . . . Greg?! Greg?! I said SIX!'

'I fucking heard you the first time!' I wail. 'I'm trying!'

'Try harder! And SIX!'

'My arms don't work any more!'

'Bollocks! And SIX!'

'Stop screaming "six"! I feel like I'm watching the Hulk play cricket!'

'I'll stop screaming "six" when you give me another press-up!' Alice takes in a deep breath. 'And SIX!'

Somehow, my trembling arms manage to push me back up again. I maintain the position for a good three seconds before all the air goes out of me and I collapse.

'And SEVEN!'

'Oh, do fuck off,' I say with a mouthful of grass.

The hands go back on the hips and the eyes bulge at their very bulgiest. 'That's it, is it? Six press-ups?'

'It would appear so, yes.'

'I thought you used to play rugby.'

'I used to fit into a pair of size thirty-two jeans as well.'

Alice gives me a look of utter disgust. 'I got the impression from your email that you'd be fitter than this.'

'I may not have realised the depths of my unhealthiness.'

'I should say so.' She sits on the bench. 'Let's take a five-minute break and see where we're at after that.'

'That sounds like heaven.'

I slowly edge myself up once more onto the bench and hang my head.

I knew I was pretty unfit, but this is frankly ridiculous. I had no idea things had got this bad over the past few years.

It's amazing how your mind can play tricks on you . . . and convince you of things that are patently false. These twenty minutes of hell have well and truly opened my eyes to the size of the task ahead of me.

I say as much to Alice.

'You're not alone. The number of clients I have who come to me thinking they're in better shape than they are would astound you. That's why I get the money up front these days. I've been stung too many times.'

'Fair enough.'

She smiles at me. 'I tell you what, though. If you just want to pay me for what little we've done today, we'll call it quits on the rest of the week. I don't want to put you through more than you're capable of doing.'

This sounds like a fantastic idea. My aching bones and muscles agree wholeheartedly.

But where would it leave me? How the hell am I supposed to help Zoe win the fifty grand if I give up so quickly?

I'll never get another blow job for as long as I live!

'No. I don't want to quit.' I give Alice a sheepish look. 'But maybe we could take it a bit easier?' My head swims. 'And stop for today at least?'

'Sure. No problem, Greg.' Alice is genuinely pleased that I haven't taken her up on the offer. I'm sure this is mainly due to the fact that she gets to keep my money, but I bet it can get quite disheartening when people keep quitting on you all the time. I've probably surprised her a bit.

'Shall we meet here tomorrow when I get out of work at half five?' I ask her.

Alice grins and whacks me on the knee. This hurts more than I care to show. 'Excellent! I'll look forward to it.' Her expression of delight falls away at the speed of light in a way that I'm already becoming familiar with. 'But for now you can get off your arse and do some warm-down exercises, you lazy bastard.'

It's like I'm being trained by someone suffering from severe bipolar disorder.

Still, I feel quite proud of myself for sticking with it, and as I walk home (alright, limp home) a short time later I can't help thinking what a brave little soldier I am.

Did I say brave little soldier? What I mean is *colossal fucking idiot.*

I could have just quit. Could have gone home that day and considered easier, less painful ways to lose weight.

But *oh no*, I had to take the macho route, didn't I?

Had to *prove myself* to Alice.

I feel like I've had every single muscle in my body removed via painful surgery and replaced with porridge.

Alice Pithering's idea of 'taking it a bit easier' is obviously very different from mine.

I was expecting to join her in the park the next day after work to take part in some gentle calisthenics, with maybe a bit of light jogging thrown in for good measure.

If anything, though, it's worse than Sunday.

We did the bloody circuit of the park again, this time followed by squat thrusts, star jumps, and various other hideous aerobic activities that can surely only be enjoyed by people who go in for extreme sadomasochism at the weekends.

Alice is obviously a bloody good trainer though, as she always manages to keep the routine at a level that never gets too difficult and causes me to stop. It's always just the right side of debilitating.

Sadly, it's not the right side of humiliating, distressing, and agonising.

This hideous process is inflicted on my poor wobbly body all week long. My life consists of two daily hours of hell, and twenty-two hours trying to recover from it. I can barely concentrate on anything at work thanks to the constant state of agony I'm in, and Zoe has problems getting more than one or two sentences out of me before I slope off to bed and sleep like the recently deceased.

Miss Pithering's years in the armed forces are readily apparent thanks to the litany of foul-mouthed abuse I'm subjected to during the week-long course. It acts as a charming accompaniment to the physical torment I'm being put through.

It's one thing to struggle to do your twentieth star jump; it's quite another to have a small bulgy-eyed woman questioning your parentage while you're doing it.

I'm sure I've seen at least three people hurry by us sketching the sign of the cross and speed-dialling 999.

'Did your mother have any children that lived?' Alice screams at me as I struggle to finish my star jump by leaping a scant two inches into the air.

'I don't know! Did yours have any that weren't pure evil?' I retort breathlessly.

'Don't be a smart-arse, you chubby twonk!'

This is another disconcerting aspect of Alice's 'motivational' style of command. She has a never-ending supply of ways to describe me through the medium of my body fat.

In the past few days I've been lard-arse, jelly-tits, jiggle-puffs, porks-a-lot, the gutmeister, flabbington, Jabba, wide-load, Nelly the Elephant—and most bizarrely, Captain Love Handles.

I thought she'd run out of insults mid-week but by first thing Saturday morning she's still going strong.

'Come on Mr Plump! Get those legs up!'

Mr Plump does indeed try his hardest to get those legs up, but he's now had a week of this constant torture and while the mind may still be willing, the body has finally decided it's had quite enough of this shit for one lifetime. It wants to do nothing more than lie in a dark room and force tears of shame from my eyes until sweet unconsciousness overtakes me.

There was a time in the dim and distant past when this kind of regular exercise was something I enjoyed—but I was young, healthy, and blessed with a brain completely devoid of rational thought.

The darkened room may beckon me, but I still have a weigh-in to do over at Stream FM this morning. The loving, healing embrace of sleep is a good sixteen hours away at least.

'Come on you horrible little toad! Another two minutes!'

'I can't!'

'You can!'

'No I can't!'

'Yes you can!'

'I can't!'

Arguing over whether I can jog on the spot for a further two minutes actually gets me to the end of those two minutes more or less intact.

'Well done!' Alice screeches and stops her watch. 'There's no way you could have done that on Sunday.'

'Possibly. But I could walk with no pain and blink without wincing on Sunday too, so I'm not sure the trade-off was worth it.'

'It will be when you get on those scales later,' Alice replies with a conviction I'm not sure I can get behind.

'Let's hope so. If I've put on weight I may kill myself.'

'Just to be on the safe side, why don't you give me fifty star jumps one last time?'

'You are kidding, aren't you?' I lift up one arm. 'You see how much that's shaking, don't you? I look like I have early-onset Parkinson's.'

Alice sighs and looks across the park. She turns back to me and shakes her head. 'You know, if you'd have put as much effort into exercising over the years as you've done making excuses *not* to exercise, you probably wouldn't be in this state.'

I try to respond with a witty retort, but am stymied by the very annoying fact that Alice is absolutely right. I *have* spent years making excuses not to make an effort to stay fit, and so I find myself vastly overweight, unhealthy, and generally unhappy with my lot. I think back on all those times I didn't go to rugby training because it was too cold, too hot, too dark, on at the same time as the football, on at the same time as lunch . . . and so on.

When did I stop *wanting* to make an effort?

Five years ago?

Ten?

'Fifty star jumps, you say?' I ask, puffing my cheeks out.

'Yep.'

'Right.'

I painfully haul myself to my feet for what feels like the thousandth time that week (probably because it is) and assume the position.

'One!' I shout as my flabby carcass achieves a momentary break with the Earth's gravity.

'Two!'

'Three!'

'Four!'

'Fi—*SHIT*!'

'What is it?' Alice says and comes over to support me.

'My back,' I whine. Pain—proper pain this time, not just the chronic aches I've been party to for the past seven days—shoots across my upper back. I felt something go *twang* around my right shoulder blade as I hit the fifth star jump.

I explain this to Alice.

'Sounds like you've pulled a muscle.' She slaps me on the arm and steps away. 'You'll be fine.'

'It's agony!'

'Nothing a couple of ibuprofen won't fix,' she says and wipes her sweaty brow. 'I'm quite relieved actually. I thought from the way you screamed like a little girl there that you'd ruptured a disc in your spine or something.'

I haven't as yet had the courage to ask Alice if she has a husband, but if he does exist then I pity the poor man more than words can say. His wife has the sympathy and bedside manner of Darth Vader with a head cold.

'We have to stop,' I implore.

Alice looks me up and down carefully. I'm sure I look a right state. My face is red and puffy, my sweaty hair sticks on end, my rugby top is badly creased, and my hairy gut is hanging over my tracksuit bottoms in plain sight. I'm stooping like an old crone on her way to Snow White's house, and wobbling around uncertainly on legs that could give out from under me at any moment. In short, I look like a fat, out-of-shape technical writer who's done more exercise in the past week than he has in the past decade.

'You're probably right,' Alice concedes. 'I did want a last warm-down jog around the park—'

'For the love of God, please, no.'

'No. On second thoughts, I think you're pretty much done, Greg.' She puts one leg up on our favourite bench and starts her warm-down exercises. 'Do you want me to give you a lift home?'

'No. I think I'll try to walk.'

'You sure?'

'Yes.' Partially because there's a Tesco Express on the way home where I can buy painkillers, and partially because I'm afraid that if I do get in a car with Alice, she might think of some last-minute training I can do before we reach my front door. I really don't want to be running along the high street with her beeping her car horn and shouting 'Faster, you tubby bitch!' at me until something prolapses.

'Okay.' She stands up. 'Well, it's been fun.'

'Has it?'

'I think so. If you feel like another course—maybe a longer-term commitment—then give me a ring.'

'Okay, I will.'

No, I bloody won't.

'Great. I'll email you the de-brief that I send to all my clients. It'll contain advice and help for what you should do next in your exercise regime.'

Never hire a personal trainer again?

'Thanks, Alice.'

She thrusts out a hand. 'Best of luck with the weigh-in session today, Greg. I'll be listening in.'

'Thank you very much.'

I hope I bloody have lost weight. I can see Alice storming the radio station and taking several innocent bystanders hostage if I haven't.

'See you later then, Greg.'

'Yeah, goodbye, Alice.'

And with that she's gone again.

My tormentor of the past seven days jogs down the path towards the car park, leaving me in abject misery, and standing next to a park bench I will never visit again for as long as I live. In fact there's a very good chance I'll never visit this *park* again.

Or anywhere else where there are trees, birds, grass, or sky.

Ten minutes later and I'm walking slowly through the doors of Tesco Express. The pain in my upper back and shoulder is so acute now that it's making me a little light-headed.

I stand in the medicine aisle for a good minute trying to decide on which painkillers to buy. There are the brand names and the cheaper superstore equivalents. I plump for a pack of these as I've never been one for trademarks.

I pick up a box of 200 mg ibuprofen and take it over to the girl at the counter.

'These are quite strong, you know,' she says as she puts them in a bag for me.

'That's what I'm hoping,' I tell her.

I don't know what she's on about, though. The last time I took these pills was when I twisted my ankle last year. Two didn't touch the pain, so I had to take three in the end to even get a little relief.

The pain I'm in now is far worse, so I dry-swallow four of the little white pills as I walk back to the house. This should be enough to take the edge off.

'Hi, honey,' Zoe says as I come through the door. 'You look awful.'

'Thanks, baby.'

'Have you been run over?'

I think of Alice's bulgy eyes and stern expression. 'Yes, I rather think I have.'

'Well, we're due at the station in an hour so you'd best go have a shower and get dressed. Remember to wear decent shorts—we're being weighed today with hardly any clothes on.'

'Okay,' I agree and slope off upstairs.

The shower is invigorating and by the time it's finished I'm actually feeling pretty good about myself. The pain in my back is almost completely gone. Those painkillers are better than I thought!

I even start to whistle as I get dressed, and by the time I walk back down the stairs I've got a broad grin on my face.

'You look better,' Zoe says as I enter the kitchen.

'Yeah . . . yeah, I feel better,' I reply in a dreamy tone of voice.

Actually, it's not a dreamy tone of voice, it's a *stoned* tone of voice. Those pills must have been a *lot* stronger than I thought.

I amble over to the medicine drawer where I'd put them earlier and inspect the packet.

Oh no.

I picked up the wrong ones in the shop.

I thought I'd bought the 200 mg, where in actual fact they are *400 mg.* Twice the fucking strength.

No wonder I'm a bit spaced. I've ingested enough anti-inflammatory medicine to stun a gorilla.

'You alright?' Zoe inquires from right beside me. I hadn't noticed her enter the room.

'Yes. Why do you ask?'

'Because you've been staring at that packet for five minutes.'

'Have I?'

'Yes, Greg.'

'Oh.'

'Are you going to be alright to go out?'

I put my hand on her shoulder. The softness of her jumper under my fingers is amazing. 'Mmmmmm. 'Course I am, baby.'

'What the hell is wrong with you?'

'Nothing. I may have just taken a little too much ibuprofen.'

'Oh, Greg!'

'Sssshhh,' I tell her and put my hand on her soft, warm cheek. 'It'll be fine. I'm fine. It's all fine. Fine and dandy. Dandy wandy.'

'Oh, good grief.'

'You have lovely skin. I don't tell you that enough.' I stroke my finger up her face. 'Lovely, lovely skin. Skin, skin, skin, skinny, skin.'

'I'm driving,' Zoe says, breaking away from this disturbing analysis of her epidermis.

'Okay, sweetheart. You drive. I'll . . . I'll . . .'

I drift off to somewhere warm and bouncy for a moment.

'I'll not drive,' I eventually say.

'Oh, this is going to go well,' my wife says with a level of exasperation I am completely oblivious to.

'That's the spirit!' I cry happily and then walk straight into the kitchen door.

On the drive to Stream FM I've decided that 'kumquat' is the nicest word in the dictionary.

By the time I'm stripped down to my t-shirt and shorts and am waiting in the green room I've changed my mind. 'Albumin' is in fact the nicest word in the English language. 'Kumquat' is a distant second, with 'moleskin' crashing in to third place, slightly ahead of 'wombat.'

'I can't believe there's going to be a bloody audience for this,' Zoe says from beside me.

The weigh-in is to be conducted in the large conference hall here at Stream FM's offices. They've converted it into a temporary studio for this very purpose. A specially selected audience of a couple of hundred have been invited along to lend a certain atmosphere to proceedings. The weigh-in will go out live on air and will also be streamed on the website.

This is all making Zoe understandably nervous.

I couldn't give a rosy, red fuck. I'm too busy thinking of words that rhyme with *albumin.*

I glance around at the other five couples, unable to wipe the dumb smile off my face. Frankly, it's a miracle I haven't started dribbling.

Most of them are looking as terrified as Zoe—other than the two scumbags whose names escape me right now. She's taking pictures of her enormous child on her iPhone and he's picking his nose with the kind of enthusiasm you'd normally see from a dwarf in a gold mine.

I do remember Shane's name, the largest of all of us. Even in my creamy ibuprofen torpor I can tell he's lost a fair bit of weight, even in the past week. This sharpens my foggy mind a bit. If he's lost some of his enormous bulk, I'd better have as well.

My male pride has taken a right kicking in the past few days at the hands of Alice Pithering, but standing here sizing up the competition has kick-started it again in no uncertain terms.

Sadly, I'm also still as high as a fucking kite, so my competitive edge is dulled again fairly quickly as I realise the word 'albumin' is quite close to 'album.' As in 'Have you heard the latest Green Day albumin? It's great . . . no yolk.'

This awful, awful pun sends me into a giggling fit that passes only when Lottie the production assistant comes into the room and tells us that it's show time.

And what a show it is! A veritable cornucopia of razzle, dazzle, and glitz!

It's either that or I'm off my tits on over-the-counter drugs, and the weigh-in is actually just a set of large scales, an LCD scoreboard above them, and two hundred vaguely bored-looking people sitting in chairs waiting for something fat to happen.

We're paraded in through the large set of double doors to the side of the conference room, and I have to resist the near overwhelming urge to start mooing.

Elise and Will, who look very shiny this morning, are speaking to the crowd and the wider listening audience, as they wander around the temporarily erected stage at the back of the conference hall.

A large sign on canvas—one that must have cost a fortune—is hanging behind the stage and reads FAT CHACE! Somebody has come along and attempted to change the misspelling by squeezing in the N, but everyone in the room can see where the cock-up has occurred. It's obvious that the sign was knocked up by the reprographics department during their lunch break.

'And here they are!' exclaims Will as we file in. 'Our twelve contestants, ready to join us on stage for the first weigh-in!'

'That's right! Let's give them all a big round of applause!' Elise adds.

The crowd is suddenly energised. They've been given their cue, and by golly, they're going to provide a heartfelt contractually obligated response if it kills them.

A roar of applause rolls over our heads as we take to the low stage. There's even a few whoops and cheers going on too. I swear I hear somebody make a mooing noise, but that's probably just the ibuprofen talking.

Twelve seats are arranged for us at the back, and we each take a pew as Will and Elise tell the audience how the weigh-in will go.

Each couple will step up to the scales and will be weighed one after another. Our combined weight will be totalled up and put on the elaborate scoreboard, along with the combined weight loss percentage. When all six couples have had their turn, whoever has lost the most body fat will win the first weigh-in—and the weekend break in London to see a show.

This is all a very neat way of assessing which of us is doing the best job of shifting the fat. However, I can't help thinking there's something of a loophole. If I just cut one of Zoe's legs off, that'll win us the weigh-in no problem.

In fact, the only issue that arises then is that there are *nine* weigh-ins altogether over the course of the competition. By the time we reach the final Zoe will be down to just a head, provided I've chopped the torso up into several pieces.

I have visions of placing my wife's disembodied head on the scales and have to suppress my mirth as I take my seat at the end of the row. In my painkiller-addled daydream, Zoe's head is still very much alive—and berating me for not wearing clean boxer shorts from where it sits on the scale's platform.

'What are you laughing about?' says the complete version of Zoe Milton by my side.

'Nothing, baby,' I reply and stare at her face. 'You have very nice hair. Can I stroke it for a bit?'

'Oh for fuck's sake, Greg.'

'For fuck's sake indeed. Fuckity fuckity fuck pants. Fuuuuuuuucccck. It's a great word, *fuck*, isn't it?'

'Just sit there and be quiet so we can get through this.'

I chuck off an ugly salute. 'Yes ma'am.'

Will and Elise are still talking. They've now moved on to thanking all the sponsors who are footing the bill for this entire debacle.

As I slump in my chair awaiting my turn in the spotlight, I become uncomfortably aware that my dreamy, happy buzz is slowly being replaced by the overwhelming urge to sleep.

My eyelids have become very heavy and my head feels like it's stuffed with cotton wool.

I try to concentrate on what our DJ hosts are saying to bring myself out of it, but their identical, manufactured disc jockey tones are actually having a soporific effect on me, making the situation even worse.

If I can just get through this weigh-in, we can go home and I can crawl into bed.

A dopey smile reappears on my face as I think about the soft white sheet beneath me, the warm, cosy duvet wrapped around my body, the comforting feeling of the pillow against my cheek . . .

'GREG!'

'Wsftgl?'

'GREG!'

'Hmnmnnm?'

'Wake up, you idiot!'

I regain consciousness to find Zoe shaking me violently.

'It's our turn on the scales. Snap out of it!' she hisses.

With bleary eyes I look up and see two hundred expectant faces peering at me. From the front of the stage, Elise is staring, less with expectation and more with blind panic.

I wave my hand. 'S'fine everyone. Just restin' my eyes.'

I stand up and rub my face.

Taking a deep breath, I steady myself, smile at the crowd, and walk forward.

At least it feels like forward, but the direction I actually go in is *right*.

. . . as in right off the edge of the stage.

A collective gasp erupts from the crowd as my left foot drops off the side of the stage, swiftly followed by the rest of me.

'OH FUCK!' I cry in such a loud voice that I'm sure it will end up with Stream FM being fined again for swearing.

Luckily the drop is only about six inches; otherwise they'd probably have to call an ambulance. As it is, my foot painfully jars on the carpet and I stumble forward like a newborn elephant.

I've lost a bit of weight, but I'm still pretty damn huge, so coming to a halt is going to be something of a problem at this juncture.

So much so, that by the time I've managed it, I've actually passed back out through the large open double doors to the conference room.

The audience must think I've fled in terror of the scales. As far as they're concerned, they've just seen a man get to his feet uncertainly, take one look at proceedings, and immediately run away like a frightened six-year-old child.

I turn myself around and scurry back into the room. 'Sorry! Sorry, everyone!' I apologise as I retake the stage next to Zoe, my cheeks burning bright with embarrassment.

'We thought we'd lost you there for a second,' Elise says and laughs in that unpleasant staccato way people do when they think things are beyond their control.

'Ha! No, no I'm fine,' I tell her. 'Just had a little smumble.'

'A what?' Elise asks.

'A stud . . . stundle . . .'

'Pardon?'

Oh great. The ibuprofen has now decided to attack the speech centres of my brain. I concentrate hard. 'A . . . a *stumble*. I had a *stumble*, Lisa.'

'Elise.'

'If you say so.'

Understandably, Elise terminates our conversation and bids Zoe get up on the scales. My wife does as she's told.

Her starting weight of fourteen stone, seven pounds appears on one side of the over-complicated scoreboard. We all wait with bated breath as the scales do their job. Someone plays cheesy countdown music over the speakers until Zoe's new weight appears with a triumphant blast.

Fourteen stone dead.

The sound of a wet fart would have been more appropriate. That's just seven pounds in six weeks.

The look of catastrophic disappointment on Zoe's face is heartbreaking. Right now, I want nothing more than to grab her hand, lead her off stage, and have nothing more to do with this stupid circus.

'Your turn, Greg!' Will tells me as Zoe steps down and off to one side.

Feeling nauseated from my mild drugs overdose and sick to my stomach thanks to my wife's distress, I take to the scales.

I couldn't give a fucking toss how much weight I've lost, to be honest.

That is until I see that I've dropped well over a stone.

From twenty stone, two pounds to a pound under nineteen stone.

Bloody hell.

I can picture Alice at home right now jumping around the place and kicking her cat.

'That's an excellent loss Greg—congratulations!' Elise says and claps me on the back as she leads me off the scales.

I can't help but smile. I wasn't expecting to have lost a whole stone!

My temporary pride is quashed the second I look at Zoe. She's trying to smile as best as she can, but I can see the disappointment writ large in her eyes. 'Well done, honey,' she says and takes my hand.

'It's nothing sweetheart,' I reply, trying to minimise her distress. I squeeze her hand. 'I have a lot more to lose than you, remember?'

She nods, but I know for certain my words haven't helped. The quicker this farce is over today, the better.

Needless to say, we don't win the weigh-in. That honour goes to the oldest couple in the competition, George and Valerie. They've both managed to drop over a stone each. It's a fantastic result for them. Just behind them are Frankie and Benny. When Benny sees they missed out on winning by only two percent, he looks crestfallen and furious all at the same time.

Zoe and I end up coming third, so our performance can be considered decidedly average.

'We could have won,' Zoe says to me forlornly as we're leaving the green room about half an hour later. 'If I'd managed to lose more, we could have won.'

'Stop thinking like that,' I reply as I put my jacket on. 'This is supposed to be about making our lives better. There's no point in doing it if it's just going to make us miserable.'

'You did alright.'

'Yeah, well, I had a skinny maniac torturing me for a week. You ate cabbage and farted a lot.'

This has the desired effect. Zoe giggles.

'I guess I have to find a better diet,' she says with a rueful grin.

'I'd say so!'

By the time we get home Zoe's mood has lifted enough for her to suggest a walk in the forest this afternoon. I could really do with just lying down and pretending to be dead, but if she needs a walk to clear her head, then so be it.

We set off after a healthy lunch of chicken and salad. A bacon sandwich would have gone down a treat, but Alice would murder me in my sleep if she ever found out.

Zoe thoroughly enjoys the two hours we spend traipsing through the countryside, but I spend the entire time thinking about that look of disappointment she had on her face at the weigh-in—when I'm not trying to ignore the dull ache in my legs, that is.

I don't think either one of us can take it if this experiment with our lives ends in failure. If Zoe doesn't lose the kind of weight she expects to, the stress and anxiety it will cause her will be too much for me to bear.

The scale of the challenge ahead hits me for the first time as we walk through the sun-dappled woods.

If we succeed and lose the weight, it will be positive and life changing.

. . . but if we fail, the harm to our already damaged self-esteems could be very high indeed.

Right at this moment, I just don't know if the risk is worth it.

ZOE'S WEIGHT LOSS DIARY
Monday, May 19th
13 stone, 1 pound (1 stone, 5 pounds lost)

I got recognised in the street today.

I'm ambling down the road to post a letter when a small grey-haired woman of indeterminate age holding a teacup Shih Tzu bustles up to me and says, 'It's you, isn't it?'

'I'm sorry?'

'It's you! You're part of the fat show on Stream FM. You're the one who can't have a baby.'

'Yes. Yes, that's me,' I sigh. 'Part of the fat show and childless.'

'I'm really enjoying it. Ladybird and I listen to Elise and that gay chappie all the time.'

'Ladybird?'

She holds up the constipated-looking miniature dog, who gives me a rueful look. 'This is Ladybird.'

'It's a dog.'

'Yes.'

'You named your dog Ladybird.'

'Yes!'

'Okay.' I shake my letter in her face. 'Well, must get on. Nice to meet you, though.'

'When do you think you won't be fat?'

'I beg your pardon?'

'When do you think you won't be fat?'

This is the most depressing question I've ever been asked. 'I don't know.'

'I hope you're not fat soon.'

'Well, thanks for that.'

'I really want you and Shane to win.'

'I'm married to Greg.'

'Oh, I thought you were Shane's wife.'

'No. I'm married to Greg.'

'Oh. Well, I don't really like you two, to be honest.'

'Really? Your dog has a stupid name and it looks like a toilet brush. Goodbye.'

And with that, I'm gone up the street before this lunatic can accost me further. I would try to run away from her as fast as possible, but achieving much more than a hurried scuttle would be impossible right now thanks to yesterday's Fat Chance challenge.

Allow me to explain . . .

You see, it's not enough for Stream FM to pit each couple against one another in a race to see who can lose the most weight. That would be far too easy.

Not only do we have the indignity of the weigh-ins, we also have to take part in a couple of challenges over the next two months that are designed to test our levels of stamina and endurance as we continue down the path to a healthier, happier lifestyle.

The first of these is a 'spinning' challenge.

You know what spinning is, of course. It's become extremely popular with people who think spandex is fashionable. Quite why they just can't call it what it is—communal exercise biking—I have no idea. I guess it wouldn't look as snappy on the promotional leaflets.

The challenge has been organised in conjunction with Fitness4All, the gym chain that's one of the sponsors of the competition—the main one, in fact. They've donated the use of their facilities and a pot-load of cash in exchange for constant, unremitting wall-to-wall publicity across the whole of the radio station's output for six months. Every break is loaded with their adverts; every poster is emblazoned with their garish logo.

It doesn't end there. Human beings are being press-ganged into being walking billboards for Fitness4All. I should know, because I'm bloody one of them.

'There's a big box just been delivered!' Greg calls up to me on Saturday morning.

'Yeah, that'll be the uniforms,' I reply as I yawn my way down the stairs.

'Uniforms?'

'Yeah, you know. Elise mentioned it Monday. Fitness4All have requested we all wear t-shirts from now on for the show, starting tomorrow at the challenge.'

Greg tries to hold up the box. It's enormous. 'I don't think this just contains t-shirts, love.'

And he's absolutely right.

'Oh, good Lord,' I say under my breath as he cuts open the top of the box and starts to pull out its contents.

There *are* t-shirts. Many, many t-shirts.

'They go down in size,' Greg remarks.

'For when we lose weight,' I surmise.

Greg holds one up. It's a hectic shade of red, and covered in a variety of brightly coloured blue and white writing. I inspect it closely as my husband waves it around.

'Mine are different to yours,' Greg comments.

'How so?' I respond.

He holds up another shirt and I see what he's on about. 'You have got to be fucking kidding me,' I say.

Emblazoned across the front of the t-shirt is a huge Fitness4All logo, written in one of those stupid swooshy fonts that's supposed to denote speed, but just ends up giving everybody with dyslexia a screaming headache. The Stream FM logo sits in the top left-hand corner, giving the shirt the unmistakable appearance of a cheaply made football jersey.

On the back things really go downhill.

Much like football shirts, our names are writ large across the top. We don't get numbers assigned to us below this, though, like you'd see on your average premier leaguer.

Instead, Fitness4All and Stream FM have decided we all need our own catchphrases. In BIG BOLD LETTERS right across our backs.

Greg's reads: I'M LARGIN' IT.

Mine is even worse. It says: FAT BUT FABULOUS.

I see several shades of red, all darker than the shirts.

Not fat AND fabulous. *Oh no.* That would just be wrong on every level.

After all, fat people are social rejects who can't be fabulous *and* fat—even if we're decorated head to toe in sequins and shine with the light of a thousand suns.

No, I'm apparently fabulous *despite* the fact that I am the size of a fucking hippo.

I have somehow managed to overcome my hideous deformity, and have achieved a degree of fabulousness hitherto unreachable to anyone with a waistline over a size fourteen.

I am a miraculous person. To be cheered and applauded throughout the streets.

How absolutely insulting. How totally crass.

How completely and utterly *unsurprising*.

Greg knows me very well, so it only takes him about half an hour to peel me off the ceiling.

'Don't let it get to you,' he says. 'It's just a silly t-shirt.'

'Easy for you to say. You spend your entire time *largin' it*. I'd have no problem with that.' I hold up one of my shirts. 'But Greg, I am not fucking *largin' it*, am I? No, no, no. I'm fat *but* fabulous. I'm huge *but* happy. I'm chunky *but* cheerful.' I throw the shirt across the room. 'You know what Fitness4All are, don't you, Gregory?'

'No dear, what are they?'

'Fit *but* full of shit.'

'Yes, dear. Shall we have a look at the rest of this gear before you rupture something important?'

'I suppose so.' I hurl the t-shirt back into the box. 'I'm not letting this go, though.'

'No, I wouldn't think you were for a moment.' Greg pulls another garment out. 'Oh, look, they've put hoodies in as well. We'll look like the local scumbags who hang around the high street.'

'Great. I can be fat but fabulous *and* hang around bus shelters worrying old people.'

'There are hats, too.'

'Are there, Greg? And do they also announce to the world that even though I have an arse the size of a houseboat, I am still able to maintain a respectable level of fabulousness?'

'Nope, they've just got the swishy Fitness4All logo on them.'

'Thank heavens for that.'

A scant few minutes later, both Greg and I have changed into our new duds and are inspecting one another.

'I look like Timmy fucking Mallet,' Greg points out.

He's not wrong. The big red baseball cap, combined with the red t-shirt, red hooded top, and red tracksuit bottoms, do all conspire to make him look like the unholy offspring of a children's TV presenter from the eighties and a tomato.

What am I saying?

We both look like it.

Two red tomatoes standing in front of one another trying not to burst into tears.

The next time we have to go to a fancy dress party we can just stick beaks on our noses and go as the Angry Birds. Specifically the big fat biffer you get after several rounds, who can wipe out loads of piggies with one twang of the catapult.

'I can't go out in public like this,' Greg says in a small voice. 'People will think I'm broken.'

'We won't have to. We just have to wear it for the show tomorrow.'

'What? The live challenge that's being streamed across the planet via the internet?'

'Yes.'

'Where there will be photographers who will take pictures for the local paper?'

'Yes.'

'Oh well, that's fine, then.'

'Shut up, Timmy. I'm no happier about it than you are.'

. . . and I'm really not.

Tomorrow I get to be a fat but fabulous tomato on an exercise bike. I can't wait.

❦

Fitness4All tries its best to look like the kind of place you'd want to hang out even if you weren't trying to burn five hundred calories.

It has a bar, for instance.

Not a *proper* bar, obviously. There's no alcohol here. But if you want to grab yourself a low-fat soy milkshake or a smoothie that's mostly ice water, then this is the place to come.

There's a nice lounge where you can sit and chat with other people who are also attempting to burn five hundred calories. A flat-screen TV dominates one wall of the lounge, hooked up to Sky Digital. The Food Channel is blocked, of course, but you can watch hours upon hours of The Active Channel and Fitness TV if you should choose to do so.

Most of the interior is decked out in a variety of pleasing shades of pink and mauve. What's left is brushed chrome or glossy black, including the shiny marble floors and sweeping staircases.

What you resolutely *can't* see any sign of is anyone engaged in exercise. There are no windows through to the gym and no obvious signs of activity of any sort. Standing in the foyer at reception you could be forgiven for thinking you were in a swanky London hotel or a particularly posh cinema.

This is deliberate, of course. The last thing the proprietors of Fitness4All want you catching sight of from the front door is a bunch of sweaty, unattractive people trying to burn off five hundred calories. The looks of pain, misery, and hopelessness on their faces might put you off coming in and handing over a month's wages for the dubious privilege of joining them.

'Nice, isn't it?' Greg says as we walk in.

'Yeah. *Nice*,' I reply, not willing to commit myself to a more complete answer at this moment. Then I catch sight of what's lurking over in the corner and the niceness of the gym interior becomes largely irrelevant. 'What the hell is that?' I spit.

Just off to one side of the reception area is a large cardboard standee, the kind you get in the cinema advertising the latest releases. Only this one is a good fifteen feet wide and features every person involved in the Stream FM competition. Above all our gurning faces are the competition and Stream FM logos, along with a strapline that reads 'MEET THE FAT CHANCERS HERE SUNDAY MAY 18TH! Come and see the challenge!'

They couldn't have chosen a worse photo of me if somebody had threatened their first-born sons.

I am making what I can only describe as a horse face.

You can see I've attempted to smile, but the process has got stuck somewhere in the middle, leaving me showing my teeth and my lip curled upwards like I'm expecting a sugar lump.

I'm also standing in a slight stoop, so I'm not even a proud upright-looking horse . . . but a trembling spavined nag, ready for the glue factory.

Greg doesn't come off much better. He's sporting a cheesy grin that makes him look ever so slightly retarded. Also, his hair is sticking up on one side, indicating that presenting himself for public consumption is beyond his skills as a human being.

The rest of our motley gang look as bad as we do, but I'm not concerned with their appearance given that I hardly know any of them and therefore couldn't give a shit.

The only two bastards who look clean, happy, and attractive are Will and Elise, who have been badly Photoshopped over the lineup of fatties behind them. Will's teeth shine with the light of a supernova and Elise has hair bouncier and more alive than a kangaroo on performance-enhancing drugs.

'Oh dear, I don't look at all well,' I hear a voice from behind me. I turn to see Valerie and George, the winners of the first weigh-in, inspecting the standing display with the same horror Greg and I are.

'Morning,' I say to both of them, as does Greg.

'Good morning, love,' Valerie replies. 'I don't normally look like that,' she adds, pointing a finger at the cardboard version of herself.

I look back and see that for some reason Valerie is a rather sickly shade of yellow, like she's had an attack of jaundice. The rest of us look fairly pink and more or less healthy, so I can only imagine it's another failing of the Photoshopped nature of the display.

'You look a bit Oriental, dear,' George says, betraying a slight element of racism in his character.

'They're all awful, don't worry,' I tell Valerie. 'I look like Shergar and Greg appears to have had a lobotomy.'

'They certainly could have consulted us before using such horrible photos,' Valerie says.

'From the way things have been going so far, I don't think our opinions hold much water,' Greg observes accurately.

'Good morning, guys!'

We all swing around to see two tanned and spandex-clad staff members walking towards us in a sprightly manner. One is male, the other female. Both are blonde and don't appear to have an ounce of fat on their bones. I don't need to look at Greg to know he's trying very hard not to stare at the girl's breasts, which have been neatly put on display thanks to the tight spandex t-shirt she's wearing. I take a swift look to see if I can catch the outline of the guy's willy, but he's either hung like a shrew or the spandex shorts he's wearing offer more comfort and support than they appear to.

'You guys are here for the challenge, right?' the girl says in a chipper fashion.

'Indeed we are, my dear young thing,' George replies. By the smooth tone of his voice he's obviously clocked a good look at her boobs as well and doesn't want to miss the opportunity to charm their owner.

'That's fantastic!' the guy replies.

I'm sure as far as he is concerned everything in the world is fantastic. Spandex is fantastic. His calorie count is fantastic. His body fat index is fantastic. His blood pressure is fantastic. In fact about the only thing that might not be fantastic is the size of his genitals, but he's probably too concerned with his fibre intake to worry about it. 'I'm Tristan and this is Hayley,' he continues.

'Nice to meet you,' Greg says, looking directly at Hayley and completely ignoring Mr Fantastic.

'If you ladies would like to follow me to our changing rooms,' Hayley says. 'Tristan will take the gents to yours.'

'Lead on, MacDuff!' George says, in a phrase I've never really known the origin of.

'I'll see you in a bit baby,' Greg tells me and gives me a kiss on the cheek. Now, my husband is not one for the public display of affection, so I can tell he's feeling nervous about this challenge and needs a bit of TLC. I give him a hug before taking my leave with Valerie and the spandex queen.

Hayley takes us up the stairs to the left while Tristan takes the boys up a set to the right. She leads us through what can only be described as a labyrinth of weights rooms, saunas, plunge pools, and massage parlours until we arrive at our destination, the main ladies' changing rooms.

'If you'd just like to get into your kits,' she tells us, 'you can then walk through into the main gym where they have the challenge set up for you guys.'

'I can hear the crowd. They don't sound very big,' Valerie says— a little note of relief in her voice.

'Oh don't worry, there are loads of them!' Hayley says excitedly. 'They're just waiting for the show to start.' She looks at her watch. 'Which will be in twenty minutes.'

'Great,' I say. 'Can't wait to parade my big fat arse in front of them.'

Hayley squeezes my arm. 'That's the spirit. Good for you.' The tone is as patronising as it possibly can be.

I bite back a response and head into the changing room with Valerie in tow.

'I'm starting to feel like the main attraction at a zoo,' Valerie points out as we both zip up our hideous red hooded tops. Valerie's slogan is 'LOSING IS WINNING.' The fact that I'm quite jealous is testament to just how dreadful my catchphrase truly is.

'I know what you mean,' I say. 'If there's a guy standing out there with a big stick and whistle I wouldn't be surprised.'

Valerie smiles. 'You think they'll make us jump through hoops?'

I pat her on the shoulder. 'Valerie, love, we've been doing that for two months already.'

Large brightly coloured signs indicate the exit to the main gym at the other end of the changing room, so I take a deep breath, mentally cross myself, and head out to face the crowd.

Who, it turns out, don't really care much about us fatties at all, judging by their rather lacklustre response to our arrival.

We walk out to find a row of six exercise bikes in the centre of the gym. The crowd sits in a semicircle around them, giving the impression of an amphitheatre. The scoreboard from the weigh-in has made its way here, hanging above our heads and ready to record our time and speed on the bikes once we get on them.

Off to the left-hand side is the temporary radio desk set up for Elise and Will, along with the production assistants who go everywhere with them. Hundreds of wires snake away to God knows where from the array of important- and complicated-looking black and grey boxes.

I sidle over to where Greg is already sitting down. As I join him, I look up at the crowd, which is about two hundred strong. Most are chatting amongst themselves or playing on their smartphones, but some are staring at us like we've just been created in a Petri dish. The low murmur of conversation can be heard above the hum of the air conditioning.

'Well, that's disconcerting,' I say to Greg.

'What do you mean?'

'I thought they'd be a bit more excited.'

'Yeah, me too. Just spoke to Dominica. You know, one of the lesbians? She got here pretty early and said they've all been sitting here for over an hour. I guess they've got a bit bored.'

'I don't like it. It feels like they're discussing what to do with us.'

'I know what you mean.'

'Any second now they're going to decide between burning us at the stake or having themselves a good old-fashioned lynching. We won't stand a chance.'

Luckily our saviours arrive in the shape of my friend the bouncy female DJ and her camp on-air partner.

'Hi all!' Elise smiles and waves as she makes her way across to the desk. Will minces along behind her, smiling broadly and also waving.

The crowd erupts into cheering and clapping. It's evident that a dozen anonymous fat people are nowhere near as exciting as two thin local celebrities . . . as is right and proper, I suppose.

Elise sees me and gives a little nod, which I return like we're two spies in a downtown Karachi liquor joint.

We're trying to keep our friendship secret while the competition is running, so she can't get accused of favouritism. This is fair enough, but it still feels very strange to be treated like a stranger by someone whose hair you've held back while she throws up into your toilet.

We've just about made up after her on-air outing of my inability to get pregnant. It took a lot of swift talking on her part—and many, many skinny lattes—but I've forgiven her for her trespasses, on the proviso that the next time she even thinks about exploiting our friendship, I will divulge all her secrets to as many people as possible. I've known Elise long enough to know that she's a good person—but she does tend to suffer from a distinct lack of good judgement when placed under pressure.

Picking up their microphones, Elise and Will say hello to the crowd and us contestants. They spend a few minutes providing some relatively bland off air warm-up material, before the clock hits eleven and we go live to the listening public.

As the show gets underway I start to feel butterflies taking flight in my chest. As the two DJs whip the crowd into a frenzy of excitement I feel Greg's hand close over mine and give it a squeeze.

Elise and Will then let everyone know what will be happening at the challenge today. I mean *everyone* as well, because even *we* don't really know what's going on yet.

We've been told that the challenge would involve some kind of race on exercise bikes, but that was about it.

With mounting horror I listen as Elise and Will fill in the blanks.

We'll be racing as couples—one per bike. The object will be quite simple. The first couple to reach fifteen kilometres wins.

I'll just say that again.

The first couple to reach fifteen KILOMETRES wins.

Fifteen fucking kilometres.

I'm flabbergasted. Do these people not see how big we all are? How out of shape we must be?

That distance is a big ask for someone thin and relatively healthy, but for a crew of people who are no strangers to an all-you-can-eat buffet, fifteen kilometres on a bicycle is *absurd*.

I look to my left at poor old Shane. He looks like he's about to have a heart attack.

Okay, Shane *always* looks like he's about to have a heart attack, but for once he has good reason.

The only saving grace here is that it'll be one bike per couple, and we'll be able to take turns whenever we like. That still means doing seven and a half kilometres each, though, more or less.

I have never hated Elise more than I do now. I wish I'd shoved her head down the toilet.

And the prize for this torture? Free membership to Fitness4All for two years after Fat Chance has finished.

That's rather like giving a man suffering from third-degree burns a holiday in the Sahara to cheer him up.

'Before we get started, we'd like to welcome a special guest,' Will says over the noise of the crowd.

'Yes, it gives us great pleasure to introduce the man who's made all of this possible,' Elise adds. 'Would you please welcome the owner of Fitness4All, Adam Edgemont!'

To the rather perfunctory applause of the audience—it seems that successful businessmen are about as exciting as a row of fat people to this lot—a young, handsome, and gleaming man steps out onto the gym floor in a suit that probably cost more than my car.

He makes his way past us, without so much as a glance, I might add, and joins Elise. He shakes Will's hand and gives Elise a warm, lingering hug. I can see her face flush red as he does this.

With a clear and certain knowledge born of thirty-seven years on this planet, I know that these two will be having all kinds of energetic sex with each other before the month is out.

Elise manages to control her hormones long enough to engage Edgemont in the single most corporate conversation I think I've ever heard. The shiny young entrepreneur manages to advertise his business, promote their summer sign-up campaign, compliment Stream FM for working with him, flirt with Elise, and wish all of us luck with the challenge in under a minute. I'm surprised I can actually pick up what he's saying. Such is the smoothness of every word coming out of his mouth, it's a wonder the sound waves don't just slide off my eardrums without making an impression.

I glance over to look at Will's face while Elise converses with their benefactor. The heightened look of jealousy on his face is something to behold.

Edgemont finishes his carefully rehearsed monologue, hugs Elise again, and makes his way over to a seat near the DJ desk. I have no doubt that he'll disappear from view in very short order. I'm sure a man so concerned with running a successful fitness empire has no interest in watching a bunch of fat people use his equipment.

With the pleasantries done, Will bids us come forward to get the challenge under way.

'I'll go first,' Greg tells me. I don't argue.

'You be careful,' I warn him as I unzip my hoodie and park it on my chair. 'Don't go out too hard—you'll kill yourself.'

'Thanks for the vote of confidence, sweetheart.'

'Just be careful.'

Greg mounts up alongside Valerie. Next to her is Benny, then Shane's wife Theresa, then Dominica. Finally Pete the chav mounts the bike at the other end of the row. I see him look over at the doors to the gym. There's every chance he's sizing up his chances of nicking the exercise bike.

'The challenge begins at the sound of the klaxon,' Elise tells everyone.

Greg leans forward in the saddle a bit, a look of determination on his face. I sigh and roll my eyes. I see the application of a lot of ice packs in our near future.

The klaxon goes off and the crowd roars.

Greg starts to pedal as if the hounds of Hell are nipping at his heels. Next to him Valerie is also pumping her legs up and down like a mad thing.

Benny is taking a slightly different tack, though. He's pedalling at a more measured pace, as is Dominica.

Poor old Theresa is forced to pedal at a much slower rate given her size, while Pete is pedalling erratically while flicking V signs at a group of lads down the front of the crowd who are obviously his mates.

A couple of minutes go by. Greg's face is already as red as his t-shirt. I glance back at Benny, who looks a lot more comfortable at his slower pace.

'Greg! Greg!'

'What?'

'Slow down a bit!'

'What?'

'Slow down a bit! You're going to knacker yourself out way too quickly at the pace you're going.'

'But I want . . . I want to win!'

'So do I, you pillock, but it's not going to happen if you can't keep going. Look at Benny—he's got the right idea.'

Greg looks past the feverishly pedalling Valerie and sees how Benny is handling things.

'Alright,' he puffs and draws his pace back down to a more manageable level. 'I hope you're right . . . right about this.'

'I am. We're going to be here for the best part of an hour. Let's not screw it up in the first few minutes.'

I feel quite proud of myself.

I've never been one for tactics . . . or patience, for that matter. The idea of taking a more measured approach has never struck me as a good idea before. When I've wanted something in the past, I've gone out of my way to get it as quickly as possible. Zoe Milton has been all about the instant gratification up to this point in her life.

You mean you've been greedy, a rather annoying voice pipes up in my head as I watch Greg pedal his way past the first two kilometres. *Maybe that's why we got fat?*

I bite my lip. When uncomfortable realisations like this dawn on you, it's never a pleasant experience.

'I might . . . might need you to take over in a minute,' Greg tells me, wiping sweat from his eyes.

'Okay.'

'How are the . . . the others going?'

I look to my left again. Valerie is still pumping away as hard as possible, but her relentless pace has slowed nonetheless. Benny is breathing hard but still maintaining a methodical cycle. Dominica looks pretty puffed and is going slowly, while Shane has already replaced Theresa. Pete is picking his nose and has got his iPhone out.

I look up at the scoreboard. Greg's currently in second place behind Valerie, but Benny is getting closer and closer.

'No-one's screaming into the lead, if that's what you mean,' I tell him. 'Chris Hoy's got nothing to worry about.'

'Right. Swap time?'

I nod my head and Greg jumps off the bike.

Sitting on a saddle already damp with the sweat of another human being is not a joyful experience, even if it is your husband's. I try to ignore a slight tingle of revulsion and start to pedal.

Bloody hell, this is harder than I thought it would be.

They've obviously set the bike's resistance quite high to maximise the difficulty of the challenge.

By the time I've gone through four kilometres my thighs are starting to hurt.

In my peripheral vision I see George replacing Valerie, swiftly followed by Frankie taking over from her husband Benny. Frankie looks to be pedalling at about the same pace as me, while George has gone out quickly like his wife did. I've pretty much disregarded the other three couples at this stage. Dominica and Angela really don't look like their hearts are in it, Shane and Theresa aren't going to win this thing in a million years thanks to their size, and Lea and Pete are . . . well, being very Lea and Pete. She's on the bike now and is also on her iPhone. She's probably texting the rest of her family the security codes to get into the gym after we've all left so they can come back tonight and rob it blind.

'How long have we been going?' I say to Greg, who's now sitting down on the gym floor beside me, head lolled back.

He looks up at the scoreboard. 'Nearly fifteen minutes.'

'And how far have we gone?'

'Just over five kilometres.'

'Is that good or bad?'

'Not a clue. You're ahead of George now, though. In second place.'

Woo hoo!

My tactics are working. George has puffed himself out already and is going slower and slower by the second. Frankie and Benny are the main competition now.

I look up to see Elise bounding over with a microphone. A groan escapes my lips. She's going to bloody interview me.

'Hello, Zoe!' she says and thrusts the microphone under my nose.

'Hello, Elise,' I say breathlessly.

'You're only just behind Frankie on the leader board, so you're doing well. How are you feeling?'

I give her a withering look. 'Just peachy, thanks. There's nothing I like more than the smell of my own body odour,' I pause to catch my breath before carrying on, 'the feel of my hair plastered against my forehead,' another breath, 'and the clammy sensation of a pint of sweat running down my back.'

Elise rolls her eyes and glares at me, before re-applying the fake DJ smile of enthusiasm. 'It looks like you've already lost loads of weight, Zoe!'

'Er . . . thanks.'

'No worries! I'm sure all the weight loss you're experiencing will really help you and Greg to have a baby very soon!'

Oh, you utter cow.

I almost open my mouth to deliver a suitable insult, but hold myself back. There is a better way to return the favour. 'I suppose you're right,' I say through gritted teeth. 'And how are you doing?' I ask.

This throws Elise. She isn't used to have the interviewee turn the tables and ask her a question. 'Er . . . I'm fine, thanks.'

I smile like the devil. 'Arranged that date you've been desperate to go on with Adam Edgemont yet, have you?'

Elise's eyes go wide. I've just broadcast the fact that she fancies our sponsor to the entire listening public, to her utter humiliation. Let's see her mention me and pregnancy again, eh?

Elise pulls the microphone away from me. 'Well, thanks for chatting, Zoe . . . Let's go see how George is doing next door!'

And with that she hurries past me to the next bike along.

It's these small victories that make life worth living, I find.

'Greg! Time to change over!'

'Already?'

'Yes! Get your arse up here!'

I jump off the bike and allow my reluctant husband back into the saddle. He sets off at a fairly measured pace, passing through the eight-kilometre mark as he does so.

I try to ignore the feeling of jelly in my legs and look up at the scoreboard.

We're still in second, but the gap to Frankie has increased a bit. Disturbingly, Lea and Pete are now in third.

How the hell did that happen? They both look more concerned with playing Angry Birds than winning this challenge. I look down to their bike and realise that while they both appear completely disinterested in the competition, they have both been pedalling at a fast, consistent rate.

'The chavs are catching us,' I say to my husband.

'What?'

'You'll have to speed up.'

Greg groans and begins pumping his legs up and down a bit faster.

Suddenly, the jelly feeling in my legs gets a lot worse. I hobble over to the chair, slump into it, and start massaging my thighs.

It really is quite ridiculous how unfit you can get if you're not bloody careful.

After a few minutes of leg massage and pained grimacing, I look up at the clock. We've been engaged in this madness for nearly thirty-five minutes now. Unbelievably, Lea has pushed past both Greg and Benny and is now in first place. It must be all that running away from the local constabulary.

In fact, Greg is now neck and neck with Benny, who is looking increasingly tired. His plan to go slow and steady was a good one, but even the best-laid plans go awry when the body you've got to work with isn't up to the task. I watch him virtually fall off the bike absolutely exhausted, to be replaced by Frankie, who isn't looking much healthier, despite the rest she's had.

The other three couples have really fallen by the wayside.

As we pass into the final five kilometres, George and Val have slowed to the point where they are over a kilometre behind, Dominica and Angela are even further back, and Shane is currently receiving oxygen from the gym's medical team, while Theresa sits in the saddle of her bike with her head slumped forward and her legs barely moving the pedals.

So it comes down to this: it's us versus the chavs.

Greg is about two hundred metres behind them as we head towards the three-kilometre mark.

My legs ache, my eyes still sting with sweat, my head pounds. But I have to get up out of this chair, replace my husband on the bike, and win this fucking challenge.

I can't remember when I last felt so strongly about something.

It's like this stupid competition has awakened something in me today that has been buried beneath a pile of neuroses and self-hatred for far too long.

I am Zoe Milton.

I am old. I am fat. I am unhappy.

But I'm going to win this bike race if it's the last thing I do.

I stand on wobbling legs and walk back to where Greg is puffing and panting.

'Get off the bike, Greg,' I tell him in a flat voice.

He doesn't argue. 'Are . . . are you okay, sweetheart?' he asks.

'Yes. Yes, I am.'

I climb onto the bike and start to pedal. It's agony. The heat of built-up lactic acid screams through my muscles.

And yet I begin to pedal harder.

And *harder*.

My head goes down and my grip on the handlebars tightens.

'It's coming down to just two couples!' I hear Elise roar over the noise of the crowd. 'Pete on bike number one and Zoe on bike number six!'

'Zoe? Take it easy, baby!' I just about hear Greg say through the thunder of blood pounding in my ears.

I daren't look up at him. Daren't say one word. If I break my concentration now I'll surely fail.

'Only three hundred metres to go!' screams Will. 'Zoe is catching all the time! The gap is down to fifty metres!'

There's nothing in the universe right now except the fire in my legs and the thunder in my ears.

In the hours to come I will thoroughly regret this. I will have to take the day off work tomorrow and spend it writing my weight loss diary, thanks to the pain I'll be in.

But right here, right now, none of that matters.

I'm going to win.

'Nearly at the finish line!' screeches Elise.

'Come on, Zoe!' I hear Greg cry from beside me.

A hundred metres to go.

Seventy-five.

It's getting harder and harder to breathe. I can hear the hoarse rasp in my lungs even over the cheering crowd.

Fifty metres.

Thirty.

'They're neck and neck!' Will bellows. 'It's too close to call!'

Twenty.

Ten.

Five.

Zero.

I cry out in a combination of pain and relief.

'And it's over! The race is over!' I hear Elise say. She shouts something else but I'm so exhausted I miss it. The world's gone a bit fuzzy around the edges.

I feel Greg's arms around me, helping me off the bike.

I put my head on his shoulders. 'Who won?' I ask him in a hoarse whisper.

I feel him squeeze me tight. 'You did, baby. You won.'

What a lovely combination of five words that truly is.

'I did?'

'Yeah.' He kisses me with a passion I don't think I've felt in a long time.

The ferocity of the kiss brings the world around me back into focus. I look up into the crowd to see people actually standing on their feet.

For me.

People are standing on their feet for me.

I see both Elise and Will run over.

The rest of the couples are clapping and cheering my victory. Well, those who are capable, anyway. Shane is still on the oxygen mask and Pete is doubled over his own bike looking like he's about to pass out with Lea punching him on the arm, no doubt in disgust at his failure to beat me.

'Congratulations!' Elise shouts. 'Well done, Zoe! Well done, Greg!'

'That was absolutely fantastic!' Will adds. Both of them are so excited now it's a wonder their heads don't pop off.

'How are you feeling?' Elise says and thrusts the microphone in my face.

'Mrfble,' I reply helpfully.

'We're great!' Greg interjects, seeing that I'm in no fit state to speak right at this moment. 'Zoe did a fantastic job. I'm so proud of her!'

'I bet you are,' Elise says, before turning to the crowd. 'And I bet you guys all agree, right? Didn't she do a fantastic job?'

The crowd, happy for the chance to make a contribution to the proceedings, screams and hollers its most heartfelt affirmation.

As I continue to regain full consciousness, I notice that Adam Edgemont and his suit are making their way over to us. He's got a look of delight on his face that can only be because of all the free advertising he's had this morning.

'And here comes our sponsor Mr Edgemont to congratulate our winners,' Will says to everyone, as if it were actually important. 'He's got those wonderful two-year passes to Fitness4All to give to the Miltons in his hand.'

Oh yes, the *wonderful* two-year passes. I'm sure they'll look very nice tucked away in the kitchen drawer for the next decade.

'Congratulations!' Edgemont says, beaming a smile of colossal insincerity our way.

'Thanks,' I half mumble.

Before I know it, Edgemont has got himself between Greg and me. I see a photographer line up a shot of the three of us, with Elise and Will on either side.

Great, now I get to have my picture taken. What a delight it'll be to see myself hot, sweaty, exhausted, and nauseated in tomorrow's newspaper.

'Here are your free passes to the gym for two years,' Edgemont says, trying not to breathe in too much. Greg and I are pretty ripe, so I can't say I blame him.

The world swims out of focus again as I take the passes from his immaculately manicured hand. 'Thanks very much.'

'How did you enjoy riding the bike?' he asks.

'Whaa?'

'The bike? It's state of the art. Did you enjoy riding it?'

'I guess,' Greg replies.

'Excellent!'

Elise thrusts the microphone under my nose again. 'Anything else you'd like to add, Zoe?'

I look up at her. A fierce wave of nausea washes through me.

'Yes, Elise. I think I might throw up a bit, if that's okay with you?'

'Pardon?'

Adam Edgemont wails in horror as I up chuck all over his expensive shoes. I hope for his sake that there's a dry cleaner's open somewhere, so he can get rid of the contents of my stomach, which are now swilling around in his trouser cuffs.

And so here I sit, some twenty-four hours later.

My thighs ache terribly, my chest feels incredibly tight, and I've burst a blood vessel in my right eye. Basically, I look and feel a right fucking state.

On the table in front of me is a copy of the local paper. On page four there is the story summing up yesterday's challenge, featuring a picture of me throwing up over Adam Edgemont, along with the headline 'FAT CHANCE THROWS UP A WORTHY WINNER.'

All of these things should conspire to make me feel awful about myself.

I should be crying my eyes out with embarrassment, humiliation, and pain.

But I'm not.

In fact, I'm the happiest I've been in a long time.

Because I *won*.

Because Zoe Milton didn't give up, give in, or give out. I started something . . . and I finished it.

For the first time I'm actually starting to enjoy being part of Fat Chance.

And to top it all off, the Fitness4All passes are up to three hundred quid already on eBay!

GREG'S WEIGHT LOSS DIARY

Thursday, May 29th

17 stone, 11 pounds (2 stone, 5 pounds lost)

Well, I've done the one thing that no straight man with any ounce of self-respect should even contemplate.

Dieting.

Urgh.

Even writing the word down makes me cringe.

Yes, I know I don't sound particularly twenty-first century, but I don't care. I come from a time when men simply did not allow the concept of dieting a place in their prefrontal cortex. It was also a time of crippling emotional detachment and repressed feelings about anything other than the football scores, but we'll try our best to gloss over that.

As far as the cavemen of my generation are concerned, the word *dieting* goes hand in hand with words such as *sissy* and *poofter*.

And yet, fifty thousand of your finest English pounds are at stake, so I've resigned myself to the fact that I'm going to have to undertake some kind of dietary change, if I'm ever going to lose the required amount of weight and win all of that lovely money.

I certainly can't do more exercise than I am already. In the few hours between work and bed I manage to squeeze in at least an hour of jogging—or various indoor aerobics like sit-ups and press-ups if the weather is nasty. I'm following a less restricted version of the regime Alice Pithering put me on for that week from Hell.

The weight loss has been noticeable from all of this, but I'm still not dropping the poundage as fast as I'd like.

More and more as the weeks have gone by I have come to realise that strenuous activity alone is not enough to shift the fat: you also have to cut back on the calorie intake.

This is irritating in the extreme.

It's one thing to have to haul your arse round the park for an hour a day. It's quite another to deny yourself some of life's absolute necessities—such as bacon sandwiches, a prawn biryani with chips, and the After Eight Mint McFlurry.

Nevertheless, I'm committed to this now, so have to bite the bullet and accept that—like a prostitute who works the docks—I will enjoy nothing I put in my mouth for the foreseeable future.

The main problem is that I don't want to try any diet that might make me look even the slightest bit effeminate. As most diets are geared around the fairer sex, this is not easy.

Obviously I'm not getting within five hundred miles of any diet where you have to go to a meeting on a regular basis. I can't think of anything I'd rather do less than sit in a circle with a bunch of other fat people talking about how my girth has ruined my sex life. People would be *crying*, of that there is no doubt. I know some people attend these horror stories for motivation, but I have the carrot of fifty grand dangled in front of my chubby little cheeks, so am as motivated as I could possibly be, without having to listen to Tracey telling us all that she can't mount her husband any more for fear of suffocating him.

Then there are all the diets they talk about in those strange women's magazines that anyone with a penis has trouble understanding at the best of times. You know, the ones that are always named after their inventors. For example: Atkins, Dukan, and Stillman.

This sounds like the kind of legal firm you'd have to employ to sue said inventors for the damage done to your vital organs thanks to severe starvation caused by their stupid diets.

I can't get behind any of the weight loss programmes designed around eating one particular kind of food either. The cabbage soup thing was right out of the window the second I smelt Zoe's first night-time fart, the grapefruit diet sounds like a recipe for severe stomach acid reflux, and the cookie diet just sounds completely counter-intuitive, given that I can consume an entire packet of Maryland Double Choc Chip with no trouble whatsoever.

I was beginning to despair of ever finding a manly, serious, no-nonsense diet to call my own.

Then, like buses, two came along at once.

Both of them sounded about as hard, manly, and tough as is it possible to get: The Russian Air Force Diet, and the Israeli Army Diet.

When it comes to being hard-nosed, severe, and completely free of frilly bits, you can't get much better than the Russian and Israeli armed forces. One spent years frozen solid on the eastern front protecting it from the Germans, while the other has spent decades in the baking heat dodging explosive devices lobbed at them by a bunch of surly Arabs. Such hardships breed *real* men— and real diets, *dammit!*

Looking at the two options, I decided to try out the Russian Air Force one first, as it looked the slightly less awful of the two.

I say slightly, because neither is exactly what you'd call pleasant. Both call for a severe restriction of calorie intake, along with the consumption of an extremely limited number of food types.

One thing that both share in common, however, is that you can drink a shitload of black coffee. I can only surmise that avoiding

German patrols and Palestinian RPGs at night calls for a lot of caffeine.

Breakfast on the Russian diet consists of coffee and toast. Dry toast, mind—don't be thinking you can sling some peanut butter on it or anything.

Now, I normally drink only one cup of coffee or tea a day on average, but when your stomach is still rumbling like a freight train because you've only eaten a solitary slice of dry toast, you have to fill it up with something, so my coffee intake immediately went up to three cups before even getting into the car for the drive to work.

The commute is a lot more stressful when you've got a massive hit of caffeine running around in your system, it has to be said. I'm usually fairly placid about dealing with bad driving (for a man, anyway) but after three cups of your finest java, I want to tear the fucking head off every single bastard on the road beside me, whether they've done anything to incur my wrath or not.

By the time I roll into the car park at work I'm livid with the entire universe. I usually give Malcolm the security guy a friendly hello on my way into the building, but on this day I can only summon a low grunt. Xpert—the electronics company I work for—is one of those progressive organisations that likes to foster a laid-back atmosphere in its offices, like a great many Silicon Valley tech firms in the USA. As I said, I'm normally a pretty laid-back kind of guy, so I fit in quite well. On this caffeine-riddled day, though, I'm finding the soft furnishings and attractive wall art to be incredibly annoying. You know you're in a bad way when inanimate objects have the power to irritate you just by their existence.

Even my usually comfortable office chair feels hard and unyielding as I lower my big backside into it.

I simply am not used to having this much coffee swilling around my system, and as the clock reaches 11 a.m. I'm just about ready to batter myself to death with one of the cushions from the lime-green sofa that sits in our office relaxation area.

I'm also not used to being this starved of sugar. Usually by mid-morning I've eaten a big bowl of crunchy nut cornflakes, a bacon sandwich, and a donut from the cafeteria.

It really is quite amazing how profound an effect the chemicals we put in our bodies have on our day-to-day well-being. No sweet stuff and too much fast stuff have turned Greg Milton from an amiable fat bloke into Mussolini's less tolerant younger brother.

Still, at least I have lunch to look forward to.

. . . Oh no, wait. I don't have lunch to look forward to because I'm on the Russian Air Force Diet. This means that my lunch will consist of two dry scrambled eggs and a tomato, microwaved in the plastic container I've brought them to work in.

'What the hell is that, Greg?' Crazy Debbie asks me in the kitchen when I produce my plastic container of eggy disappointment.

'It's my lunch,' I reply.

'It looks like something my cat brought up last night,' Crazy Debbie informs me.

I don't know why my lunchtime ritual always seems to coincide with Crazy Debbie's. It's like her stomach and mine have become psychically linked over the years I've worked here. This has led to many conversations with the woman as we stand in front of the microwave waiting for our meals to warm through. Given that up until this stupid diet I used to have a rather large microwaveable lunch, these little chats would go on for quite some time, as I'd usually be nuking at least a couple of burgers or kebabs to keep me going through the afternoon.

It's the contents of these conversations that have convinced me that Crazy Debbie is in fact crazier than a box of squirrels.

Oh, she looks fairly ordinary, with her dowdy work clothes and lank brunette hair, but underneath that librarian-like exterior beats the heart of a raving lunatic.

For instance, I know all about her obsession with llamas. The llama books she reads, the llama t-shirts she wears at the weekends, the llama stuffed toys she has around her house. None of this sounds particularly crazy, I'll grant you. People fall in love with all types of animals, and llamas are no more or less attractive than horses when you get right down to it.

Then Crazy Debbie told me she'd eaten a llama's heart raw while on a walking holiday in Tibet, and I began to have grave misgivings about her mental state. 'It tasted rubbery,' she said as my chicken shish sizzled its way to edibility. She then spent ten minutes explaining that she ate the raw heart as she wanted to ingest the soul of the llama to better understand its place in the universe. I had to leave half of the chicken kebab in the end.

Crazy Debbie also likes to have sex with strangers in a car park, owns a collection of samurai swords, and speaks fluent Yiddish. She's not even *Jewish*.

No one really speaks to Crazy Debbie much around the office, so I know I'm the only one who understands the depths of her insanity thanks to our lunch time microwavey chats.

'Where's your usual lunch, Greg?' Crazy Debbie asks me, her eyes squinting.

'Er, I'm on a diet, Debbie.'

'Are you?'

'Um, yeah. Haven't you noticed I've been eating a lot less recently?'

'Not really.'

'I've lost nearly two stone.'

'Oh. I hadn't noticed.'

This is both demoralising and surprising.

Not surprising that she hasn't noticed my weight loss, but surprising that she wasn't aware that I was on a diet. My inclusion in Fat Chance has been the subject of much water cooler talk around the office. Despite her lack of communication with her fellow workmates, I'm amazed that Crazy Debbie hasn't heard about it, given that I don't seem to be able to walk two paces through the building without at least one person mentioning it to me. Even Gunta, the Latvian cleaner who hardly speaks English, knows that 'big mister Gregory is on fat radio show.'

'You don't listen to Stream FM, then?' I say to Crazy Debbie.

'What's that?'

'The local radio station.'

Crazy Debbie's face darkens into a suspicious scowl. 'I don't listen to the radio,' she says flatly.

For a second I almost ask why, but then it occurs to me that anyone who speaks Yiddish for no reason and eats llama hearts probably has a reason for not listening to the radio that I really don't want to hear about.

Crazy Debbie pokes a crazy finger at my plastic container. 'What is it?' she asks.

'Two eggs and a tomato.'

'Not much of a lunch.'

'No.'

'Why no salad stuff? Or a Ryvita? Or some vegetables?'

Or a llama heart?

'I'm on the Russian Air Force Diet.'

'The what?'

I explain to her that for seven days I'm having nothing but coffee and toast in the morning, followed by a tiny combination of meat, eggs, vegetables, and fruit for my other two meals. I am allowed to douse the whole lot in Worcestershire sauce, pepper, and mustard, though, if I so desire.

It occurs to me that explaining the diet out loud makes it sound completely barking mad.

'I see. Sounds sensible to me,' Crazy Debbie says when I've finished. She pauses for a second. 'Did I ever tell you about my Russian friend Uri? I met him in the car park at Sainsbury's one night last summer. Big chap he was. Drove an old Mercedes Benz. It had a really big, comfortable back seat that we—'

Ping!

I'm saved a lurid description of Crazy Debbie versus the mad-dogging Russian by the microwave informing me that my eggs and tomato are ready to be consumed—whether I want them or not.

'Oh, look! My lunch is done,' I say a little too quickly, opening the door. The smell that emanates from the microwave is like a triumphant fart.

I now have a choice.

I can eat the fart tomato, or I can stand here and listen to more of Crazy Debbie's life story.

The decision is ultimately an easy one. 'Well, must be getting back to my desk. Lots of work to do!' I tell Crazy Debbie and turn to leave, holding the fart tomato out in front of me as if it's a live hand grenade.

'You don't want to lose too much weight, Greg,' Crazy Debbie says, ominously.

'Why . . . why not Debbie?'

'You'll need your reserves of fat to keep you going when it happens.'

I edge closer to the kitchen door. 'When what happens?' I say, not really wanting an answer.

'You know. When the end comes.'

'Okay, Debbie! Nice to speak to you! I'll be off now. Enjoy the rest of your day!'

I hurry back to my desk and sit down, not looking up for a good twenty minutes just in case I see Crazy Debbie hovering over me with a copy of the *Necronomicon*.

The fart tomato is horrible. Microwaved eggs are never appetising at the best of times, but when you add a tomato into the equation you end up with a watery mess that does indeed resemble something a cat might produce after a night on the tiles.

The rest of my day is spent coming down off my caffeine high, dealing with my sugar low, and trying not to think about Crazy Debbie as a harbinger of the oncoming apocalypse.

By the time I get home I feel miserable, tired, and thick-headed.

. . . and this is only day one of the diet.

For tea I am allowed a few ounces of red meat and some green salad. It doesn't stipulate how much green salad, so I take liberties and eat an entire iceberg lettuce.

'How was your first day?' Zoe asks me as I sip one of the four large glasses of water the diet advises I also consume a day.

'Well, I now hate the soft furnishings at work, will never be able to eat a fry-up again, and have an overwhelming urge to donate money to the Save The Llama Foundation.'

'So you'd say it was going well, then?'

'Oh my, yes.'

Sometimes I am amazed at my own levels of stupidity.

I should have just quit the Russian Air Force Diet after day one, knowing full well that it was doing me no good. I can be an extremely stubborn person, though, when left to my own devices, so instead of packing it in, I decide that I will see out the seven days—and be damn well proud of my accomplishment at the end of the week.

The next morning I consume another three cups of coffee with my dry toast and vibrate my way to work, screaming at innocent motorists like they've attempted to have uncooperative sex with one of my elderly relatives.

We all know that nicotine is incredibly addictive, and that it can take only one cigarette to get you hooked, but I wasn't aware that caffeine possessed similar qualities.

By mid-morning I am, once again, feeling bloody dreadful. I'm currently working on a rather complex instruction manual for a medical scanner and need my powers of concentration honed to a fine point in order to put the thing together properly. Sadly, all I can think about as I crouch over the keyboard is how furry my tongue is. I also have a whistling nose. Every time I breathe out I sound like one of those old-fashioned kettles. The combination of fur and whistle are distracting me thoroughly from the task at hand.

I need something to kick-start my brain into some sort of proper cognitive function.

I go down to the kitchen and make myself a cup of Kenco. I add two heaped spoonfuls of coffee for good measure . . . which I can cheerfully admit now was a mistake.

Within twenty minutes of downing the thick, bitter concoction my mental faculties have skyrocketed. The furry tongue and whistling nose are erased from my mind and I am more focused on my work than the Hubble telescope.

My fingers are a whirl on the keyboard; the mouse flies across the pad at near supersonic speeds.

When a work colleague comes over to discuss a meeting we have the next day, I usher him away with a few grunts and squeaks, and return to my flurry of work.

When I come to look back at all this productivity about a week later it will become apparent that what I've written is complete tosh, but right now—while I'm in the zone—I feel like I'm doing my best work *ever*.

By midday two things have occurred.

I've finished all the work I'd planned for that entire day, and I've crashed down from the caffeine high like the fucking Hindenburg.

Still, lunchtime beckons. Some food should perk me up.

Today, instead of the fart tomato, I am blessed with a small beef burger and some lettuce.

Now, I'm pausing here to speak directly to any members of the Russian military who may have picked this diary up for a look.

My question to you good folk is this:

Why?

Oh good God in Heaven, *why?*

I know it is cold up there and there's not much to do once you get outside Moscow and can't see the red light district any more, but for the love of all that's holy, why would you make life even worse for yourself by eating such a ridiculous diet?

Yes, I know the Cold War was a bit of a bugger and getting a decent meal behind the Iron Curtain wasn't exactly easy, but it's been over *twenty years*, people.

Have you seen what soldiers in the American army have access to? I'm fairly sure I once heard about a McDonald's being opened on an army base.

They're allowed all sorts of tasty food, those Yankee chaps.

And you know what? So are you!

Stalin's dead, in case you hadn't quite noticed. You don't have to eat like the end of the world happened three days ago anymore.

It's not like the strict diet has helped you win many wars recently, has it? The US kicked your arse in the Cold War, those Chechnyans are still giving you a whole heap of trouble, and the less said about what happened in Afghanistan in the eighties the better.

I'm not saying that eating Big Macs would necessarily have led to a crushing victory over your various opponents, but at least you could have managed a bit of comfort eating in the aftermath of defeat. A few tubs of Ben & Jerry's might have softened the blow when the Berlin wall came down, that's all I'm saying.

Anyway.

I choose to eat my solitary burger cold at my desk. I try to imagine myself huddled over a gas stove on the Eastern Front with Germans all around, but the mental image this conjures up is rather depressing, so I dispel it with a swig of my Diet Coke and get back to work.

Diet Coke acts as an efficient caffeine delivery mechanism, just like coffee, so by the time I've finished my second can of the brown fizzy stuff, I'm back up in the clouds and buzzing like a swarm of bees. The rest of my working day passes at lightning speed.

'Are you feeling alright?' Zoe asks me as I kiss her hello when I get home that night. 'Your eyes are bloodshot and you're blinking a lot more than usual.'

'I'm fine, Zoe. Absolutely fine. Just had a little too much caffeine today, I think. It's this diet I'm on. It's making me drink a lot of the stuff, you know? Those Russians must really love their coffee. It's not too bad, though. I got a lot of work done today, and I'm not feeling all that hungry at all, funnily enough. You wouldn't think that, would you? A couple of days ago all I could think about was being hungry but today I've hardly noticed that I've not eaten much of anything. I bet I've lost some more weight. I'll have to go weigh myself this evening to check how much I've lost. I know Elise said we shouldn't do it so it will be a surprise at the weigh-ins, but I just don't think I've got the willpower not to check. What do you think, baby?'

'What?'

'Nothing. Have we got any Coke in the house?'

'There's a bottle of the cheap Asda stuff in the cupboard but I don't think—'

'That's fine! That'll do! Cheap Asda Coke is fine by me! I mean, it's not as good as the real stuff, is it? It always tastes a bit more watery to me and never quite as sugary. But then I guess that's why they can afford to make it so cheap to buy, because they don't worry about it tasting as good. I wonder where they have it made? Do you think they might make it in Russia and have it imported? That would make sense, because the Russians don't seem to be too worried about what their food and drink tastes like, as long as it's nice and cheap. You want a glass, too?'

It takes Zoe a few seconds to respond. 'No, thanks,' she eventually says, a look of deep concern in her eyes.

'Okay then, I'll go make myself a cup. Cup? Cup? You don't drink Coke from a cup, do you? I meant glass. You drink Coke from a glass! You drink coffee from a cup. Silly me. I must be hungry.'

And with that I disappear into the kitchen, leaving my wife sitting in the living room trying to disentangle that whole conversation and derive some meaning from it.

Needless to say, the next two days proceed in similar fashion.

I don't know what being addicted to heroin or cocaine is like, but if my newly discovered dependence to the legal drug caffeine is anything to go by, it must be pretty damn unpleasant.

If I'm being honest here, I would struggle to give a clear account of that forty-eight-hour period. I know I did some stuff. For instance, Zoe and I went to the cinema. I didn't see much of the film though. I had to keep getting up to go for a piss every five minutes, so I missed much of the plot. Thankfully, it was a romantic comedy starring Jennifer Aniston, so missing a majority of it was probably a godsend.

Since I started drinking all this caffeine, my bladder appears to have shrunk to the size of a golf ball. Not half an hour goes by these days without me having to get up from whatever it is I'm doing to visit the little boys' room. I'm starting to worry what damage all this is doing to my prostate.

The issue with my dependency on caffeine drinks comes to a head on day five of the diet—more specifically, that Friday evening.

This was the monthly dinner with the in-laws—an event I never look forward to with much enthusiasm, even when I'm allowed to eat what I want. This occasion promised to be ten times worse than usual, given that my hearty meal for the evening based on the Air Force Diet would be a princely eight-and-three-quarter ounces of red meat. This amounted to one rather anaemic-looking bit of steak from the Tesco meat counter.

It was our turn to host the meal this month, which was just as well, as turning up on their doorstep with my anaemic steak in a plastic Tupperware container would have been highly embarrassing.

To not make me look like such a weirdo, Zoe had elected to cook steak for everyone. That way I wouldn't feel completely left out. I might not be able to eat any of the delicious roast potatoes or steamed crisp vegetables everyone else would be having, but at least I'd be in some proximity to them as I chewed my way through my small piece of beef.

I'd be chewing the fucker pretty damn quickly, as I'd just finished off my *seventh* cup of coffee that day. Add that to two cans of Diet Coke I'd also consumed and I was so off my tits on caffeine I couldn't have stood still if you'd put several guns to my head.

∾

The doorbell rings at precisely seven thirty. The doorbell *always* rings at precisely seven thirty when Alan and Barbara Davenport come for dinner. Alan spent thirty years in the merchant navy and Babs has the kind of OCD that usually requires lengthy periods of treatment. As they've come in a taxi this evening, I don't know how they've managed to time their arrival so precisely. I can imagine Alan standing outside our front door for ten minutes looking at his watch until exactly half past seven.

'Evening, Gregory,' Alan says as I fling open the front door. I hate being called Gregory.

'Good evening Alan, good evening Barbara,' I reply quickly, thrusting out my hand. 'Can I take your coats?'

The poor buggers haven't even got in the door yet and I'm already trying to undress them.

Such is my loud, decisive, caffeine-laced tone that Alan is removing his coat on the doorstep before he even knows it. 'Er, thank you, Gregory,' he says, handing it to me as he walks into the hallway.

'No problem, no problem, glad to be of service!' I bark and waggle my outstretched hand at my mother-in-law as she follows her husband in. 'And yours, Barbara? Your coat? Can I take your coat? Give me your coat.'

Babs looks mildly terrified. She probably has some OCD-based ritual she usually goes through before removing an item of clothing, but I'm giving her no chance to do it tonight.

I more or less rip the long wool coat off her back as she hurries past me. 'Thank you, thank you, well done,' I tell them, as if they'd learned a new trick. I open the door to the cupboard and attempt to hang both coats up. The hooks are overburdened already, though, so I end up just tossing Alan's over the ironing board.

'Where is Zoe?' Alan asks as I shut the door and offer him a hectic grin.

'Zoe? Zoe? She's in the kitchen, Alan, cooking us up a lovely meal. Well, cooking *you* up a lovely meal. I'm on this diet at the moment, you see. It's called the Russian Air Force Diet. It's very good; I've lost quite a bit of weight this week. The only problem is I don't get to eat much at tea time. I'll have finished mine off before you've even popped the first potato in your mouth, probably!' I end my babbling diatribe with a rather hysterical chuckle. By the time this fades out we've reached the living room and I'm jiggling about on the spot like I need a piss. Which I actually do, of course.

Zoe appears from the kitchen and comes over to give her mother and father a hug. 'How are you both?' she says warmly.

'We're well, thank you,' Babs replies. 'Greg's just been talking at us about his diet.'

I chuckle again and jiggle a bit more. 'Yes, yes, yes, I have. Very good diet it is. Very good indeed.'

'It's certainly given you a lot of, er . . . pep,' Alan responds.

'Oh my, yes,' I say and chuckle/jiggle once again. I couldn't be more disconcerting right now if I was dressed as a clown and licking a paring knife.

Zoe sighs and rubs her eyes. 'It's the caffeine, Dad. The diet means he has to drink a lot of coffee, which he's not used to, so . . .'

'Ah, I see.'

'Yes, yes!' Chuckle/jiggle. 'Lots and lots of lovely caffeine, every day!' Chuckle/jiggle. 'I'm not hungry, though, Barbara!' Zoe's mother blanches. 'I'm not hungry at all! Well, I'm a little bit hungry, but mostly I'm just really, really happy and excited.' I have the overwhelming urge to give Babs a hug, so I do. I feel her go stiff beneath my arms. 'And I'm very, very pleased to see you both.' Now I'm chuckle/jiggling and hugging my mother-in-law all at the same time. This whole thing has descended into levels of creepiness that may require some sort of religious intervention.

'Leave Mum alone, Greg,' Zoe tells me. 'Why don't you pour us all a glass of wine while I talk to them?'

'Okay, okay, that sounds like a lovely idea!'

I vibrate my way out into the kitchen, giving Zoe a chance to explain, and no doubt apologise for my rather odd behaviour.

Not only does too much caffeine make you livelier than an electrocuted cat, it can also make you incredibly indecisive. I discover this rather unlovely side effect as I'm standing in the kitchen attempting to pour my in-laws a drink.

We have wine in all three shades in our house. Given the weight loss regimes that Zoe and I have both been on, not much of it has been drunk recently, but that hasn't stopped people giving it to us over the past few weeks at parties similar to this one. This has led to something of a build-up, so I'm faced with having to decide between no less than three bottles of white, two of red, and one rosé.

I spend a constructive couple of minutes jiggling in front of them before I narrow my choices down to just the whites. This only partially helps matters, though, as I still have to decide between Chardonnay, Pinot Grigio, and Sauvignon.

I'd better ask.

'Excuse me?' I say from round the kitchen door.

'What, Greg?' Zoe answers.

'Just wondering which wine they'd like to drink. Only we have quite a lot. There's Chardonnay, Pinot, or Sauvignon. I thought maybe the Pinot as the Chardonnay looks a bit cheap—you know, dear, it's the one the company gave you for hitting those targets. Well done on that, by the way. Did I say well done already? I can't remember if I said well done. Well done! The Sauvignon's the same as that one we bought from Tesco at Christmas. The one I didn't like. Remember? It was too sweet I thought, for a Sauvignon. Not that I'm much of a wine drinker, anyway. Always prefer a beer myself, but you can't just drink beer at a dinner party, can you? It just wouldn't be *right*, I don't think. So I'll go with the Pinot, shall I? Yes, I'll just pour you all a glass of Pinot. That'll be for the best.'

Without waiting for an actual response from anyone I disappear back into the kitchen again. It turns out you *can* make decisions on your own when high on caffeine; you just don't realise you're doing it at the time.

Ah, but will they want big glasses or small glasses?

Shit.

Um.

Er.

Big!

Big is always better!

I pour Babs and Alan the kind of measures that get you thrown in prison if you so much as look at a motorcar after drinking it. I've emptied an entire bottle with two glasses.

As we're both trying to lose weight, I prepare two tiny glasses for Zoe and me. What I'm basically saying with my choices here is that I think my wife's parents are a couple of raging alcoholics.

Judging by the shocked expressions their faces as I hand them the drinks, they think so too.

The next half an hour is agony. For the other three people in the conversation, anyway. I'm happier than a pig in shit.

The combination of caffeine and alcohol mixes nicely in the speech centre of my brain and I spend thirty minutes verbally bashing my extended family over the head with a series of conversation topics I can barely recall now.

From what I remember, I started off educating them about how much sugar there is in wine, then I moved on to how much sugar there is in cheese. Then I moved on to a story I'd read about a chair made of cheese, and *then* I moved on to a story I'd read about a chair made of beer cans. Then I moved on to how saying 'beer can' sounds like you're saying bacon in a Jamaican accent, then I moved on to how Zoe and I want a holiday in the Caribbean—or maybe the Seychelles, or maybe Key West, or maybe China . . .

The rest is a bit of a blur, but by the time Zoe ushers me out into the kitchen to help her dish out the dinner, I have for some reason started singing the Ying Tong song, as made famous by The Goons.

'Ying tong, ying tong, ying tong, ying tong, ying tong tiddle-eye poh,' I merrily sing as I vibrate my way across the lounge with my incredibly irate wife.

'Will you stop it!' she hisses at me once we're out of her parents' eye-line.

'Stop what?'

'You're acting like a drug addict. They probably think you're really on cocaine, not just drinking too much bloody coffee.'

'Well, you know technically, the original Coca-Cola drink did have cocaine in it, I think, so I guess that's probably where the name comes from, so—'

'Shut up!'

I do as I'm bid, though it takes a great deal of effort.

I manage to keep my verbal diarrhoea under control while Zoe and I prepare the meal. By the time we sit down to eat the food, though, I'm back on the babble train.

It would be fine if I had a decent amount of food to stuff in my gob and keep me quiet, but I wolf down the small steak in about ten seconds flat, leaving me plenty of time to flap my lips while my wife and her parents try their best to enjoy their meals, with my incessant talking as an unwanted accompaniment.

Things reach their final and shocking denouement as Alan and Babs finish off the crème brûlée Zoe had made especially for them.

'Crème brûlée is a fascinating pudding,' I jabber. 'Caramelising the sugar properly is particularly difficult and takes a great deal of skill. Zoe's very good at it now, but you should have seen some of the disasters she's come up with in the past. Oh my, yes. Many times I've stood with her in the kitchen while she's attempted another batch. The smell of burnt sugar really is quite horrible, I think. Our extractor fan could barely cope with it. Still, she's got it down to a fine art now, as you can probably tell from the ones you're eating. She's a very talented cook, is your daughter. Much better than me, anyway. I'm sure she probably gets it from you, Barbara. I always look forward to coming round to you for a meal. She's certainly a chip off the old—'

'Shut up, Greg,' Barbara says in a small, exasperated voice.

'Sorry?'

'Be quiet. Please, *please* be bloody quiet, just for a moment.'

I'm stunned. Barbara is usually a very polite, gentle woman. All that obsessive compulsive stuff leads to the kind of temperament ill-suited to confrontation.

'I'm sorry, Barbara,' I apologise. 'I was only complimenting you on your cooking. I wouldn't have thought you'd be offended by that. Mind you, it's strange what some people can be offended by these days. I was watching the news the other day and there was this woman on there who was up in arms about something on the BBC last week. A show about religion it was. She was really unhappy about—'

'Can't you just stop talking?' Alan interjects. 'We've hardly been able to get a word in all evening!'

'Haven't you? *Really*? I thought we'd been having a lovely conversation tonight. After all, we've talked about cheese, and the Chinese, and The Goons, and beer cans, and China. Did I already say China? Well, we've definitely talked about it . . .'

I can't stop myself. I am simply unable to prevent words from spilling out of my big fat mouth at an absurd rate of knots.

I'm also aware of a thunderous headache starting to form at the back of my skull.

'Greg!' Zoe snaps. 'For God's sake go and calm down upstairs!'

And so we have the final ignominy.

I have been ordered to go up to my room like a badly behaved child.

Alan and Barbara are silent as I push my chair back and stand. I start to apologise for talking at them so much, but I pause with my mouth half open. If I start speaking again now I'm likely to launch into yet another ramble and make things even worse.

I bend down and give Zoe a kiss on her red forehead before backing away from the table and leaving the lounge.

As I climb the stairs I can hear Zoe giving her parents the apology and explanation I was unable to provide. '. . . it's the caffeine,' she is saying. 'He's just not used to it. It's like giving too much sugar to a five-year-old.'

I close the bedroom door for fear of hearing any more. The humiliation of it would be too much to bear.

I spend the next hour or so jiggling around the bedroom until I hear Zoe call up to me that her parents are leaving.

Like the aforementioned badly behaved child, I slope back down the stairs with my head hanging.

'I'm sorry I was so silly,' I tell Barbara and Alan as they put on their coats.

Babs puts a conciliatory hand on my shoulder. 'It's alright, Greg. Zoe explained how much of that stuff you've been drinking because of the diet.'

'You do appear to have lost a lot of weight, though,' Alan remarks, which puts a smile on my face for the first time since I was banished to the top floor.

'Do you really think so?' I say. 'I'm so pleased you've noticed. After all, that's why I'm on the diet. There wouldn't be much point in drinking all that coffee if I didn't lose any weight, eh? No, no. It would be a complete waste of time. It's not *that* bad a diet, really. I haven't felt all that hungry in days. Which is surprising for me, because the amount of food I used to pack away would suggest that I really would miss it more than I have. I guess coffee must be something of an appetite suppressant. Bit like cigarettes, I suppose. Not that I'd ever try cigarettes as a way to lose weight. I mean, all you'd be doing then is swapping one bad thing for—'

'Greg!' Zoe snaps.

'Sorry! Sorry!'

I clamp my lips shut and give the parents-in-law a final goodbye that consists largely of hand gestures. Once Zoe closes the front door on them, I start chewing on one knuckle, knowing that the next few minutes of my life are going to be all about getting told off.

'Well, thank you, Speedy Gonzales,' Zoe begins. 'Here I am trying to convince our loved ones that these diets are worth all the time and effort and you start acting like a heroin junkie.' I open my mouth to respond. 'Don't say anything!' Zoe barks, and slaps my arm. 'Just keep your mouth shut and listen. God knows, your jaw could probably do with a rest. It's a wonder it hasn't fallen off with all that motor-mouthing.'

And so, Gregory Milton's evening comes to an end with having a stern finger pointed at him, and the kind of verbal abuse no man with a caffeine addiction should have to suffer.

That's a complete lie. My evening does *not* come to an end at that point at all, given how much coffee I've drunk throughout the day.

My evening *actually* comes to an end at about three in the morning, a good four hours after Zoe has gone to bed.

I spend most of that time shaking in the corner of the living room, flicking the TV repeatedly between a 'Location, Location, Location' marathon, and four episodes of 'Australian MasterChef,' both at a very low volume.

By the time I feel tired enough to go up to bed, I could easily have told you how long you need to cook a three-bed semi in the Lake District to get the right consistency, and exactly how large a mortgage you should be paying on a chocolate and maraschino cake with excellent views of Windermere.

. . . or something like that anyway. By this time my brain is crashing from the caffeine high and I may have become a little confused.

I climb out of bed the next day at about ten fifteen. My eyes are glued shut for a good twenty minutes after that.

I stumble into the kitchen and immediately start looking for the Kenco Finest.

'Oh no you bloody don't, pal!' Zoe snaps at me. 'You're not drinking another cup of that stuff unless it's decaf.'

'But the diet . . .'

'Fuck the diet! Have some orange juice and we'll buy a jar of caffeine-free coffee later.'

Which, when you think about it, is something I should probably have done at least three days ago.

The change to decaf is painful. Very, *very* painful.

Withdrawing from the chemical I've become so quickly dependent on is a trial I never intend to repeat. Within forty-eight hours I am lethargic, confused, irritable, and suffering from the worst constipation of my life.

It's now been five days since I last had any caffeine, and I only took my first decent crap this morning. It was like a war zone down there.

I'm still bloody tetchy, and have been snappy with everyone I've come into contact with.

Still, better I walk around like a bear with a sore head, and not the Tasmanian Devil. I may have been pretty rude to people over the past few days during my withdrawal, but at least I haven't told them my entire life story in five minutes while showering them with spittle.

I have to confess that I just couldn't take on the Israeli Army Diet after my experience with the Russian Air Force equivalent. It called for even more coffee consumption, and even less food.

I just didn't think my brain or my bowels could take it.

There's a very good reason why diets like these don't become more popular in the mainstream. It is because they are incredibly *stupid*. Stupid and highly detrimental to your well-being.

A reliance on coffee and very little else may be good for members of the Russian and Israeli armed forces, but for a fat middle-aged bloke in England they are a distinct no-no.

I am absolutely *done* with these diets.

I may eat my words and live to regret this decision if we're ever invaded by hordes of screaming Chechnyans and grenade-flinging Arabs, but it's a chance I am most definitely willing to take.

ZOE'S WEIGHT LOSS DIARY
Tuesday, June 10th
12 stone, 5 pounds (2 stone, 2 pounds lost)

I can't believe we've been at this for three months now. Time seems to be slipping away as fast as the inches around my waist. Despite the horrors of the cabbage soup diet, and some of the other methods of weight loss I'm employing (which I can't bring myself to write about here yet; it's too disturbing to my fragile mental state. Check back with me when I'm not so calorie starved) I'm managing to just about maintain my sanity.

I think I've reached the stage where both my body and mind are getting used to the massive change in lifestyle . . . but it's touch and go sometimes. Yesterday, for instance, I spent a good twenty minutes fantasising about going for a swim in a lake of double cream. At the centre of the lake was an island made of Jamaican ginger cake. The swimming wasn't easy—double cream is quite thick, after all—but I managed to make the going a bit easier by opening my mouth and eating as much of it as possible.

When a telephone call snapped me out of the fantasy, I was miserable for the rest of the afternoon. I would quite happily have lived the rest of my life out on that brown squidgy island.

To make myself feel better, I picked up some holiday brochures for Jamaica on the way home from work. It looks like a nice place, but the sea is far too blue, not at all double cream like, and the island itself doesn't look edible in the slightest.

. . . As I say, it's touch and go sometimes.

I tell you one thing all this dieting is definitely doing, though.

It's making me horny.

Nymphomaniac levels of horny.

I've now lost two stone, Greg's dropped over two and half, and by golly, that collective weight loss is enough to set a woman's thoughts to all kinds of dirt.

I never realised that going on a strict diet could be such a kick-start to your libido.

Before the competition started, my sex drive was well and truly in the doldrums, and to be honest, our unhealthy lifestyles have put the dampers on our bedroom activities for the past few *years*.

When Greg and I first met at college we were, and I'll put this as delicately as my near-constant state of sexual arousal will let me, *fucking all the time* and absolutely *everywhere*.

I was nine stone and fit as a fiddle. Greg was thirteen stone— most of which was muscle thanks to all the rugby he played.

Frankly, we were both beautiful and we knew it.

We met when we were both eighteen years old, and high on being young and stupid. The head of the college rugby team wanted me to model a ladies' version of the new kit he'd just wasted most of the sport department's budget on, and I was more than happy to oblige given that the hundred pounds he'd promised me would set me up nicely for clubbing at the weekend. The photo shoot was arranged with me alongside one of the rugby team modelling the men's version of the kit. The guy chosen to do this was Gregory Milton.

Gorgeous, gorgeous Gregory Milton.

I still remember to this day the sharp bolt of electricity that passed through my whole body when I saw him for the first time.

I was sitting on a bench in the sports hall, pulling up the long white socks that came as part of the kit, when I looked up and saw him walk in through the double doors across the hall from me. Thankfully he wasn't high on painkillers that day, so didn't come stumbling in like a drunkard. No, back then Greg Milton strode everywhere with a confidence and poise that was enough to make this girl's heart thump very hard indeed.

He was carrying a rugby ball, casually tossing it in the air and catching it again without even looking. By the time he'd made it across to where the camera was being set up for the shoot, I was having trouble taking my eyes off him.

It later transpired that he felt the same way. 'The way you were playing with those long socks,' he would tell me weeks later, 'and the tight blue shorts? It was a miracle I didn't trip over my own penis.'

The photo shoot was conducted by Lionel, one of the photography department lecturers. Lionel was the kind of man who really shouldn't be let near a telephoto lens—especially when around other human beings. He had a reputation for being a right pervert.

Legend had it that his house was full of black and white photographic 'art' featuring young women in a variety of compromising positions. Legend also had it that he was on the registered sex offenders list, but that kind of rumour springs up very easily and is always almost impossible to verify.

The way Lionel had me seductively posed on and around Greg during the photo shoot gave me the distinct impression that there was something funny going on with him, though, I can tell you that.

'Now, Zoe, why don't you wrap your hands around Greg's bicep and press yourself up against him?' Lionel suggested.

'Really?'

'Yes, yes, I think that would look lovely.' He didn't quite wipe the dribble from his lips, but he was close, I could tell.

Now, had Greg not been six foot of walking sex I wouldn't have gone along with Lionel's request. As it was, I gave my future husband a speculative look and moved a bit closer to him. 'You okay with this?' I asked him.

Greg swallowed hard. 'Er, I think so. If Lionel reckons it'll look okay.'

'I'm sure it will.'

I couldn't actually give a toss what it looked like, of course. I just wanted a grope.

I snaked my arms around Greg's hard bicep, pressed myself up against him, turned to the camera, and smiled.

Greg smelled absolutely *amazing* and it took all my self-control not to fall on the floor in a gooey mess. A sight like that wouldn't have made a particularly good photo.

'Now, I think you should stand in front of Greg and hold his ball,' Lionel instructed me.

I assumed Lionel was referring to the rugby ball Greg had brought along, though at this point I think I would have happily stuck my hand down his shorts and had a good old rummage.

'Put your arms around her, please,' Lionel said to Greg as I got into position.

I felt his strong arms gently rest across my shoulders and the breath was sucked right out of my body. I nearly dropped the bloody rugby ball.

By the time Lionel finally wrapped up the photo shoot I was so aroused it was a miracle I didn't rape poor old Gregory Milton right there and then on the sports hall floor.

'Thanks for doing this,' he said to me as we walked back towards the changing rooms. 'Selling these kits at the games was my idea and this will really help flog a few, with any luck.'

'My pleasure.'

'You certainly look a lot better in it than I do,' he said awkwardly as we reached the two separate doors leading to each changing room.

'I wouldn't say that,' I replied. 'You look pretty good in it, I reckon.'

The hormones were so thick between us by now you could almost see them floating in mid-air.

Greg licked his lips. I knew what was coming.

'Are you doing anything now?' he asked, 'I mean, would you like to maybe get a coffee with me in the canteen?'

Okay, so it wasn't exactly an invitation to join him at the Ritz, but I was eighteen and a coffee in the canteen sounded *wonderful.*

'Sure. That'd be nice. Meet you on the other side?'

'Yeah, yeah. Great. That'd be great. *Great.*'

With that settled, Greg was off through the changing room door quick as a flash.

'Greg!' I called after him.

'Yeah?

'Don't you want your ball back?' I held it out, smiled, and cocked my head to one side in the most outrageously flirtatious way I possibly could with my clothes still on.

It had the desired effect.

Greg took the ball back. Dropped it. Picked it up again. Gave me a sheepish smile and disappeared from sight.

I, on the other hand, walked calmly and slowly into the girls' changing room, feeling very smug indeed.

Look, I'm not going to beat around the bush here or lie to you: Greg and I wound up having sex for the first time about four hours later.

I am completely unapologetic about it as well.

My sexual experience up to that time had been with one guy called Chris, whom I'd dated the year before for a couple of months. As first-time sexual partners go, Chris was a fine introduction into the world of carnality, but he never really managed to knock my socks off. The only times I'd achieved an orgasm before the first time with Greg were on my own, and generally resulted in cramped fingers.

Greg had been with a couple of girls prior to me, but both had been one-night stands, so we were really on a par experience-wise when it came to that sort of thing.

The coffee in the canteen turned into a couple of alcoholic beverages in the local pub, which in turn led to a rather unsteady walk in the park, a good hard snogging session on a bench, and the aforementioned sex back at his parents' house.

It was just as well they were out at the cinema, as the sounds I made during the huge, rushing orgasm I felt as Greg came inside me would have disturbed them to an enormous degree, had they been downstairs watching 'Corrie.'

I felt a small pang of shame as I lay next to Greg on his single bed, as I tried to recover my wits. There's a name for girls who sleep with guys on a first date. It rhymes with hut, nut, and rut.

That small pang would stay with me for another couple of weeks until I realised I had fallen in love with Greg at first sight. When that happens to you, all bets are well and truly off.

Over the next few months, we embarked on a marathon of sex that only two teenagers in love can possibly maintain without serious injury. In fact, as I sit here looking back on it now, I can safely say that our sex life was always incredibly healthy, varied, and very regular throughout the first few years of our relationship.

. . . right until we got married and both fell into full-time jobs. But even then, we always made sure that we had sex at least once or twice a week, unless I was on my period, or either one of us was working lates.

In fact, our sex life was very healthy until about seven years ago, when we both hit our thirties and started to put on weight.

A funny thing happens to your metabolism when you reach thirty. It decides that it's had quite enough of burning off all that energy at a fast rate of knots, and figures it's time to take things easier from now on. Where once you could stuff away over two thousand calories a day and care not a jot, now the ounces and pounds start to slowly pile on.

You don't notice this happening, of course. If you did, you'd probably take steps to avoid it. But when you work thirty-eight hours a week and have things like mortgages and car insurance to worry about, it's amazing how fast you forget about your health and physical well-being.

So there comes an inevitable day when you go to put on a pair of jeans that you haven't worn since last summer . . . and discover that the bastard things won't button up anymore. Then you rush into the bathroom, brush the dust from the electronic scales that have sitting behind the laundry bin for two years, and stand on them with your heart thudding in your chest.

That day was the first time I'd ever looked down at the scales and seen a weight reading of over ten stone.

Needless to say I went on a diet right there and then. And for a while it worked. I went back under ten stone and called it a victory.

But then more years went by. Thirty turns very quickly into thirty-three, then thirty-four.

And the metabolism keeps slowing.

And the mortgage payments keep coming out of the bank.

Life becomes all about staying financially afloat and the constant drudge of commuting to the office.

Sex unfortunately becomes a rare monthly treat, rather than a daily recreational activity.

It becomes less and less of a treat the more you start to notice your love handles getting in the way. Marry that with the sound of your newly acquired body fat slapping together and your libido doesn't really stand a chance.

Where once you whispered filth into each other's ears and dressed up for some sexy role play, you now just go through the motions with one another before falling asleep—and are frankly surprised anytime you actually manage to achieve an orgasm.

If a couple has been together for a long time and their sex life has gone off the boil, they will often try to inject a little excitement back into their relationship, either by trying something a bit risqué or by attempting to recapture the magic of their early lives together.

Greg and I made the mistake of trying the latter option.

It was about six months before we started the competition, and we were both at what you could describe as our lowest ebb, in terms of our sex life and our lifestyles in general.

January is never a good month when you're fat. You've just had all the excesses of Christmas to deal with. And boy, did we get particularly excessive this year. Tins of Quality Street were consumed with abandon, turkey sandwiches were crammed in our mouths like there was no tomorrow. I drank my way through what felt like an ocean of red wine and Greg did much the same with the lager.

I confess that this edible debauchery was largely my fault. The embarrassing horror of getting stuck in the green dress the month before still weighed heavily on me, and I tried to cheer myself up in the only way I knew how: by eating.

What a cruel and idiotic thing the human brain truly is.

When faced with this kind of adversity through addiction it should prompt you into doing something *positive* about it. Logic suggests that if you're hooked on too much fat and sugar, there should be a part of your cerebral cortex ready and willing to metaphorically slap you around the face a few times until you come to your senses and start eating tofu. But *no*, the little sod doesn't do that. Instead it tries to cope with the misery of addiction by plunging you *even further* into the mire of the very obsession you need to get away from!

It's the equivalent of burning your hand in the fire and going back repeatedly to see just how crispy you can make your skin before the entire appendage drops off.

So during Christmas I salved my wounded self-esteem by making myself even fatter, in a glorious downward spiral that would have seen me washing myself with a rag on a stick and unable to walk if it hadn't been for Elise and her radio competition.

Between Christmas and the third week of January I'd put on half a stone and Greg three-quarters. We also hadn't had sex for over a month. More specifically, we hadn't had sex since I'd attempted to fit into that green dress—a fact that should come as absolutely no surprise to anyone.

This meant that for the first time in our fifteen years of marriage we hadn't made love over the Christmas period even once. Not one romantic session in front of the Christmas tree, not one quickie while the Queen was on, not one drunken shag after a Boxing Day party.

Nothing at all.

I'm sure Greg had wanked off a few times, given that no man can go a month without at least one incident of self-abuse, but my sex drive was utterly dormant for the first time in my life.

I've always enjoyed sex.

No, scratch that: I've always *loved* it.

From the first time with Greg, and on through the years until the weight really piled on, our sex life has been the cornerstone of what has by and large been the best relationship any woman can hope to have.

My husband is kind, thoughtful, intelligent, and loving. He also sports a large penis. This by no means has any influence on how much I love him, but when somebody serves you up a delicious cake, it's always nice to find a big, juicy cherry on top.

In all our time together a month has never gone by without sex, not until last Christmas.

Not even when Greg broke his leg and we had to employ a hastily constructed pulley with block and tackle so he could perform. Not even when I came down with a bout of influenza that would have pole-axed a rhino. I finished that particular session by being sick all over the carpet, but damn it, it was still some good, hard sex we had that night . . . what I can remember of it thanks to the delirium.

The realisation that we've gone so long without a shag dawns on us one night in front of the TV. We're watching 'Game of Thrones,' a program that seems to delight in the depiction of fantasy people going at it hammer and tongs on a fairly regular basis.

As a gorgeous thin redhead bounces up and down on a ruggedly handsome man in the kind of medieval castle bedroom that every girl dreams about staying just one night in, Greg turned to me and said 'When's the last time we did that, baby?'

'We've never stayed the night in a castle, Greg. I wanted to last year, if you remember, but you made me go to the Goodwood Festival of Speed instead.'

'I didn't mean that. I just meant . . . you know . . . what they're doing.'

'Oh, right,' I say and flush red. 'It's been a while.'

Greg starts counting on his fingers. I know full well how long it's been since we've had sex, but I'm interested to see if he'll come up with roughly the same figure. 'It's got to be over a month,' he eventually says.

'Thirty-four days,' I reply.

'Really? That's a lot for us.'

'Yes Greg, *it is*,' I sigh, and start picking at one corner of the cushion.

Greg sits up and looks at me closely for a few moments, before pausing 'Game of Thrones' in mid-shag and moving over on the couch to put his arms around me in a comforting manner. My husband knows how to read my moods very well.

'What's wrong, sweetheart?' he says and kisses my cheek.

'I'm not sexy.' I reply, downcast.

'What?'

'I'm not, Greg. I'm big and fat and ugly.'

'Don't be so bloody ridiculous!'

'Yes, I am. That's why we haven't had sex for ages.'

'It's only been a month! And we've both had lots of work on our plates. It's got nothing to do with how you look! You always look gorgeous to me.'

I can feel tears in my eyes, which I'm extremely annoyed about, but there doesn't appear to be anything I can do about it. 'But it was almost a month before the last time as well!' I cry. 'We do it less and less, Greg. And it's because I'm getting fatter and fatter!'

'No, no. That's not . . . it's not . . . I don't think you . . .' Greg blusters. I know he's trying to come up with an excuse that'll make me feel better, but I know he won't find one. He hangs his head and runs a hand through his hair, before grabbing one of his love handles and giving it a shake. 'I don't think it's down to you getting fatter anyway, baby.'

Oh, great. Now we're both depressed by our combined weight gain. This is turning into a truly *wonderful* evening.

Greg unpauses the TV and we watch the two thin, healthy people bouncing up and down on the bed for a few more moments.

'Turn this off, will you?' I eventually say when I just can't suffer the comparison any more.

We sit in silence for a few minutes before Greg utters the line that most people who have been married for over ten years probably say at some point. 'Maybe we could do something to . . . you know . . . make it more exciting?'

'What like? Do it on roller skates?'

'Not quite.' He lapses into silence again. Then I see the light of an idea spark in his eyes. 'I know! Let's do a bit of dressing up!'

'Dressing up?'

Greg waggles his eyebrows. 'Yeah, you know. Get some sexy stuff on and role play a little.'

I give him a withering look. 'You think Ann Summers caters for a woman of my size, do you? If I try to wear one of those tiny G-string and bra combos I'll end up looking look a rolled pork joint.'

Greg has the decency to not argue.

Another few silent minutes go by. I pick up the iPad and start mindlessly web surfing until Greg pipes up again.

'How about . . . how about what we were wearing when we first met?'

'You mean the rugby kits?'

'Yeah.' His eyes are gleaming. 'Yeah, the rugby kits. I can still picture you in it now.'

I consider his idea for a moment.

It's a *good one*.

For the first time in God knows how long I feel a faint rush of sexual desire.

The idea of recapturing the thrill of our first time together, from the photo shoot to his bed a few hours later, is one that I can well and truly get behind. Also, rugby kits come in all different sizes, so even we should be able to find a pair of matching kits that will fit our larger frames.

Greg walks his fingers along the couch. 'Maybe . . . maybe we could even take a few photos?'

Blimey, I hadn't even thought of that! It sounds *great!* And pretty damn *dirty* into the bargain.

'Okay,' I say to him, a little breathlessly. 'I'll go online and get us the outfits. You try to find the digital camera.'

It takes just three days for the rugby kits to be delivered. They're not exactly the same as the ones we wore all those years ago, but they are more or less the same shade of blue, and the shorts are the same crisp white that I remember from nearly two decades ago.

Greg does manage to track down the camera. It's not the newest, but it will still take some decent timed pictures when propped up on the chest of drawers at the end of our bed.

There's no Lionel the Pervert this time around, of course, which can only be considered a good thing.

Greg and I both change into the rugby kits and join each other in the bedroom. He is holding a photo album, the page open at the rather tatty print of our first picture together. Lionel had made us pay through the nose for a copy, the little weasel, but it had been more than worth it.

'Shall we recreate our first photo, then?' Greg suggests, putting the album on the bed before giving me a lingering kiss.

'Why not?' I reply with a cheeky smile.

Greg goes over and sets the camera timer running. He comes back and I try my best to place myself in the same position I was in all those years ago.

The camera shutter goes *click*. 'Let's have a look, shall we?' I say, heart racing. This is all very exciting. My mind is already fast-forwarding to what happened later that day and I'm feeling more turned on than I have in a long, long time.

Greg retrieves the camera, and fiddles with the settings until the shot that's just been taken appears in the display.

We sit on the end of the bed and take a good, hard look.

My libido is immediately snuffed out as soon as I take in what the photo has to offer.

The problem is that we've managed to recreate the pose we were in back at college a little *too* well. This gives rise to an immediate and painful comparison to the original photo.

Frankly, it looks like the two young sexy kids in the original shot have had hoses rammed up their arses and been pumped full of jelly.

You'd need a good couple of hours in Adobe Photoshop and the constant use of the Bloat Tool to otherwise illustrate the change from young Greg and Zoe to current Greg and Zoe.

Rather than recapturing the erotic vibe of our youth, all we have served to do with this little experiment is hammer home just how blubberous we've both grown in the intervening years.

'Oh, good God,' Greg whispers.

'I know. I look like a whale in a polo shirt.'

'I have tits, Zoe. Look at my big floppy tits.'

Greg holds up the old photo and we look from one to the other with jaws agape.

'Delete it,' I order.

'Okay.'

Greg fiddles with the buttons on the camera and the hideous picture is irrevocably wiped from existence. It will, however, take up near-permanent residence in my mind's eye for the foreseeable future.

'I think I'm going to take this gear off,' Greg says. 'I don't feel up for it any more.'

'Yes. I think that's a very good idea,' I reply. 'Then I think we should burn them . . . and never speak of this again.'

Needless to say, the sex did *not* happen that night.

Nor did it happen for many more nights after that, until we started Fat Chance. It would take the crazy diets and exhausting exercise regimes to get me horny again.

It wasn't an immediate thing.

I didn't just wake up the morning after I started dieting to find myself ravenous for sex. I was too busy being ravenous for food at the time.

Slowly, though, as we both started to drop a few pounds here and there, I started to admire Greg a lot more when I looked at him, and I even started to hate my own body a bit less as the weight loss went on.

It's amazing what only a small change can do for you psychologically.

And it isn't just the actual weight loss. Replacing all those fats and sugars with vitamins and minerals does wonders. Your skin starts to look healthier; your hair starts to look fuller.

A lot of incremental little changes add up to big ones.

And your sex drive eventually returns . . . in fucking spades!

So much so that I nearly got us both chucked out of B&Q the other day.

It really isn't a good idea to go to a hardware store when you have a rampant libido and your husband is dressed as a burly workman. I had no choice, however, as we needed to replace some of the flagstones in the patio.

Greg had put on his old work t-shirt and tatty black combat trousers to do the job and I stood and watched appreciatively as he lifted the heavy stone squares onto the trolley. His biceps rippled under the thin t-shirt material as the sweat ran down his back, staining the shirt. You know you're really horny when a sweat-stained shirt is doing it for you.

We were right out the back in the exterior part of the superstore where they sell all the garden stuff. There was no-one around.

I watched Greg shift three of the flagstones onto the trolley before I couldn't stand it any longer.

'Hey, baby,' I say to him.

Greg stands straight and wipes a sweaty arm across his forehead. 'What?' His face is flushed red and his hair is sticking up like a peacock's tail, but he still looks adorable as far as I'm concerned.

'There's not that many people around, is there?' I point out and I move closer.

He swivels his head about and returns my gaze. 'Nope. What's your point?'

'Well, I was just thinking that behind the row of bushes over there looks quite private.' I squeeze one of his biceps.

'Yeah? So? Are you feeling alright, Zoe? Only I was going to ask you to help me push this trolley back to the cash desk, but if you're feeling a bit—'

'Greg! I am absolutely *fine*. I'm just saying that there's nobody about and *it looks really private behind those bushes.*'

This is still greeted with confusion. 'Are you saying you want those bushes in our garden? Only they look bloody expensive and the fence is fine as far as I can tell.'

Good grief.

Sometimes men can be denser than liquid hydrogen.

I wrap my arm around Greg's neck and stare him in the eye. 'Gregory, I want you to take me behind those bushes and fuck me. Do you think you can do that?'

The light dawns. 'Er . . . are you serious?!'

I grab his crotch. 'No Greg, this is all one big joke and I'm not really massaging your cock at the moment.'

'We can't, Zoe!' His head darts about. 'What if somebody catches us? We can't!'

Big Greg says no, but little Greg is most definitely saying yes. Usually it's a bad sign when a man thinks with his penis, but in this instance I'm more than happy for it to take charge.

Without brooking any more argument, I yank my husband behind the row of privets. Handily, there's a pile of relatively soft-looking compost and bark chipping sacks behind it. It's almost as if the Gods of DIY *want* us to shag in the middle of this garden centre.

It takes me precisely three nanoseconds to whip my jeans and knickers down. Therefore I have plenty of time to help my husband fumble his combat trousers open. This is just as well, as if the job had been left to him on his own I'd still be sitting on that pile of compost awaiting entry.

When Greg is eventually ready for action, I turn around and bend over the compost sacks. He slides into me, and it is completely and totally delicious in every single respect. Okay, I can feel several bark chippings prodding me in the tits and gut, Greg actually smells like three-day-old cheese, and I'm going to have horrible friction burns from the plastic I'm sprawled out on, but by crikey it's a fuck I won't be forgetting in a hurry.

Sadly, necessity dictates it doesn't last that long. We both reach a more than satisfactory climax in less than two minutes. This is officially the quickest I've reached orgasm since I bought that Rampant Rabbit seven years ago.

I used it once, and climaxed so hard I needed two fillings replaced. It went into a cupboard and never saw the light of day again, because the idea of repeating that intense a sensation filled me with horror. I'm also with a private dentist, so it would have got extremely expensive in the long run.

Having done his duty, Greg flops onto my back, as is standard operating procedure at a time like this.

Before I let him withdraw, I must remember to move my legs back a bit, as my knickers are around my ankles and the last thing I want is a gusset full of semen when he pulls out. If I can just make sure my underpants are not directly below my bum I should—

'Are you folks okay?'

Oh dear sweet Jesus.

'Is that man hurting you, Miss?'

He is, bless him, about seventy years old. The poor bugger probably isn't used to seeing two overweight people slumped in post-coitus over the bark chippings and has reached the conclusion that I'm being attacked.

'Oh, fucking hell!' Greg shouts and backs away from me like I've just been wired up to the mains. This, of course, deposits all that semen I was talking about right into my knicker crotch.

Nevertheless, a wet undercarriage is better than a charge for indecent exposure, so I reach down and yank my jeans up, trying my hardest to keep my nether regions from sight behind the pile of compost and chippings.

Have you ever tried to pull up your underwear and jeans while leaning forward in a prone position? It's a lot harder than it looks.

I have to rest my full weight on the sacks of earth and wood, while thrusting my legs out backwards to allow the jeans to ride up my thighs properly.

Now, I'm proud to say I've lost quite a bit of weight recently, but I'm still a heavy girl. Heavy enough to send the big bulging plastic sacks sliding away from me and onto the ground. I follow them in short order with a plaintive squawk.

'Oh dear!' the old fella cries, and comes over to help me up.

Where my bloody husband is right now—when I need him most—I have no idea.

I turn my head.

Oh yes, there he is, standing in dumbfounded shock like a naughty boy who's been caught with his hands in the sweet jar.

'Greg! Help me, will you?!' I implore him.

'Sorry, sorry,' he mumbles and comes to my aid.

Both husband and decrepit sales assistant help me to my feet.

'Thank you,' I say and try to ignore the uncomfortable damp feeling between my legs.

'Yes, thank you very much, sir. It's very kind of you to come over,' Greg tells the pensioner.

What? And watch us fucking for a couple of minutes?

'Do you need any assistance?' he asks, a bit unsure. He's obviously been pre-programmed by the senior staff to always be polite and helpful to customers. I can't imagine that there was a training session designed to help new sales staff deal with people shagging on the landscaping products, though.

'Ah, no. I think we're fine,' I reply.

'Yes! Absolutely fine!' Greg adds, in the highest tone of voice I've ever heard him use. 'We're just buying some new paving stones,' he embellishes. The old duffer looks down at all the sacks now lying haphazardly around our feet. 'And bark chippings of course!' Greg throws in. He bends down to pick up a sack. It's the one I've just been screwed on top of. 'We always need bark chippings!'

No-one *always needs* bark chippings. Bark chippings are rarely *needed* by anybody, unless you happen to be half termite.

Still, it seems to do the trick. He believes the ruse. 'Okay, then. Well, if you do need anything then please don't hesitate to come find me,' the old bloke says. 'My name is Roger.'

Of course his name is Roger. Why wouldn't it be?

Given what I'm carrying around in my undercarriage, the next fifteen minutes of my life are *delightful*, as I'm sure you can imagine. Especially the fantastic moment I have to sit in the car.

Despite that, I'm in a cracking good mood as we arrive at home and get to work laying those flagstones. After I've had a quick shower, that is.

To have your sex drive restored and purring like a well-oiled engine is a wonderful and unexpected side effect of being on a strict diet. I'll take a soaked gusset and friction burns over self-loathing and a barren sex life any day of the week.

I should also note before I close this diary entry that Greg and I revisited the mail order rugby kits a couple of nights ago.

I hadn't burned them in the end, just stuffed them at the back of the wardrobe.

We still both looked utterly ridiculous once we had them on, but this time it was because neither of us could get the shorts to *stay up*. The tops billowed around our smaller frames like sails.

We had sex in them, though.

It was terrific!

The story of the rugby kit doesn't quite end there, either.

You see, I now have a goal to strive for. One that even eclipses the fifty-grand prize that's waiting at the end of the competition in September.

All those years and unhealthy meals ago, when Zoe Milton was a svelte size ten, she was also something of an accidental thief.

The rugby kit I'd been given to wear in Lionel's photo shoot never got handed back. It went in my rucksack and stayed there until I discovered it about a week later when I emptied the bag out. By that time I was head over heels in love with Greg Milton. This meant that the outfit had a huge amount of meaning for me. It symbolised our first meeting, our first time together in bed, and the start of what I hoped would be a long-term relationship.

So I kept it, and put it somewhere very safe.

For nearly twenty years—unbeknown to my husband and the world at large—that rugby kit has sat folded up neatly in a variety of wardrobes and cupboards, waiting for me to put it back on again.

There is my goal.

There is my challenge.

I will fit into that rugby kit again, I wholeheartedly promise you.

GREG'S WEIGHT LOSS DIARY

Thursday, June 26th

17 stone, 1 pound (3 stone, 1 pound lost)

I hate running.

I *loathe* jogging.

I *detest* sprinting.

'But it's what our bodies are designed to do!' a well-meaning spandex-clad maniac told me the other day in the gym. 'It's how we used to get across the African plains.'

I have never visited the African plains, nor do I ever intend to.

But if events conspire against me and I end up having to go there, it will be by modern conveyance. I will fly to the continent in a plane, and once there I will cross the bloody thing in an air-conditioned jeep. This will allow me ample opportunity to take photos of the local wildlife and chat to my friendly guide Akibu about his Manchester United football shirt. I can hardly do those things if I am having to jog through the tall grasses and worry about the nearby lions, can I?

Running provides me with no pleasure whatsoever. I am too tall and too bulky to do it efficiently. There's a good reason why Paula Radcliffe and Mo Farrah are such skinny little buggers. If you're carrying too much weight your equilibrium is thrown off and you risk crashing to Earth painfully with almost every step. I know this because I have fallen over more times since I started running than an alcoholic with an inner-ear infection.

Bearing all this in mind, you can imagine my delight when Stream FM announced the second Fat Chance challenge at the weigh-in on the Sunday before last.

Yep, it's a sodding fun run. An entire eight kilometres of ambulatory hell.

Not only that, but the fun run will also be open to several lucky members of the public, picked from out of a hat by one of Elise's production assistants. Alongside us poor fatties will be thirty cheerful—and probably thin—people from the Stream FM audience, no doubt included to increase the size of the spectacle.

. . . and it's an audience that seems to be growing larger with every passing day. Fat Chance has really picked up steam popularity-wise in the past month or so.

I reckon these extra runners have been crowbarred into the race so that the poor spectators along the route don't have to constantly look at a load of fat people sweating their way into an early grave. If one of us keels over from a severe myocardial infarction, I'm sure the specially chosen extra runners have been ordered to conceal the bloated corpse until the coroner arrives.

The run will start by wending its way through the park, carry on through some of the quieter streets in the town, and eventually end up at Stream's broadcast building eight kilometres down the road.

The first couple across the line will win the challenge—and two tickets to see England play at Wembley in a friendly against the Ukraine. I can't stand football and nor can Zoe, so our motivation levels for this one are in the basement.

'Can't we just feign serious injury on the start line and pull out?' Zoe suggests as we mull over the email we've just received from the radio station.

'Possibly, though I think it may come across as something of a coincidence if we both collapse in agony twenty yards from the start pistol.'

'Maybe I'll just feign injury, then.'

'Oh no. Not bloody likely. If I have to run this thing then so do you.'

Zoe sticks her tongue out at me and takes another bite of her green salad.

'And this thing is on Sunday?'

'Yep.'

'Less than a week away. I wish they'd give us a bit more bloody notice.'

'What? And let us get too prepared for it? Not likely. Unsuspecting fat people make better entertainment. The look of confusion and misery on our chubby little cheeks is good box office.'

'True.' Zoe taps her fork on the kitchen counter thoughtfully. 'So that gives us six days to get as prepared as we can for the longest run either of us has ever done.'

'Even when we were young and thin.'

'Absolutely.'

'That's about the size of it.'

'Joy of joys.'

'And we get to do it with a bunch of skinny idiots who will probably run us into the ground in three seconds flat.'

Zoe points her fork at me. 'That's not the worst thing that could happen.'

'It's not?'

'Nope. What if they decide to *cheer us on*? Encourage us with useful motivational phrases and hearty clapping.'

The horror of this sinks in. My face goes an unhealthy shade of white. 'They're going to, aren't they? That's really why Stream have picked a load of punters to take part. Not to beat us . . .'

'. . . but to help us across the finishing line.'

I grip my wife's arm. 'I can't do it, Zoe. I can't have healthy people running around me in circles shouting *You can do it, Lard Arse!* It'll finish me off.'

'If you want the fifty grand at the end of this thing you'll do it. After all, we're in second place right now. We've actually got a chance of *winning* this competition if we keep it up the way we have been.'

Zoe's logic is unfortunately unassailable.

At the weigh-in the previous day we were shocked and amazed to discover that we were in second place in terms of the competition overall, just behind Frankie and Benny, who both look noticeably thinner as each week passes. They're half a stone in front of us, while Valerie and George are a mere four pounds behind. If we can keep going the way we are, as Zoe says, we could pull clear of the tea shop twosome and close the gap on our biggest rivals.

This means running eight kilometres in public in those stupid bright red outfits, though. Over five miles dressed like a sweaty fucking tomato.

Oh joy of joys.

The kind of weather you want for a fun run is mild, sunny, and without much of a breeze, so Sunday of course dawns cold, drizzling, and gusty. Not only do we have to wear our idiotic red Fitness4All outfits, we now get the pleasure of them sticking to our clammy skin thanks to the constant rain and wind.

The inclement British summer weather doesn't appear to have put off the crowds. Not in the slightest.

The audience at the cycling challenge was limited by the size of the gym hall, so we didn't really get much of an inclination of how popular this competition is becoming. The park is open to all and sundry, though, and the size of the crowd that has turned out this morning is shockingly large. It numbers easily in the thousands.

Zoe and I are flabbergasted as we walk over to the start line, pushing our way through a heaving mass of bodies to reach the guys from the radio station, who are huddled in a semi-circle of grass that's marked out with metal barriers to keep the crowd at bay.

As we push our way through I can hear my name being shouted from several people in the swarm, as well as Zoe's. There are over a dozen banners and placards being waved. One reads 'Frankie & Benny rock!' Another says 'Go Angel and Dom!' Most disconcertingly, I see a third saying 'We love the Miltons!' I peer at the teenage girl holding it. I've absolutely no idea who she is.

A complete stranger is holding up a placard in support of me and my wife . . . and I have never laid eyes on her before. What an exquisitely strange sensation.

The Miltons have fans. Honest-to-goodness *fans*.

I try to put the notion out of my head as we enter the cordoned-off area. The last thing I need is my ego running away with itself before my feet have had a chance to get going.

I spy Elise by a stack of electronic equipment. She's having a radio pack fitted over an outfit of tight white spandex, indicating that she too will be running in the race. The spandex leaves nothing to imagination. Usually at a time like this my brain would indulge in a nano-fantasy about a drunken threesome with Zoe and Elise, but I'm still so shocked by the idea of my local celebrity that it completely forgets to do it.

'I thought you were going to start the race and Will was going to run?' Zoe says to her as we get to where she's standing.

Elise rolls her eyes. 'He twisted his ankle in training last night.' She points over to where Will is enjoying a pre-show latte and chatting to some of his adoring listeners. 'From the amount of whinging he's been doing you'd have thought his foot had been bitten off by a passing badger.' Her eyes narrow. 'He doesn't appear to be having any trouble standing up today, though.'

Elise then rubs her eyes and yawns. 'You sure you're up to this?' I ask her.

'I think so. I was out late last night and have a hangover of epic proportions, so I'm not exactly happy about having to run all that way with this thing strapped to my hip.'

Zoe grins. 'How are things going with Mister Wonderful?'

'Adam is a lot of fun,' Elise replies, somewhat defensively. Her relationship with the main sponsor of Fat Chance has been well documented in the local papers. You can tell the unwanted attention is smarting a little. 'Anyway, the show's starting soon. You'd both better go over and stand with the others.'

'Oh dear, we've been dismissed,' I say to Zoe, with mischief in my voice.

'Sounds like the blonde bombshell local radio DJ doesn't want to talk about her love life with us anymore,' Zoe agrees.

Elise gives us the finger discreetly and hurries off over to where Will is standing. My wife and I go over and join the rest of the contestants to await the start of the race.

We're joined by the lucky thirty punters who have been picked to run alongside us all the way to the Stream FM building. As feared, most of them look intolerably healthy. To add insult to injury, they are all decked out in rather tasteful white running kits emblazoned with the Fitness4All logo. This getup looks a lot more dignified than the hideous red ensemble I'm forced to wear once again.

'Hi Greg!' a middle-aged woman wearing a headband says to me. Like the girl with the placard, I have no idea who this person is, yet she seems to think she knows me well, judging from her friendly greeting.

'Morning,' I say a little uncertainly.

'Looking forward to running with you today!' she tells me happily.

'Yes. Me too. I guess.'

'That's the spirit!' she crows, and gives me a playful punch on the arm, before performing several painful looking warm-up lunges right in front of me.

Everyone else dressed in white has the same cheerful, expectant look about them.

Everyone dressed in red looks altogether less sure of themselves. Other than Frankie and Benny, that is. They both look so determined to win they could be German.

Benny has even joined in with the warm-up exercises, and is staring down the course like a Formula One driver on the grid waiting for the lights to go out. I realise at that moment that there is simply no point in trying to win this race—the Jamaican couple already have it sewn up mentally before the start gun even fires.

The rest of us clad in bright red just look scared. Eight kilometres may sound like nothing if your BMI is healthy and your ankles don't have to support an extra five stone, but when you've been at the kebabs too much over the past ten years, eight kilometres feels like eight thousand. I can already feel the tightness in my chest and the burning in my thighs.

Shane and Theresa look the most worried of all of us, which hardly comes as a surprise. While it looks like they've lost quite a bit of weight between them, they both still look incredibly large when compared to the rest of us.

Looking at Shane's concerned face I'm instantly reminded of just how crass this entire enterprise actually is. A baying crowd have come to gawp at a bunch of fat people pushing themselves to the limit.

And if that limit gets passed? Well, that would be just terrific for the ratings, wouldn't it? I'd imagine the sight of Shane face down on the ground and once again requiring medical attention would be just what the doctor ordered.

I'm brought out of my cynical reverie by the sound of Elise and Will firing the crowd up. It doesn't take much effort. They're all excited about this race, even if we're not. I catch Shane's eye and give him an encouraging smile and a thumbs-up. He returns it slowly. I can see how much his hand is visibly shaking.

'Okay guys!' Will shouts into his microphone. 'Everyone to the start line. Let's get this race underway!'

We shuffle forward into position as Will tells the crowd more about the route we'll be following. Elise comes over and stands between me and Zoe.

'If you intend to interview us,' Zoe says to her, 'I'd do it in the first two hundred yards. After that all you're likely to do is get covered in sweat and phlegm.'

'No worries,' Elise replies, gripping her microphone tightly in one hand. 'Any interviews I do will be kept short anyway. I feel like I'm about to throw up any minute.'

I feel a small pang of sympathy for her. I once played a rugby match with the kind of hangover they sing about in songs.

Will starts a countdown from ten and holds up a starting pistol. The noise of the crowd ratchets up to an almost painful level.

I set myself and wait for the off. If I was a religious type I'd probably be sketching the sign of the cross on my chest right now. As I look to my left down the row I see Valerie doing that very thing.

The countdown reaches zero, Will pulls the trigger, and with the gun's sharp report ringing in my ears I start to run.

Well, I say *run* . . . a fumbling jog is a more accurate description of what I'm doing.

All the white shirts take off a brisk pace, including Elise, who, despite her hangover, is still able to trot off at a lightning rate compared to me.

Frankie and Benny take an early lead out of the competition couples, which comes as no surprise.

Benny's pretty much keeping up with the white shirts as we hit the first three hundred metres. Frankie is struggling, though, so I can see some marital strife occurring about seven kilometres down the road if she's not able to keep up with her husband. It's the first *couple* across the line, not the first *person*.

I will have no such problem with my betrothed. Zoe looks about as enthusiastic about this as I am. Her pace mirrors mine and we run along shoulder to shoulder in a delightful show of matrimonial solidarity.

Frankie and Benny's determination to win this challenge has filtered down to most of the other couples as well. Valerie and George are jogging no quicker than we are, the two lesbian girls are a bit faster but not by much, Pete and Lea are plodding away twenty feet back, and Shane and Theresa are walking so slowly they've barely got away from the start line. No-one seems to have the stomach for a fight with the Jamaican couple up ahead—who have put even more distance between us.

In fact, we're all so slow that it's giving a healthy percentage of the enormous crowd ample chance to follow alongside the race route, hollering and shouting at us as they do so.

I hear a lot of encouraging shouts of 'Come on!', 'You can do it!', and 'Keep running!' However, I also pick up quite a few less-flattering cries. 'Run, you fat bastards!' is a lovely thing for someone to shout, as is 'You're so fucking slow, you fat cunt!' These witty epithets are accompanied by a great deal of laughter coming from the more boisterous members of our entourage.

I grind my teeth. That sense of being a performing monkey, sent out to prance and frolic for the delight of the crowd, returns to me as I plod my way towards the park's exit.

As we reach it, I notice that a lot of the white t-shirt wearing brigade have slowed their pace and a few have even stopped at the park gates. They are looking back down the course at us, waving and clapping their hands in encouragement.

I now feel like a dog being called by its master.

'C'mon Greg! C'mon, boy!'

I'm amazed to realise this is actually *worse* than being called a fat cunt. Insults are easy to deal with when you get right down to it—you can either ignore them or hit a bastard in the face. But heartfelt support laced with good-natured pity? What the hell are you supposed to do with that? You can hardly punch somebody in the mouth for cheering you on, can you? It might come across as a little ungrateful.

Grind, grind, grind go my teeth, making it quite hard to effect a fake smile as I lumber past our well-wishers and onto the road leading out of town.

'This is not what I'd call a fun way to spend a Sunday afternoon,' Zoe pants from beside me.

'No, not really,' I reply. 'You might think being patronised and insulted from every angle would be bags of fun, at least in theory. But it's surprisingly unpleasant in reality, isn't it?'

'Yep. If another prick in a white running kit tells me I'm doing well, I might just kick them in the giblets.'

'They'd probably just congratulate you on how strong your kick was, and that doing it helped you burn five more calories.'

Zoe laughs, which is probably not the best use of the oxygen in her lungs at the moment, but it puts a smile on my face. Any time I can make my wife giggle is time well spent.

The smile drops off my face when I hear somebody shout 'You fat tosser!' from the crowd. I don't know if the comment is directed at me specifically, but it hardly matters at this juncture.

Zoe picks up on my mood change. 'Don't worry about it, baby. They're idiots.'

'It's not them I'm mad at. Some people just love being pricks if you give them half a chance. It's the bloody radio station I'm pissed off with for putting us in this situation.'

'Well, try not to think about it.' Zoe points ahead. 'Elise is jogging back this way and she's got her microphone out.'

I groan and look from the crowd to where Zoe's mate is coming back towards us, an expectant look on her face.

Elise stops in her tracks and allows us to catch up, slotting herself in between the two of us as we jog along. 'Will's going to throw over to me in a second for a quick interview with you both,' she informs us. 'Have you got enough puff to talk?'

'Just about,' I tell her.

This, in and of itself, is a rather amazing thing. I must have jogged well over two kilometres by now and I can still hold a conversation with relative ease. This would have been unthinkable a few months ago. About the only conversation I'd have had with anyone at the end of this much running back in January would have been the one conducted with St Peter while standing at the pearly gates.

This thought cheers me up no end, and the idea of being a source of public amusement seems a little less awful. If being called a fat cunt and treated like a puppy are the price I have to pay for a decreased chance of getting heart disease, then so be it.

'*Do not* ask me about wanting to get pregnant again, Elise,' Zoe says to her. 'Unless you want a discussion live on air about how good Adam Edgemont is with his tongue.'

Elise groans. 'Don't worry, I'm in no mood for anything like that,' she says and takes a deep breath. 'Frankly, all I want is a hot bath and a nap.'

'Great, then by all means . . . interview away.'

Elise talks into her headset for a second, indicating that we're ready to go. A few moments go by and she suddenly changes from a tired and hung over friend to a bouncy and enthusiastic DJ in a split second. It's quite the sight to see.

'Thanks, Will!' she exclaims into her microphone. 'I'm here with the Miltons, who are proving to be one of the most popular couples in the competition so far.'

We are?

'They're currently just passing the three-kilometre mark of the run and are looking good!'

We are?

'How are you feeling, Greg?' she asks me and thrusts the microphone in my face.

'Um, yeah, pretty good I suppose. My feet are hurting a bit.'

'That's great!'

It is?

'And Zoe, Frankie and Benny have motored off well into the lead. You think you have any chance of catching them?'

'I don't know,' my wife replies. 'They looked pretty up for it at the start line. You'd have to stick a rocket up my arse to catch up with them now, I reckon.'

Zoe sometimes just can't resist making her friend's life more difficult, no matter how hard she tries.

Elise administers an irritated punch to Zoe's shoulder, and the microphone is swept back in my direction. 'And what do you think of the support today, Greg? Aren't all these runners great for coming along?'

I figure I'd better sound a little more lively, just to give the poor girl a bit of a break. 'Yes they are, Elise!' I blurt out. 'I've never felt so supported and encouraged!'

'Fantastic!'

'I know! I can't wait until we reach the finish line when I can thank them properly . . . and then hopefully one of them will give me a dog treat!'

Confusion is writ large across Elise's face.

'Also,' I carry on, just because I'm in that kind of mood now, 'I really can't thank the crowd enough for following us along the route!'

'Okay . . .'

'Oh yes! Why, if they weren't constantly reminding me that I'm fat, I might have completely forgotten in all the excitement!'

Elise isn't a genius, but even she knows when an interview has gone south. 'Well, thanks for your time, Miltons!' she says, and hurriedly pulls the microphone away from us before we can embarrass her further.

'Pleasure!' Zoe and I echo.

'We'll throw back to Will, who's now driven up to the finish line,' Elise tells the listeners, ending her broadcast. She drops the microphone into the holster on her hip and glares at us both. 'You pair of tossers.'

Zoe and I both laugh out loud.

Elise spits a few more exasperated insults at us for few moments, before jogging ahead to no doubt collar some other unfortunate for a chat.

'That was a bit mean,' Zoe says after her giggles have died down.

'So is making fat people run for the amusement of the masses,' I counter.

The next kilometre passes in more or less the same way as the first three.

While my breathing is fairly laboured and my legs are a bit rubbery, I'm otherwise in pretty good shape at the halfway point, and feeling positive about finishing the fun run without disgracing myself. I might even beat a few of the white t-shirt brigade if I'm very lucky!

It is at this stage in proceedings that the gods of over-confidence decide to pay me a visit for my towering hubris.

Their punishment is meted out via the running shoes I've currently got on my feet. They were purchased specifically for this race from one of the local sporting goods shops.

My old trainers had reached the point where the soles were starting to come away, thanks to all the exercise I've been doing recently. I didn't particularly fancy the idea of them falling off my feet before the finish line, so thought I'd better pick up another pair for the eight-kilometre run.

So on Saturday I went in to the gigantic DC Sports store on the retail estate just outside town, with the express purpose of finding replacements. Having never been one for labels, I walked straight past all the expensive brands like Asics and Nike and into the section containing the cheap no-brand alternatives.

This proved to be a mistake of *Herculean* proportions.

You see, wearing cheap running shoes is fine when all you're doing is walking down the street to get a pint of milk and a kebab. When you're actually *running* in them, though, it's a completely different story. There's a lot more pressure and friction going on, and if you've picked a pair of trainers that even the impoverished Bangladeshi children who make them wouldn't stick on their feet, you know you're going to have a really bad time of it.

Badly made, cheap running shoes don't fit properly, don't cushion your feet adequately, and allow a lot of uncomfortable rubbing. This leads to every jogger's worst nightmare: *blisters.*

And how long does it take for cheap, badly manufactured running shoes to cause painful and debilitating blisters, you might ask?

Oh, about four kilometres into a fun run, I'd have to say.

I'm first aware that something is wrong as we jog up the hill that goes past the train station. This is the first stage of the race that's been uphill, and the change in gradient is enough to start those shoes rubbing in lots of uncomfortable places.

My feet have been aching and a bit tender ever since we set off, but I'm well used to this sensation by now from all my daily exercise, so have been able to more or less ignore it. However as the road climbs, I start to feel a sharp, stabbing pain in both of my little toes, my left big toe, and my right heel.

'Fuck,' I wince as we run past one of the local pubs, where about twenty people are cheering us on from the beer garden.

'Are you okay?' Zoe asks.

'I'm not sure. My toes are hurting for some reason. It feels like someone's stuck a hot needle into them.'

'Ouch. Do you want to stop for a second to have a look?'

The next words that tumble from my mouth are the most unwise to have ever sprung forth from my lips. 'Nah. I'll be fine. I'm sure it can't get any worse.'

It absolutely *does,* of course, but my brain's gone into 'ignore it and it'll go away' mode so I manage to convince myself that the pain isn't increasing for the next kilometre of the race. But by the time we've run back down the hill and have hit the suburban sprawl that rings the city centre, every single footstep has become agony.

It feels like I'm running barefoot across hot coals.

I'm now sucking air in through my teeth with every step I take, and I'm starting to sound like an overworked steam engine.

To mitigate the pain I try to run in as ginger and light a fashion as possible, in order to keep the weight off my poor battered toes.

Have you ever tried to run in a light, ginger fashion when you're seventeen stone and five kilometres into a fun run?

'Greg?' Zoe asks.

'Yeah?!'

'Are you alright?'

'Yeah?!'

'Then why are you running like that?'

'Running . . . like . . . what?'

'Like somebody else has just shit your pants?'

'Feet . . . are . . . hurting!'

'Then stop!'

'No! I . . . want . . . to . . . finish!'

Zoe grinds to a halt, leaving me to stumble up the road a few more feet.

I notice she's not by my side any more and come to rest myself. 'Why have you stopped?'

'You need to look at your feet, Greg. You can't keep going like this. Come over to this bench and sit down.'

'But —'

'Now, Greg!'

I look around the street. Miraculously, we seem to have temporarily dropped all our fellow runners and followers from the crowd. Taking this as a good sign, I do as I am told and limp my way back over to where my wife has sat herself down on the bench.

The relief when my backside hits the wood is indescribable. The instant the bench takes my body weight, the ache in my thighs slackens off, and the intense agony emanating from my feet reduces to a dull roar.

What's going on underneath those cheap trainers isn't going to be pleasant to look at, though, so I put it off for a few seconds.

I lean back against the bench and let out a groan of pleasure. Such a simple thing it is to sit down and not move. I must try to do it more in the future.

'Come on,' Zoe says and punches me on the arm. 'The race isn't over yet. Let's see what the damage is.'

I sit up and groan once more, this time in utter despair, and unlace my left running shoe. This is the foot that's hurting the most, so I figure I'd better take a look at it first to see the extent of the injury.

With the shoe removed I tentatively pull my sock off.

The simple act of removing one's sock should never be accompanied by the kind of pain I feel as I pull it over my heel. It's like someone has taken a rusty cheese grater to my skin and is giving it a vigorous rubbing.

'For fuck's sake!' I cry in distress.

'Oh, good God,' Zoe says and clasps a hand over her mouth. I'm not sure whether this is just in shock or to prevent vomiting.

My foot is a horror show. One that makes *Hostel*, *Saw*, and *The Evil Dead* look like *Finding Nemo*.

To start with, the whole foot has gone a very strange colour. It's a mixture of hectic red and pallid white, with several disconcerting small patches of purple thrown in for good measure.

This is all merely background, however, to the real awfulness going on around my toes and heel.

To start with, my little toe has basically turned into one big blister. It extends from the nail, down to where toe meets foot, and wraps its way underneath. The blister is a milky white, and when I prod it with my finger I can see the pus moving around under the semi-translucent layer of skin.

A second enormous blister about three inches long runs down the side of my big toe. It is another bulbous cushion of skin and pus, formed by the constant friction of five kilometres of running.

Things are even worse on my heel, though. At some point over the race another gigantic blister must have formed. However, such has been the pressure applied to it every time I put my foot down, it has burst, creating a mess of such nastiness I can barely bring myself to describe it here.

Firstly, the pus has soaked my sock and created a kind of biological glue that has managed to stick sock to skin, resulting in the hideous pain I felt when I pulled the damn thing off. Doing so has ripped the skin that formed the blister, which now flaps around in two sagging halves. Underneath is a large patch of fresh pink skin, which is incredibly sore and tender when even lightly touched.

'Everything alright?' I hear a cheerful voice say from in front of me. It's the middle-aged woman in the headband from the start line. She's seen us sitting here and has jogged over to lend some moral support.

'Fine, thanks,' I say quickly.

'Having a break, are we?' she asks, jogging up and down on the spot. Behind her I see Valerie and George pass us by. Headband has obviously broken off from the pack surrounding them to come over and see what's going on with the Miltons.

I hide my foot under the bench so as not to distress her.

'No, not really,' Zoe tells her, in that dismissive tone people use when they just want the other person to fuck off.

'There's no shame if it's got too much for you, you know!' Headband says and continues to bounce up and down on the spot.

I'm instantly enraged. She automatically assumes that we've stopped because we're big fat twats.

These people may have turned up to this fun run to support the cause, but it doesn't mean they're not still as prejudiced as the ones calling us fat cunts while safely hidden in the crowd.

'We've stopped because of my foot,' I tell her. 'Come here and I'll show you it.'

Headband smiles in an agreeable fashion. 'Okay.'

As the woman leans in, I produce the Foot of Horror and wave it at her, giving her the full impact of the double blisters and torn flesh.

'Oh, good God!' she exclaims.

'That's just what I said,' Zoe replies.

I point at the rapidly diminishing Val and George. 'You should get back to the others, you know. Like . . . *now?*'

Headband backs off, getting the message. 'Yes, yes, you're right,' she says a little queasily. 'Well, best of luck with the rest of the race!' she finishes and bounces away.

I look down at my swollen foot. 'I think the chances of there being a rest of the race are slim to none,' I say with inevitable gloom.

'Let's look at the other foot and see how bad it is,' Zoe suggests.

I flip the other shoe and sock off, and am pleased to see that the damage is less extensive. There's another small blister on my little toe, but other than that it's not too bad.

What's more, my left foot has returned to a rather more healthy colour now that it's had a few moments out in the air. I can't run any more, though. The idea of putting my sock and cheap running shoe back on over my wounds and plodding up the road is unthinkable.

Zoe puffs out air. 'I guess that's that, then.'

'Yeah, sorry, sweetheart.'

I put an arm around her as we watch Pete, Lea, and the two lesbians jog past us with another gaggle of white-shirted fun runners. I am reminded of the pilot fish that constantly hang around whales in the ocean.

'Don't worry, these things happen,' Zoe says, patting me on the leg. 'We did quite well anyway.'

'I would have liked to beat that lot, though,' I say, nodding my chin at our passing competitors.

'We won the last one. That's good enough for me.'

I let out a snort of disgust and sit back against the bench. A few blissful, peaceful minutes go by as I let the light drizzle cool my brow and bare feet. We'll have to get up and arrange some sort of transport away from here soon, but just for the minute I'm enjoying the relative quiet away from the madding crowd. Now all the runners have gone ahead of us, there's nobody about other than the two of us and a few pedestrians.

'Greg . . . *look.*'

Coming down the road are Shane and Theresa. They are completely on their own. Not one of the thirty white shirts run alongside them. It's quite a pathetic sight. Theresa is puffing and blowing, dragging one foot in front of the other. Shane has his head to the sky, his neck strained upwards almost as if he's actively fighting the colossal weight he carries around with him. Their pace is incredibly slow, but they are still going.

'I'd forgotten all about them,' I say.

'Me too. I thought they'd given up ages ago.'

'Everybody else certainly seems to have given up on them.'

I feel the anger that Headband sparked off returning.

Everyone wants to support the fatties—providing the fatties aren't *too* fat, you understand. Nobody wants to hang around with the slowest and biggest of the bunch. Where's the fun in that?

Shane and Theresa reach us as the bench. Shane gives me a thumbs-up and looks back up the road. Theresa attempts a smile, but it comes across as more of a grimace.

As they pass us, I feel a powerful compulsion to join them wash over me.

I look down at my battered feet. There is no way in hell I can run in these cheap, shitty shoes again.

But if Shane and Theresa can keep going, then I can sure as hell keep going too, even if I have to do it in my ruined, sweaty socks.

'Greg? What are you doing?' Zoe asks as I painfully slip the socks back on and get to my feet.

I throw both running shoes into the bin next to the bench and look back at Shane and Theresa. 'I thought I might go and keep them company for a bit.'

'You can't run any more!'

'No, but they can't run at all, and they're still going, aren't they?' I extend a hand down to her. 'Let's go with them, baby. They shouldn't be doing this alone.'

Zoe takes my hand and stands up. Her eyes look a bit watery. 'There are times when I am very glad I married you, Greg,' she says, her voice cracking a little with emotion.

'Let's see if you still think that when this race is over,' I tell her and start to hobble off down the road.

When we catch up with Shane and Theresa, there isn't a lot of conversation exchanged. They're both too puffed out to speak much and I'm in too much pain from my blisters. It's up to Zoe to ask if they'd mind us accompanying them to the finish.

It's hard to tell under the hectic red faces and sweat, but I think they are both grateful for the companionship.

The final three kilometres of the race are absolute hell. We have to stick to Shane's pace, as he's the slowest of all four of us, so it takes us nearly an hour to get in sight of the Stream FM building. In that time I feel the blister on the side of my left foot burst and the whole of my right foot goes numb thanks to the fact I'm now running with no shoes on at all.

During the last five hundred metres of the race I'm only able to limp slowly up the road, so it's just as well Shane can't go any faster himself.

The crowd begins to build again as we head towards the finish line. They can see what distress we're in and react to it with an up-swell of cheering that actually lifts my spirits, and helps fog the pain I'm in enough for me to keep going.

As we get nearer to the line I can see Shane really starting to struggle. He starts to weave across the road erratically, his shoulders slumped from the effort.

His legs have gone.

If I don't do something, the poor sod will collapse in front of all these people and tomorrow's front page story will be written.

I limp over to him, curl one arm under his, and lift him upright again. This adds a huge amount of pressure to my already ruined feet, but there is no way in hell I'm giving this crowd the thrill of watching an obese man fall to his feet in failure.

'Tha . . . thanks,' Shane says and lifts his head. With my help he's able to jog in a straight line again and the finish line gets ever nearer.

With only fifty or so metres to go, I tap him on the shoulder and say 'Can you do the rest on your own, mate?'

He looks at me out of the corner of one eye and nods his head.

I remove my supporting arm from his and slow my pace even more, letting Shane and Theresa get slightly ahead of us.

'They deserve to cross the line first,' I say to Zoe, who nods in agreement.

To the sounds of thunderous applause, Shane stumbles his way across the finish line with his wife, his arms held high above his head and an exultant—if exhausted—expression his face. With head held high he emits a long, loud cry of what I can only assume is a combination of agony and triumph.

The ovation from the masses is no quieter when Zoe and I cross the line as well, I have to say.

I don't feel like raising my arms over my head and shouting, though. All I can think about is getting off my feet and sticking them in some warm, soothing water.

We are instantly surrounded by the other couples and the white shirts, all of whom take turns in clapping us on the back and telling us how incredible we are.

Funny, just an hour and three kilometres ago nobody gave a toss.

Elise interviews both Shane and Theresa, while Will talks to Zoe and me. I try to make light of the fact I finished the race in my socks, but Will is having none of it. My blisters will be the subject of some discussion on the radio station and in the local paper for a couple of days to come, it seems.

The real heroes are Shane and Theresa, though, as is right and proper. The DJs and reporters can see how much of an effort they put in to finish and are extracting all the human interest they can get out of it for their airwaves and column inches.

I spot Frankie and Benny standing over in one corner looking a little disgruntled, and feel a fair bit of pity for them. They won the race, after all, and yet the guy who came in last is getting all the attention.

Sorry . . . the guy who came second to last. The honour of the wooden spoon falls to yours truly and his blisters.

'I bet Shane and Terrie will be the ones featured in the paper tomorrow,' I point out to Zoe in the taxi back home a little later.

'Probably. I'm sure they'll get a shot of him crossing the line with his arms up. It was like something out of *Chariots of Fire*. Only with more wobbling.'

When I do see the paper the next day, though, I am amazed to see that the image they've gone with to illustrate the dramatic end of the fun run isn't one of Shane crossing the line. Instead, it's a shot of me and Shane just before the finish with our wives alongside us. My arm is tucked under his, and the strain and effort is writ large across both our faces.

The caption that goes with the story is *He ain't heavy, he's my brother.*

You couldn't ask for a better cliché than that, could you?

Cliché or not, I can't help but feel a bit proud of myself.

Zoe was *certainly* proud of me, as by the end of the day she'd already got the cutting from the paper framed and on the kitchen wall. She also had the kind of sex with me that night that most men only dream about, or watch late at night on the Sky channels near the top end.

The blisters on my feet still haven't completely healed and I think a trip to the doctor's is in order for my left heel, but I'm still extremely glad I saw the fun run out.

If nothing else, I got the chance to help another man lift his arms above his head and cry triumphantly into the sky.

I also learned a valuable lesson.

Sometimes, you really do get what you pay for . . . especially when it comes to footwear.

ZOE'S WEIGHT LOSS DIARY

Tuesday, July 8th

11 stone, 4 pounds (3 stone, 3 pounds lost)

My life has become very peculiar.

I would even go so far as to say quite bizarre.

One minute I'm boring old Zoe Milton, sales co-ordinator and wife of eighteen years; the next, I'm a local celebrity.

In the past four months, since the beginning of Fat Chance, I've had to get used to seeing my face on a variety of billboards, posters, websites and leaflets. This was initially the worst thing to ever happen in the history of the universe, given that the last thing a self-conscious fat person wants is for her grisly visage to be plastered up all around town. When it's hard to look in the mirror every morning, it's downright impossible to walk past a poster of you posing like one of the special kids without breaking down and crying like a little girl right there and then in the street.

After a few weeks I got to a point where I could block out all the pictures mentally, in the same way really rich people block out the homeless folk they walk past every day on their way to their six-figure-salary jobs. Where once I would see my fat face and all its chins staring down at me as I drove past on the dual carriageway, now there would merely be a large hole in the fabric of the universe, an area of dull negativity with absolutely nothing worth looking at in it.

This happy state of affairs continued until a couple of weeks ago, when my relationship with all those awful pictures underwent an interesting and unexpected change. Where once I would look up at them and feel self-loathing and despair, I now looked at them and felt a strange mixture of pity and pride. Pity for that poor obese girl staring back down at me, and pride because I wasn't that poor obese girl any more.

I am a whole three stone lighter than I was when those pictures were taken, and if I ever needed proof of the difference that makes in the way you look, all I need to do is look in the mirror, then look at that billboard on the dual carriageway on the way in to the office.

Of course dealing with inanimate objects like billboards (or cardboard stands in a gym reception area—that bloody thing is still there and taunting me every time I go in for a workout) is one thing. Coping with the unwanted attention of my fellow human beings is entirely another.

Be they family, friends, work colleagues, or complete strangers, everyone's attitude towards me is coloured by Fat Chance.

The competition has become a massive hit, much to my disgust.

Listening figures have skyrocketed at Stream FM, visits to the website to watch the videos have gone up over one hundred percent, and the Breakfast Show now attracts the biggest audience of any local radio morning programme. This is especially true every Monday when we all troop into the show for the weekly check-in.

These have become an unlovely constant in my life.

Monday mornings are never much fun, but when you add the joy of speaking to several thousand people over the radio, they become ever so much *worse*. I am not by nature the type who likes to perform on any kind of stage, even one where nobody can see my face—so trying to be entertaining and interesting on a weekly basis is about as easy as pulling somebody else's teeth. Thankfully a lot of the other contestants have warmed to the job now and are 'giving good radio.' This means that Elise no longer has to bully me into saying something interesting, as she constantly had to do in the first few weeks of the show.

In fact, the Monday morning chats have exposed a couple of real entertainers in our midst. Dominica is a hoot to listen to when she talks in her broad Spanish accent about her dieting and exercise programmes, getting more and more animated with every passing week. George and Valerie have formed a mild-mannered comedy double act that I could see them taking to the Edinburgh Festival Fringe if they so desired. It's not so much what they say, just the way they say it—in a laconic, dry style of humour that everyone gets a kick out of. You only need to hear the routine about a visit to the funfair that ended with George trapped in a seat on the teacup ride to get a good idea of how they bounce off each other.

'It was rather bloody uncomfortable,' George tells us.

'And him in his new trousers,' Val adds.

'Yes indeed. Nice ones, too. Burton's they were. Seemed a pity to rip them.'

'That lovely young fireman was very insistent, though.'

'Indeed he was. Reminded me of Gareth.'

'Gareth?'

'Yes. Boy from up the road. Big lad. Shoulders like a side of ham.'

'You mean Grant.'

'Do I?'

'Yes. Gareth was Paul's best friend in school. Had a squint and the kind of haircut your mother warned you about.'

'Ahh. You're right, of course. Fruity lad, he was. I can't see him being much of a fireman.'

'No. His hands were too floppy.'

'Without a doubt . . . Er, sorry Elise, what were we talking about again?'

I can't decide whether the absent-minded back and forth is natural or deliberately executed. Either way it's highly entertaining.

If the weekly check-ins are a ratings hit, then the monthly weigh-ins are the kind of audience bonanza that the station executives must be having kittens about.

One weekend in every month people huddle round their radios and wait to hear who's leading the competition.

. . . at least they would if this was 1952. I know that most people listen to the radio now on their smartphones but I'm a romantic at heart, and I like the mental image of a family gathered round a big box in the corner of the living room. It helps to visualise all those people taking an unhealthy interest in how many pounds I've lost recently, and I choose to do it in a way that's appealing to me. There's nothing romantic about a bloody iPod.

The weigh-ins may be great entertainment for the listening public, but they're nerve-wracking experiences if you're actually taking part. Partly because you have to strip down (more or less) in front of a crowd to do it, and partly because the weigh-ins are the one time when you get to find out how well you're doing compared to the other couples.

Lest we forget, there are fifty thousand pounds up for grabs here, and the monthly weigh-in gives you a great idea of how near you are to getting your grubby mitts on them.

Greg and I have never actually been in the lead as yet, but we've been in either second place or third place every time we've stepped off the scales and the scoreboard has tallied up our combined weight loss. Frankie and Benny have consistently been at the top of the leader board, with only one weigh-in not being won by them. This went to George and Val, who were having a particularly good month thanks to a weeklong visit to a weight loss spa arranged for them by their son Paul.

We have the next weigh-in coming up next week and I'm really hoping that Greg and I will have closed the gap to Frankie and Benny enough to keep us in the competition as we head into the last few weeks.

I find myself in a period of my life where at least one major aspect of it is a matter of great local public interest. Never has one woman had so much attention paid to her waistline. Not since Kate Middleton fell pregnant, anyway.

My weight loss is now the main topic of conversation whenever I'm with my friends and family. I hear the same old questions over and over. *'How much have you lost this week?' 'Do you think you've lost more than that nice black couple?' 'Do you have to wear those bright red outfits? Only they make you look like a tomato.'* . . . and so on, and so forth.

My mother and father are extremely proud of me, I'm pleased to say. 'It's lovely to see you blossom like this,' Mum said to me a few days ago, making me sound like a tulip.

Dad's contribution has been more blunt. 'Just bloody glad to see you lose weight, darling. You were a coronary waiting to happen.' His words would have held more meaning if he hadn't been smoking a Marlboro at the time.

The strangest change in my life thanks to my newfound local fame has been the relationship I have with my co-workers. The dynamic among us has shifted . . . and unfortunately not for the better in some cases.

Zoe Milton has always been something of an 'under the radar' kind of girl at work. I like to think I've always done my job well, but I've never tried to stand out from the crowd, or bully my way into positions of power and influence. I'm the first to admit I don't take all that well to confrontational situations, so have never done anything risky to climb the corporate ladder. I'm happy being a sales co-ordinator, and as long as no one tries to take it away from me, I'm equally happy not to make a fuss.

However, it's a little hard to maintain your flight path under the radar when you're part of a highly successful competition and promotional campaign being run—at least in part—out of the same bloody office as the one you work in.

Of course I've been kept away from any of the actual promotional and marketing work for Fat Chance. That's being handled purely by Stream FM's dedicated communications team, so there's no conflict of interest. This doesn't stop them annoying me on a regular basis for feedback and ideas, though. While I try to get on with my job selling advertising space, I keep getting interrupted by people asking me if I'd mind giving them a sound bite about how great it is to use one of the four-thousand-pound treadmills at Fitness4All, or what my thoughts are on the new poster going up in Asda.

Since March I've gone from mild-mannered marketing type who wouldn't say boo to a goose, to front-and-centre valued member of the team and mascot for the radio station's success.

Most in my office are happy to support me and have no problem with my new-found celebrity.

Unfortunately, the same cannot be said for my boss.

Caitlin Marks has never liked me that much anyway.

From the first day I met her in the interview panel for my job, I got the distinct impression she wasn't keen on me in the slightest. If the decision to hire me had been purely down to her, I would never have set foot in the building again. I have no idea why she took such a dislike to me. I can only imagine it was because she either didn't like the skirt I was wearing or didn't like the flippant jokes I made during the interview. Caitlin has the sense of humour of a bag of pig manure, so the latter is more likely.

Over the years, though, our relationship has thawed a little, mainly because I've got on with my job and done everything she's asked me to on time and with a minimum of fuss. Caitlin is the kind of person who likes people when they know their place, and up until a few months ago I knew my place very well: *under her*.

Then Fat Chance started, and it all went to shit.

You see, not only does Caitlin Marks not like it when other people get ideas above their station, she is also pretty damn fat. Not quite as big as I was, but she's definitely a size eighteen—and not a particularly attractive one at that. Some plus-sized ladies carry it very well. They're all sexy curves and sass. They stride through the world proud of being a larger woman and will make every effort to let you know that.

Caitlin, however, is lumpy. Lumpy, uncoordinated, and sporting a complexion that can only be described as sallow.

All the time that meek and mild Zoe Milton was fatter than her everything was fine, but once I dropped below her dress size *and* became the office talking point, her attitude towards me plummeted.

The phrase *'You're late again'* has become her catchphrase whenever I'm around these days.

It doesn't matter that the reason I'm late is always because of Fat bloody Chance, of course!

The situation came to a head last Monday when I turned up at nearly eleven thirty, thanks to the radio show over running by a good twenty minutes. Val and George were in the middle of a smashing anecdote about their week in the health spa and nobody wanted to stop them before they'd finished describing what it was like to be covered in mud and have pebbles balanced on your forehead. This was all very well, but it led me into a confrontation with

Caitlin that the fatter, less confident version of myself would have run screaming from a mere four months ago.

'Morning, Maz. Has Pigdog been prowling around?' I say to Maz (real name Mary), one of the admin assistants who works alongside me in the office.

Pigdog is a name Mary came up with to describe Caitlin a few months back.

There's always somebody like Mary in an office environment—the one who gives nicknames to everyone, the kind that are invariably funny or clever enough to stick with their recipient through the rest of their working lives. *Pigdog* is probably the least clever of Mary's efforts, to be honest, but it does capture the essence of Caitlin's personality well enough for it to have stuck in my mind, if nobody else's.

My nickname is Zoballs. Which could be better or worse, frankly.

'Yeah, and she's got a face on,' Maz tells me.

'Yuck. Really?'

'Yeah. You remember last Halloween when Meems and I decked the place out in pumpkins and witches without getting permission from her?'

'I do.'

'Same face she made then. Only a bit more wrinkled around the forehead.'

'Spectacular. I'll just go keep my head down and get on with that email to Sanderson Construction.'

Maz gives me a wink. 'Good idea, flower.' She then looks me up and down. 'You're looking good, Zoballs. And sounding good on the show this morning, too.'

'Thanks, Maz.'

'I'm glad I've got you and Gregster in the pool.'

'The what?'

'The office pool, silly. For who wins the competition? Me and Meems have got you, and I reckon we're onto a winner.'

'You're *betting* on us winning?'

'Absolutely! Meems has you in her hairdressing pool as well. She's beside herself.'

I feel cold fingers creep across my neck. 'There are a lot of these bets going on, are there?' I say in a squeaky voice.

'Yep!' Maz says with a huge smile. 'Great, isn't it?'

Fuck, no!

'I guess.'

'You should put some money down on yourself. Extra motivation.' Maz looks over my shoulder and the smile is gone. 'Watch out. Here cometh the Pigdog.'

I turn to see my boss marching across the thin green corduroy office carpet towards me, a thunderous look on her face. I steel myself for the onslaught.

'I've been emailing you for an hour, Zoe!' Caitlin says when she gets to me.

I figure I'd better try and be as conciliatory as I can, so I affect an apologetic smile and put my hands up. 'I'm so sorry, Caitlin. The show overran and I've only just got here.'

'Don't give me that. I'm sick of your excuses, Zoe.' Her face has gone an unhappy shade of red. It looks like she's really het up about my lateness this time. I fear a shit-eating grin and a sorry tone of voice may not be enough to get me out of this one.

'Would you please accompany me to my office?' she spits and turns on one heel, marching back across the thin green carpet.

'Oh dear. Batten down the old hatches,' Maz warns me.

I take a deep breath and meekly follow Caitlin back to her office, preparing myself for the worst.

Once her door is shut behind us, I get it with both barrels.

'I've had quite enough of your attitude, Zoe.'

'But I—'

'Don't interrupt me! The number of times you've been late for work is entirely unacceptable.'

'Four times in as many months?'

'Yes! And when you are here, your attitude towards work and your colleagues has become lackadaisical.' I can actually see sweat beads forming at Caitlin's brow. It obviously took a lot of effort to use that big a word in a sentence.

'Are you saying I'm *lazy*?' I reply, not liking the slightly whiny tone in my voice.

'I certainly think your work ethic has dropped in recent weeks, yes. Your productivity has definitely suffered.'

'I'm . . . I'm sorry,' I stammer.

I look down at my feet shame-faced. I hate, *hate*, HATE being told off like this. I pride myself on doing a good job, and when someone in a position of authority questions my ability to do that, it makes me feel about three inches tall.

I guess the competition may have affected my work. Maybe my work rate *has* gone down a bit?

After all, I'm always tired these days thanks to all the exercise I'm doing, and my low-calorie diet may be affecting my levels of concentration.

Perhaps Caitlin is right?

Perhaps I haven't been doing my job as well as I should have because of—

Hang on a fucking minute . . .

What the *hell* am I doing?

I'm letting Pigdog convince I'm in the wrong . . . and for no good reason!

My work has *not* suffered because of Fat Chance. If anything it's got *better*. The new Sanderson contract I've negotiated, selling all that air time to the local cinema, the deal I struck last month with Makepeace Car Sales . . .

I've been doing a *good* job, thank you so very much, your royal Pigdoggyness!

This isn't about my work: this is all about her not liking the changes Zoe Milton has been going through in recent weeks.

The unlovely truth is that my boss is *jealous* of me right now, and intends to show her displeasure any way she can. This is a blatant power play. Caitlin wants to re-exert her authority over me—it's as simple as that.

And I almost let her get away with it.

My fists clench.

In the back of my skull I can hear the meek and mild obese girl I once was screaming at me to unclench, take the lecture, and return to my desk.

Don't rock the boat, Zoe. Don't make waves, Zoe. Don't do anything risky, Zoe. Girls like you don't get to win, Zoe. You get to take all the shit thrown at you, and then you get to go home and eat an entire trifle to make yourself feel better.

You swallow down the anger, then you swallow down the calories. That's the way it works.

Except I've lost over three stone. My face is plastered across billboards. I'm on the radio. People are actually betting on me to *win* something.

I don't have to swallow anything anymore if I don't want to.

'Caitlin,' I say in a level tone of voice. 'I don't agree with your assessment of my work.'

'What do you mean?' she asks, incredulous.

Unbelievable.

She actually can't understand how I could possibly disagree with her.

'I mean I don't agree with you. My work has *not* suffered. My attitude is *not* bad, and while I have been late for work a few times, I have a very good reason, which you are fully aware of.'

'Now listen to me—'

I hold out a firm hand. 'No, please let me finish. I don't believe you have any cause to question my work, other than because you have a problem with me on a personal level. I believe you are being highly unprofessional, Caitlin.'

Good grief. I've gone mad.

Pigdog's eyes are like saucers. 'How dare you say that to me!' she wails. 'I will have you up on a disciplinary!'

Now I've well and truly got her. 'Please do. In fact, I insist upon it,' I reply calmly, and fold my arms.

This throws an ocean of cold water over her towering anger. Caitlin's expression instantly changes to one filled with doubt. Her bluff has been called. 'I'm sorry, Zoe. That was uncalled for.'

'Oh no! Please. I think we should launch a disciplinary investigation. That way I can show that my work has not suffered in the slightest.' My eyes narrow. 'I can even talk about it—and you—on the radio next week. It should make a *really* good story for Elise and Will to get to the bottom of.'

I'm tempted to pull out my phone and take a picture of Pigdog's face. I've never seen pure terror captured in such a glorious manner before.

'There's no need for that, really,' she says.

It's nice to hear my own apologetic whiny tone of voice from a few minutes ago projected back at me.

'No? Okay then, Caitlin. Let's forget about it then, shall we?' I reply. Let's face it, I've won this argument and there's no point in pushing my luck.

'Yes, I think that would be best.' She straightens up again. 'Let's just make sure you're on time for work from now on and a bit more proactive around the office.'

Incredible. She stills wants the upper hand.

'You know what, Caitlin? Fuck you.'

'What?'

'I said *fuck you*. You're a bully. And not a very good one at that.' I point a finger. 'Come after me again for no good reason and I'll make sure *everyone* knows about it.'

This is going too far. I know it even as I say it.

Threatening her like this means she's going to be out to get me from now on. If I even put a foot wrong I'll be immediately at risk of getting kicked out of my job. The thing is, I can't help myself right now. Caitlin the Pigdog has become symbolic of all the people who have ever tried to squash me beneath their feet in the past.

I fall silent, as does my boss.

I think we both realise now that this conversation should never have happened. She's threatened me with a groundless disciplinary, and I've threatened her with character assassination on live radio. We've both stepped well and truly over the line and need to back-track as quickly as possible.

'I think you should leave now, Zoe,' she says. 'No more need be said about this matter.'

'Okay. I agree.' I pause for a second. 'Should I send you over the Sanderson contract before lunch?'

'Yes, please.'

'I'll get back to my desk, then.'

'Please do.'

I sidle out of Caitlin's office, breathing a long sigh of relief as I close the door behind me.

What an exquisitely uncomfortable few minutes of my life. Not just because of the argument, but thanks to the realisation that I've spent a majority of my life comfort-eating my problems away, instead of confronting them and dealing with them properly. Caitlin has unwittingly performed some much-needed shock therapy on me this morning. Her idiocy has made me see my own.

How many times over the years have I substituted standing up for myself with chocolate cake?

How many times has my backbone been made of the same jelly in all those trifles I've eaten whole, in one sitting?

Well, not anymore.

Those days are over.

From now on Zoe Milton is not to be trifled with.

I've had no further run-ins with Caitlin since our little private discussion in her office. An uneasy but necessary truce has formed—at least while I'm still part of Fat Chance. What happens when my brief flirtation with celebrity goes away is anyone's guess. I just hope I've done enough to assure her that screwing with me is a mistake she might live to regret.

This new-found sense of self-worth is all very well, but it doesn't help you much when you're being stalked in IKEA by a lunatic.

I only went out to buy a new wok and some decorative bookends.

IKEA is the perfect store to shop in when you want to purchase items as incongruous as that. Sling any two apparently random things together and chances are you can still find them lurking in one corner or another of the blue and yellow megastore.

Tea strainer and a gardening fork? Framed picture of two elephants and a cheese board? Bottle of insecticide and super king duvet cover in an odd shade of milky green? You can find them all, right in IKEA—if you're prepared to tackle the incomprehensible floor plan and are wearing your best walking shoes.

I don't usually like to venture into IKEA without Greg. His sense of direction tends to be better than mine, and without him there's every chance I could get lost in table lamps and never find my way out again. This Sunday, though, he is playing rugby for the first time in years with the lads down at the leisure centre, so I'm going to have to go it alone. I reassure myself with the fact my phone has GPS satellite navigation on it, and I have a clear four hours with which to negotiate my way back out again, so I should be alright. I have left instructions to call in the search and rescue teams if I am not heard from by next Thursday, though.

Like the circles of Dante's Inferno, IKEA descends through several floors towards Hell itself (or the checkout, as people with no imagination insist on calling it).

Unfortunately for the unwary traveller, you must venture through every floor no matter what item you wish to procure, whether you want to or not. For example, should you wish, like me, merely to purchase a wok and a couple of bookends to stop Greg's huge hardback rugby books from falling over all the time, you must also look at every other sodding product IKEA has on sale. You must make your way along the circuitous and tortuous route that the sadistic Swedes have laid out between you and the exit.

No one in human history has ever said the following: *'I've just popped into IKEA and picked up some meatballs. You fancy a spag bol?'*

One does not simply 'pop' into IKEA. One plans the visit like a military operation.

Make no mistake: shopping there is *not* to be taken lightly. Not if you wish to retain both sanity and a healthy bank balance.

With this in mind, I girded my loins and parked the car near to the exit. There was still every chance I'd never, ever find it again, given the mammoth size of the car park and the maze I was about to enter inside, but I figured that by putting my battered Golf as close to the exit as I could, I might stand a fighting chance were I ever to emerge again into the daylight.

The ride up in the elevator is without incident. I emerge at the top of the car park structure and make my way through the cavernous open doors into the first foyer area of the store.

Picking up one of the enormous yellow plastic bags, I start to whisper *'wok and bookends, wok and bookends'* under my breath. I find it helps to utter a mantra like this as you navigate the aisles. That way you're more likely to keep your mind on the task at hand, and not get distracted by the bright blue watering cans and very reasonably priced coffee tables.

This never works, of course. IKEA is master of the impulse buy. You may just go in for something boring, cheap, and necessary, but you can bet your bottom dollar that you won't make it out the other end without having purchased something large, expensive, and blessed with a silly product name.

Ten minutes after entering, I'm standing in the middle of level three (bedroom furniture . . . and place of heretics if you're Dante) wondering whether to buy an occasional table from the Goopli or Smerferdle range.

The Goopli looks bigger, but the Smerferdle goes better with the couch.

I've completely forgotten about the bookends and the wok, and I can assure you that I left the store that day without having bought either of them. This happens a lot in IKEA. You should probably get used to it.

No, for Zoe Milton, life is now all about Goopli and Smerferdle.

My eyes swap from one to the other in an agony of indecision. I stand immobile, letting the other shoppers flow about me like a river around an upstream boulder. I will not move from this place until a decision is reached. Goopli or Smerferdle. Smerferdle or Goopli. I must decide. *I must decide.* I MUST DECIDE.

'Oh my God, it's you!'

The voice is high, hectic, and nearly cracking with excitement.

It's also completely blown my concentration. I was *this close* to deciding on the Goopli, but now I'll have to start the process all over again.

Not that I'm going to get the chance, because I now have a high, hectic voice in my ear that shows no concern for the serious dilemma I find myself in.

'It is, isn't it!? It's you!'

I look around at my new companion.

She is a woman whose look can only be described as 'eclectic.'

That's if you're being polite.

If you're not, you're more likely to describe her as being dressed like a mental patient. She looks like a charity shop has thrown up over her.

Starting from the feet we have wellington boots. One is red with yellow spots, the other blue with green spots. The tights are nice, if a little too bright orange for my tastes. The jean shorts are fairly sensible I suppose—faded black and sporting turn-ups a good three inches wide.

Then we come to the poncho.

Now, ponchos are a bold fashion choice at the best of times, but when said poncho is a chunky, knitted number in all the colours of the rainbow, 'bold' simply doesn't do the choice justice. Nor does 'courageous,' 'valiant,' or 'daring.'

'Madder than a box of badgers' is certainly accurate, though.

Normality reasserts itself when we reach her face. It's an open, pleasant moon shape with happy eyes, and is framed by a brown bob of hair.

Then we come to the top hat.

Yes, the top hat.

The woman is wearing a top hat.

Not crazy enough for you?

Okay, the top hat has a plastic geranium sticking out of the hat band. The kind you can fully expect to squirt water at any moment.

How's that?

She looks like a children's television presenter. One you wouldn't actually leave any kids with for more than a minute.

. . . and she knows who I am.

God help me.

'Hello. What . . . er, what do you want?' I say in clipped tones. I'm annoyed that I've been distracted from my Goopli/Smerferdle conundrum and fail to keep the irritation out of my voice.

'You're Zoe Milton, aren't you? From the radio? From the competition?' She's almost vibrating with excitement.

Now, I should do the sensible thing here and lie. If I'm committed enough to it she might just go away. However, I have a stupidly accurate moral compass that precludes me from that kind of thing. This has got me into more trouble over the years than I care to remember.

'Yes, I'm Zoe Milton.' Time to effect the patented fixed smile of the reluctant celebrity. 'Are you enjoying the show, then?'

She claps her hands together three times in rapid succession. 'Oh yes! It's wonderful! I'm a little overweight myself so you're an inspiration to me!'

'That's nice.'

'It is! It is! It really, really is!' More hand clapping.

'What's your name?' I ask, trying to stay polite.

'Veronica! My name's Veronica! I can't believe I'm taking to Zoe Milton!' *Clap clap.*

I offer an uncertain smile. 'Well, you are.'

Though quite why you're so excited about it is beyond me.

I don't think I'd be this thrilled if I saw Johnny Depp standing butt naked over by the pouffes.

'I just can't believe it!' Veronica screeches and giggles like someone who's no stranger to a padded white cell. 'I love you so much!' *Clap, clap. Giggle, giggle.*

I have to wrap this up.

'Well, it's nice to meet you,' I say, starting to move away.

'Yes! Yes! I can't believe I'm meeting you!' Then Veronica lifts her poncho. 'Will you sign my tits?'

Underneath the poncho is a thin green blouse, unbuttoned enough to show what is quite an impressive cleavage. I can see a series of signatures already scrawled across them. They look like tattoos.

I'm in real trouble here.

'Er . . . er . . . I don't think so, Veronica.' I look at my watch. 'I'm really short on time and have to be going. It was nice to meet you, though!'

I try to move away, but Veronica's cleavage is having none of it. 'Oh, please sign them! It'll be a great addition to my collection.' She points at a bare patch on the left one. 'You can sign right here next to Cliff Richard and Sir Chris Hoy.'

'No! No! Sorry! Have to go!' I cry and scuttle off as fast as my feet will carry me.

Veronica inexplicably gives chase, forcing me to shift my arse even faster. I'm actually having to run away now. I have my back turned and am heading for the shortcut leading to the stairs—and hopeful salvation.

This is a thing that is happening to me.

I am trying to escape from a woman with a top hat and 38 DDs, who is now pursuing me through IKEA with crazed determination.

I'm trying, but I'm not succeeding.

Veronica is only fifteen or so feet behind me. From somewhere I don't want to think about she has produced a large black marker pen. 'Come back, Zoe! Sign my tits, please!'

'No, go away!' I flap my hands back at her.

'Please! Everybody does it eventually!'

'No! Fuck off!' This is hideously impolite, but I'm at the end of my tether.

'Sign them!'

'I said fuck off!'

I round a corner and can see the stairs ahead. For a split second Veronica has lost sight of me. This is my chance to get away.

But the stairs are too far away! By the time I reach them it will be too late. My pursuer will have caught sight of me again. I'll never be able to shake her off!

'Oi! Over here!'

I whip my head around. A tall blonde woman is beckoning me over to the open door of one of the customer lifts. A man is holding the door open, an exasperated look on his face. Between them stands a small, pretty little girl of about five, sucking a finger and looking at me with great concern.

'Come on!' the woman hisses and beckons again.

For all I know this could be yet another lunatic who wants me to sign a part of her anatomy, but at least this one isn't wearing a top hat.

As Veronica the nutcase comes round the corner, I disappear into the open lift, the blonde woman right behind me. As the doors are closing Veronica homes into view. She looks round and sees me standing in the lift. 'Come back, Zoe!' she wails and starts towards us. The exasperated man hammers the button to close the lift doors. They start to come together. I hold my breath. If they don't shut quickly enough, Veronica's going to be in here with us. I'll be trapped. There will be no escape from the tattooed tits and top hat!

Thankfully, the last image I have of Veronica is her anguished face and outstretched hand as the lift doors close, ending her relentless pursuit.

The blonde woman blows air out of her cheeks. 'Blimey, that was close,' she says and pats me on the back.

'How did you know what was going on?' I ask her.

'We heard her shout about wanting you to sign her tits, and then saw you run away. Figured we'd try to lend a hand. It looked like you needed it.'

'Yes, yes. Thank you so much.'

'To tell the truth, I was going to come over and say hello myself. I listen to Stream FM a lot.'

'You're not going to ask me to sign something, are you?' I ask suspiciously.

'Course not!'

'Great,' I put out a hand. 'I'm Zoe . . . but I guess you already know that.'

'We do!' she says with a smile as we shake hands. 'I'm Laura, and this my husband Jamie.'

The man waves and gives me a sympathetic smile. 'Pleased to meet you.'

'You're the radio lady,' the little girl pipes up in a matter-of-fact tone.

'Yes, Pops. She is. Be nice, though. She's having a bad day,' Laura says to her.

'I am rather,' I reply. 'I only came into buy a wok and it all went downhill from there.'

'Sounds about right for IKEA,' Jamie says. 'I came in for a Daim bar cake once and ended up in casualty for three hours.'

'Really? How did that happen?'

Jamie makes a face. 'You wouldn't believe it.'

I think back on Veronica, her top hat, and the choice between Goopli and Smerferdle. 'You know what? I probably would.'

The lift pings and the doors open onto the car park. 'It'll have to wait for another time, I think,' Laura says. 'You probably want to get out of here before she rides down in another one of the lifts.'

My blood runs cold. 'Oh, God! I hadn't thought of that!'

'It was nice to meet you,' Laura adds.

'You too. And thanks for all your help again.'

'No problem,' Jamie says. 'Good luck with the rest of the competition.'

'Bye, radio lady,' the little girl says.

I give the little girl a wave and walk away from all three, thanking my lucky stars that they came along just at the right time.

My pace increases somewhat when I hear the sound of another lift door opening behind me.

I daren't look back, just in case I see Veronica sprinting towards me with Cliff Richard and Chris Hoy jiggling around on her rather mountainous breasts as she comes at me with that pen.

I ordered a Goopli online when I got home.

God bless the internet.

If Caitlin and Veronica have one thing in common, it's that they've both *completely* misinterpreted my significance in the grand scheme of things.

Yes, I'm on billboards and on the radio, but that doesn't make me a star by any stretch of the imagination.

The star of this entire escapade is the competition itself. After all, no-one would be running after Zoe Milton through the bedroom furniture section if she wasn't part of the juggernaut that is Stream FM's weight loss competition. I'm just not that fascinating or charismatic—much as I'd like to think I am after a few drinks.

Achieving even a small amount of celebrity is an extremely strange thing to cope with. It elevates you in the eyes of others, no matter how undeserving you may be of that elevation.

You also seem to lose ownership of yourself to a certain extent.

Some people think that you now belong to them in a strange way, just because they know your name and can pick you out of a line-up.

It's all just a little bit too much for this girl.

I've regained a degree of self-confidence in the past few months that I thought was gone forever, but that doesn't suddenly make me want to be the centre of everyone's attention.

Still, it's all temporary, of course. Once Fat Chance is over then I can return to my life of anonymity, relatively unscathed by my brush with fame—other than a new tendency to suffer a panic attack anytime I see a top hat.

I'm also never shopping in the IKEA store again.

Say what you want about B&Q, if you do get cornered by some nutter next to the tins of gloss at least you have a clear line of sight to the nearest bloody exit.

GREG'S WEIGHT LOSS DIARY
Wednesday, August 6th
15 stone, 4 pounds (4 stone, 12 pounds lost)

Wow, less than a month until this is all over.

In a mere twenty-five days we'll find out if Zoe and I have lost enough weight to win that glorious fifty thousand pounds.

We've now shed *nine stone* between us, which was Zoe's total weight when I met her. How completely and utterly bizarre.

That kind of weight loss is immediately noticeable to anyone who hasn't seen you for more than a few weeks. I bumped into a guy the other day who'd left the company just before Christmas for a job in Dubai. He actually walked straight past me without registering who I was, despite the fact we'd worked in the same office for four years together. I caught up to him and had to spend the next minute or so convincing him I wasn't my own thinner twin brother.

Even the people you see on a regular basis can't help but comment when they see you've shifted another three or four pounds in one week. I like the look they get on their faces. It's usually a combination of amazement and amusement, born from the fact that someone they know well is changing right before their eyes.

Inexplicably, eating less makes dining out a more pleasurable experience. Zoe and I used to love going out to dinner in the first few years of our marriage. It was one of the cornerstones of our relationship. By the time our fifth anniversary had rolled around we'd pretty much become on first-name terms with most of the local restaurant managers.

Thinking back on it, maybe we became a little *too* familiar with the local restaurants. Our time and money spent in them may well have contributed to our combined weight gain over the years. The Miltons certainly never left a restaurant hungry or unsatisfied back in those days.

Needless to say, those evenings out dwindled to nothing once we had piled on enough pounds. When you realise you are very overweight, eating becomes something you'd rather do in the privacy of your own home, where no-one can look at you and make snap judgements.

In recent weeks, however, we've rediscovered a love of eating out, even going so far as a bit of alfresco dining when the weather has been good enough. The difference this time is that we choose the healthiest options on the menu and don't accompany our meals with a bottle or two of red wine. Where once we would eat and eat and eat with little time for conversation, we now both pick at our food and set the world to rights as we do so. I know more about Zoe's life outside the one we share together than I ever have. The same is true for her.

Where once a meal together was all about the food, it's now all about sharing some quality time with each other.

It's not all good, though, this dieting business.

Take clothes, for instance.

When you're on a long-term weight loss program it can play havoc with your dress sense—and your wallet. You essentially have one of two choices: either stay walking around in the clothes you've always had in order to avoid the extra expense, or pay regular visits to the clothes shops and re-buy a new wardrobe every couple of months.

I tried the first option to begin with, being a man used to a certain degree of frugality. It didn't work out well at all. By the time I'd started cutting new notches in my belt, I was starting to resemble a small boy dressed in his father's clothes. I'd have to constantly hitch my jeans up, and my vast collection of polo shirts all billowed like sails around my shrinking frame. The final straw came when I was down the pub and someone asked me with a sympathetic voice if I'd contracted some kind of serious disease.

When people are mistaking healthy weight loss for a terminal illness, it's time to change your wardrobe.

And change it I did, in one swooping attack on Marks & Spencer that my bank balance took weeks to recover from.

This was all well and good, but I was *still* losing weight and quickly found myself once again cutting notches in my belt and hitching my jeans up.

I did seriously contemplate buying a pair of those nylon trousers with an elastic waist—but decided against it, as looking like a terminal cancer patient is slightly better than looking like a guy who's just escaped from the Shady Pines Institute for the Mentally Bereft.

So back to Marks & Spencer I went.

Then I walked straight *through* Marks & Spencer and took a sharp left into Primark.

If I'm going to keep renewing my wardrobe every couple of months I'm going to be buying the cheap stuff, even if it is badly made and makes me itch.

Zoe has got it even worse than me, of course.

We men don't really hold much stock in the clothes we wear. That would just be a little bit 'fruity' and best avoided at all costs. We don't talk about clothes with other men, and we certainly don't compare wardrobes.

Women, on the other hand, seem to define their very existence based on their fashion choices, and the fashion choices of the other women around them.

Poor old Zoe is having to constantly update her wardrobe thanks to her weight loss. Sometimes she even buys exactly the same item of clothing three times over in decreasing sizes, in the kind of gross western consumption that people in the third world get justifiably upset about.

I pointed this out to her the other night. The reaction was not pleasant.

'Don't guilt trip me, Gregory,' she snapped. 'If I go out in clothes that are too big for me I'll get crucified by the other girls next time I'm out of earshot.'

'But won't they just be jealous that you've lost all that weight?' I respond, showing my complete and utter lack of understanding of how the female mind works.

'No Gregory, that will *not* be what they talk about. Losing four stone is nothing in their eyes when compared to being dressed like a bag lady.' She puts her hands on her hips. 'Just accept that for the time being our credit card is going to get pounded, and my usual sensitivity to the plight of those in developing countries is secondary to the need for my arse to look good in chiffon.'

That was the last word on the subject.

Since then I have resolutely refused to go anywhere near a shopping precinct with my wife, for fear of having to spend a good six hours sitting outside changing rooms while she tries on everything in sight.

I can't escape the hell of female clothes shopping completely, though. Zoe has taken to ordering stuff online, so I'm forever having to take delivery of a package from one website or another. So much so that I'm now on first-name terms with our postman.

'Has she gone mental?' asks Wilfred the garrulous old postie as he hands over the latest purchase. 'This is the fifth parcel of the week.'

'Quite possibly,' I reply and take ownership of the brown cardboard box.

He gives me a look of profound sympathy. 'Joan was the same with shoes. I had to threaten her with divorce before she bankrupted us both.'

'And how did that work out for you?'

Wilfred looks more glum than Birmingham. 'I got the dog in the settlement. The house went to her and the shoes.'

I didn't quite know what to say to that, so I took the conversation back in the direction of business and told him that if any more parcels come and we're not in, he should just come through the side gate and leave them in the shed. He seemed a little disconsolate that I didn't want to discuss his marital break-up in more detail.

There's no doubt about it: losing weight is an expensive business.

You may think that all that money lost on new clothes would be clawed back by the cash we're not spending on food, but you would be completely wrong in that assumption.

Yes, we no longer treat ourselves to at least two takeaways a week and have cut down on unhealthy meals and snacks in general. The problem is we have to eat *something*, and healthy food is always more expensive than the cheap, sugary stuff. Mung bean salad and a fresh fruit compote may be a one-way ticket to a smaller waistline, but they also costs four times as much as the family-sized lasagne and chips lurking a few aisles away in the frozen food section.

I always knew that a harsh weight loss program would mean a lot of physical effort, but I wasn't prepared for how much of a financial outlay it is, too. I now have a better appreciation of why so many people on limited incomes and benefits are big roly-poly people. It's hard to maintain a thirty-two-inch waist when the salads are three quid and the burgers are thirty pence.

I haven't even started on how expensive the actual diet food is. All those milkshakes, smoothies, healthy snack bars, and dried fruit snacks cost a bloody fortune.

How on earth can we ever expect our society to get thinner when no-one is making any effort to make the healthy food cheaper than the toxic, fatty stuff that's creating a nation of tubby fuckers with too many fillings?

The expense sadly doesn't end there, either. If eating healthy is a strain on your wallet, then exercising can quite easily break it completely.

Gym fees are quite frankly idiotic.

If the government wants Britain to lose weight it should make all those fitness companies charge less for the privilege of using their shiny, complicated equipment.

Let's face it, exercise can be something of a ball ache, especially if you've just spent eight hours at work, sitting at a desk feeling your vertebrae fuse together. The last thing most of us need is to then go to a hall full of sweaty people and add our own perspiration to the mix.

People need to be incentivised to get off their arses and go to the gym. Charging them fifty pounds a month on a one-year contract is not the best way to accomplish this, as far as I am concerned.

If the gym contract stated that you could stop paying if you didn't hit your target weight within six months then I'd be more likely to sign up—but I think the chances of that happening are roughly equivalent to me winning Miss World in a mankini.

I'll apologise for the hideous mental image that may conjure up, and move on.

Since March, when this whole escapade began, I've tried many different kinds of exercise in my pursuit of a healthier lifestyle and fifty thousand pictures of the Queen.

My week with Alice Pithering still keeps me up at night, but it did give me some insight into what it's like to have a personal trainer. Enough insight, in fact, to make me one hundred percent sure that I *never* want a personal trainer ever again.

Aside from this I've also tried a plethora of exercise contraptions that purport to help you shift weight at a vast rate of knots. Most of them also promise to make exercise 'fun' and easier to fit into your hectic social life.

All of them are expensive.

None of them work.

Take the following few paragraphs as both warning and consumer advice, so you don't end up making the same mistakes I did.

Like everyone who embarks on a weight loss program I went for the easy options first. This is just human nature. If we can avoid hard work, we damn well will. An entire industry has been built around this inherent laziness, one that I have contributed a great deal of money towards in the last six months.

If there is a piece of exercise equipment specifically designed for the lazy, it's the electro muscle stimulator. Not half as dirty as it sounds, these odd little contraptions are designed to send small electric charges through your body, making your muscles twitch—which apparently encourages weight loss.

How utterly brilliant! You can just attach a few pads to your body, turn on the machine, and lose umpteen calories while you're sitting in your armchair watching 'Downton Abbey.' By the time the episode has ended (usually with tea being served in the drawing room) you've dropped several pounds, all without any effort whatsoever!

Needless to say I was sceptical. But I was also grossly over-weight and lazy, so I forked out two hundred quid and ordered the Electromax 2000 from Amazon with fingers crossed.

Let's just repeat that: I spent two hundred quid on a machine that basically electrocutes me every few seconds, in order to avoid any *actual* exercise.

∾

The Electromax 2000 is promptly delivered three days later and by the time Downton starts at 8 p.m. I'm wired up and ready to rock. Two pads are stuck to my gut, a further two are placed on my thighs, and the final couple are strapped to my biceps. I look like someone about to enter suspended animation for the five-year journey to Mars.

'Are you sure about this?' Zoe asks me from the couch, doubt in her eyes.

'Of course! I did some research on the internet. The science of this thing is very sound.'

Boy, do I sound pompous when I'm trying to prove a point.

The pads are connected by wires to the big friendly blue Electromax box, which I've sat on the arm of the chair. As the Downton credits begin I turn the big friendly blue dial at the top of the box to the on position and sit back, ready to burn off the fat while watching posh people argue politely with one another.

'Ahh, Lord Poncyface, so nice to see you again . . .'

Bzzzt.

'And the same to you, Captain Sternexpression . . .'

Bzzzt. Bzzzt.

'I trust your wife Lady Furrowedbrow is well?'

Bzzzt. Bzzzt. Bzzzt.

'She is. I was so sorry to hear about your wife's tragic demise at the hands of that Irish ruffian.'

Bzzzt. Bzzzt. Bzzzt. Bzzzzzzzzzzzzzzzzzzzzzzzzzt.

'Ow! For fuck's sake!' I scream, wrenching the pads from my stomach.

'Is it painful?' Zoe asks, pausing Downton and trying very hard not to laugh.

'Is it *painful*? You fucking bet it is!' I jump out of the chair and pull the rest of the pads off. 'How the hell is this thing supposed to make you lose weight?' I hold a pad up and examine it. 'Unless the electric shocks eventually clamp your jaws permanently together, meaning you can't eat anything.'

'Well, colour me completely surprised,' Zoe says, in a derisory fashion. 'You bought a get-fit-quick contraption off the internet and it doesn't work.'

'Sarcasm does not help at a time like this, woman. Back to your period drama.'

I gather the Electromax 2000 in my arms and carry it out of the room. It goes into the cupboard under the stairs, where I have every intention of letting it rot.

Two hundred pounds is a lot of money, however, so I have another go with the stupid machine about a week later, while Zoe is out with her friends. This time I lie out on the bed and mentally prepare myself for the self-inflicted torture I'm about to put myself through.

I last about eight minutes.

Seriously, in what universe did somebody think this was a good idea? To run an electric current through your body for the purposes of weight loss?

What's next? Inhaling vast quantities of helium because it might dye your hair blonde?

About the only thing the Electromax 2000 managed to accomplish in the few minutes I did use it was to make my bowels loosen. Half the reason I turned it off was because I needed to go and take a dump.

The machine went back under the stairs, and it really will stay there until the end of time as far as I'm concerned.

Unless I come down with a nasty case of constipation.

The next contraption I wasted my time and money on was an abdominal exercise machine called the Ab Lunge. It claimed to burn fat and tone your stomach muscles using a combination of forward and lateral movement. You basically kneel down on two platforms that move along two metal runners, grip the handle, and move yourself back and forth, exercising your abs, lats, and other incomprehensible muscle groups.

I bought it after watching one of those late-night infomercials.

You see what going on a diet does to you? The madness it inflicts?

In no other circumstance would I even consider buying *any-thing* I'd seen on a late-night infomercial. Never in a million years. You will never see me purchase a miracle steamer designed to clean up everything from spilled milk to nuclear waste. Nor will you find me shelling out for a juicer that can crush diamonds and mix you up a tasty banana smoothie in three micro-seconds.

But when it comes to ways to lose weight I am a complete moron. Hence the hundred and fifty quid I spent on the sodding Ab Lunge.

I knew I was in trouble within the first few minutes of unpacking the box out in the conservatory. The instruction manual on how to put the thing together consisted of one thin piece of double-sided A4 paper. On this were a series of amateurish pictures of the Ab Lunge in various states of completion, next to the kind of instructions they would have had a problem deciphering over at Bletchley Park.

It took three hours to put the bastard together, by which time I'd sweated so much that the last thing I wanted to do was jump on it and exercise.

I had a go at it the next day, though.

Down I went into roughly the same position you'd find yourself in on a motorbike. Hands gripped tightly on the handlebars, I started to move forward and back, left and right—just like the infomercial had told me to do. The left right stuff didn't appear to be doing much, so I just concentrated on going forward and back, forward and back. The knee platforms ran smoothly up and down the metal track and in no time I felt myself building up a sweat.

'Enjoying yourself, are you?' Zoe asked as she came out into the conservatory with a cup of green tea.

'Yes! Yes! It's good!'

'Is it?'

'Yes!'

'That's just as well, as from where I'm sitting, you look like you're shagging a mountain bike.'

'What?'

'Yep. If I could get you move that enthusiastically when you're on top of me it'd be a miracle.'

'Shut up.'

'Look at those hips go! Be careful, though, you don't want to go too far with it.'

'Be quiet!'

'We don't want a lot of little mountain bikes wheeling around the house in nine months, now, do we?'

'Will you leave me alone? I'm exercising!'

Laughing her head off, Zoe leaves me to it.

But now the whole process is ruined. Now she's pointed out what I look like, I can't get the image of me sexually molesting the contents of the nearest Halfords bicycle department out of my head.

I stop after twenty minutes and try my level best to ignore my wife for the rest of the day. This proves difficult, as she's found an old bicycle bell from somewhere, and periodically rings it for the next few hours—asking me if it makes me horny every time she does it.

Like with the Electromax 2000, I have another go on the Ab Lunge a week later when Zoe is once again out with her cronies.

I do a good hour on it and get off feeling very pleased with myself.

Pleasure turns to disgust when I wake up the next morning and my stomach muscles feel like they've had a hammer drill run over them in the night. The mere act of sitting up is painful. Going for a shit is nigh on impossible as every time my bowels contract it sends pain right through my stomach region. This causes me to become constipated for the next few days.

. . . which of course gives me the chance to use the Electromax one more time.

The Ab Lunge is now in the loft. I did consider putting it on eBay, but I'm a truthful kind of guy, and I didn't think I'd get many bids based on my description of the thing:

For sale. Ab Lunge. Used twice. Ever wanted to rape a bicycle? Now's your chance! Warning—may cause severe backup of the bowels.

Having now dropped three hundred and fifty quid on these useless contraptions, I thought it best to budget a little more sensibly and go for exercise equipment that wouldn't break the bank.

I immediately discounted the trampette, as I'm not five years old and have grown out of the desire to bounce up and down until I feel sick. Similarly, the gym ball wasn't an option either. If Zoe was in hysterics at my attempts to hump the Ab Lunge, the sight of me rolling around on a giant squishy ball like it was my first lover would likely end up in her going to casualty for oxygen deprivation.

Then I saw the StretchFit resistance band.

Oh holy Hell, I really wish I hadn't.

On the surface, the StretchFit seemed like the cat's whiskers. It was cheap at twenty quid, and looked like a very simple piece of exercise equipment to use. All it consists of is two long pieces of strong rubber, with plastic stirrups and handles attached. You pull at the rubber band, which provides resistance and tones your muscles.

An overabundance of exercises is available if you buy one of these things. You can put your feet in the stirrups and grip the handles to do any number of resistance activities, such as lunges, rowing, arm curls, and overhead presses—to name but a few. But then you can also attach the StretchFit to your wall, banister, or other sturdy object and do even more stuff with it. Pull-downs, pull-ups, lateral twists—all sorts of interesting and varied workout methods are open to you. It's a whole gym in one easy package!

. . . One of these days I'm going to stop falling for this marketing bullshit. This will also be the day I stop believing what I read in the *Daily Mail* and realise that my local mechanic has been ripping me off for years every time I take the car in for its MOT.

The StretchFit resistance band duly arrives (free postage and everything!) and I immediately set to work.

Of course it turns out to be shit.

Your feet go in the stirrups; you grab the handles and pull. This does very, very little. Why? Because by the time you achieve any real tension on the rubber band, you've already stretched your arms out to their maximum limit. Unless I suddenly develop the ability to extend my limbs like Plastic Man this particular product is largely pointless.

For the sake of being thorough, I try a few more of the routines laid out on the A3 poster that comes with the StretchFit. None of them work any better than the standard arm stretch. I do work up a sweat, but it occurs to me that I'd be working up the exact same amount of sweat if I just put the bloody thing down and did the routines without it.

As a final resort I attempt to attach the StretchFit to the end of our banister. This might provide more tension and resistance than I am able to supply using just my body.

And indeed it does! With my back to the banister and each length of rubber band over either shoulder I am able to step a few feet forward and extend the bands out far enough to actually get some resistance on the go.

I spend a happy five minutes pushing my arms out in a boxing motion, and by the end of the routine my arm muscles feel like they've had a workout.

Then I swap to lateral twists. This exercise requires you to stand side-on to the StretchFit, pulling it around your body in a twist motion that's meant to work your lats and abs.

This exercise works, too, though after a couple of minutes I have to stand further away from the banister to get the full effect and maximize my workout. This strains the rubber bands to their limit. I'm not worried, though; the instructions state that the rubber is incredibly strong and will not break no matter how much tension is placed on them.

They are absolutely right. The rubber bands do not even come close to breaking.

Which is more than can be said for the end of my banister.

As I'm at full stretch and enjoying the burning sensation in my abdominals, the rounded end of the banister pole gives way in spectacular fashion. With an enormous *crack!* it flies off, catapulting both it and the end of the StretchFit across the living room.

The banister end shoots straight into one of the conservatory windows, smashing the entire double-glazed pane.

The fun isn't over just yet, though, as the rubber band now springs back towards me at an ungodly speed. The hard plastic foot stirrups fly at my head, and will do some serious damage if I don't get out of the way.

I duck as fast as possible to protect my face. I am not quick enough to stop the stirrups whacking me in the back of the head, though.

In a concussed daze I stagger into the newly ventilated conservatory and survey the damage.

I then go back inside and pull the Ab Lunge down from the loft.

I figure that once Zoe sees the damage I've done, the Ab Lunge is the only thing I'm going to have the opportunity to shag for a long time to come.

In the end, the StretchFit resistance band cost twenty pounds . . . along with another *six hundred* pounds to fix both conservatory and banister.

I considered suing the company. Zoe stopped me when she pointed out that as I'm a local celebrity at the moment, if the press found out about it they'd have a field day. It's one thing for the local population to know you're a fat bastard. It's quite another for them to know you're a fucking moron.

The experience of Electromax, Ab Lunge, and StretchFit hammers home the fact that these fad machines do absolutely nothing for you, no matter how good they claim to be.

They are all designed to make exercise seem easy and carefree. The problem is that exercise is resolutely *not* easy and it is *never* carefree. It is hard work that tests your endurance and stamina—which is kind of the point when you get right down to it. It's the effort you put in that squares with the weight you lose. The more hard work you do, the more pounds you shift. It's as simple as that. Any time you try to make shortcuts or avoid any actual exertion, all you're doing is wasting your time and draining your bank account.

Bearing all this in mind, I elected to take a more biological approach to exercise.

. . . No, this doesn't mean what you think it means. Don't be so disgusting.

What I mean is that I spent a couple of days researching human biology to get a better understanding of how our bodies function. By doing this I learned what kind of exercises we are actually *designed* to do—on an evolutionary level, so to speak. If Darwin tells me what exercise I should be doing, then I'll damn well do it!

Sadly, the main exercise the human body is designed to do is running.

Fuck it.

Long before we had cars, bicycles, and horses to ride, we got around by putting one foot in front of the other. For thousands upon thousands of years the human race relied on Shanks's Pony, often conducted at a brisk pace to either catch prey or to avoid becoming it.

Deep down I knew this horrible fact before I even started my research, but I thought I might find something else that wasn't as painful, boring, or time consuming.

I failed.

After having this annoying revelation, with a sigh and a heavy heart I laced up my (very expensive) Asics running shoes and prepared to do battle with the pavements of local suburbia.

'You look happy,' Zoe remarked from the kitchen. 'You'd think you were going off to war, rather than a jog around the block.'

This has become a very unhealthy habit my wife has developed since we started this competition. She seems to take great delight and amusement from my failed attempts to find the right exercise regime for me.

'Leave me alone. I don't want to do this, but Darwin tells me I've got no choice, the hairy bastard.'

'So you don't like jogging, then?'

'Of course not. It hurts. And I feel like a right plum.'

'How so?'

'I look like an idiot when I'm jogging. It's embarrassing.'

'Ah, so your ego is the real problem here?'

'Oh, give it a rest. What else am I supposed to do?'

'Buy a treadmill and do it at home?'

This is the irritating thing about Zoe: her suggestions and comments may be saturated by sarcasm, but nine times out of ten they're also bloody good ones.

I unlaced the running shoes, picked up the iPad, and went back on Amazon.

Four days later I had a treadmill. At four hundred quid it's the most money I've dropped on self-improvement so far, but I'm confident it will be a wise investment.

The treadmill goes in the conservatory and I embark on a daily routine of running myself into a dazed stupor, only stopping when funny white lights start flashing in front of my eyes.

And by Christ if it doesn't actually work!

I've found my niche!

Running on the treadmill is far less painful than on the street, thanks to the give in the machine's belt. The shin splints and thigh cramps that usually plague me whenever I go for a jog do not materialise. What's more, I have control over the gradient and distance I run, so if I'm having an off day I can just run a couple of miles on the flat, but if I'm Captain Enthusiastic I can do four miles on an incline.

The treadmill is very convenient. All I have to do is stick on my running clothes and saunter over to it. I can even watch the television, if I angle the machine around so it points into the living room.

Marvellous stuff!

In fact, I eventually reach the point where I don't even wear most of the running clothes.

I mean, why bother? Our conservatory is not overlooked, so I see no problem with having a three-mile jog in my boxer shorts and t shirt. No-one's going to be looking at me, so why go through the inconvenience of getting my clothes all sweaty and having to put them in the wash?

If I'd just stopped there, everything would have been alright.

But one day it occurred to me that there was no real need even to wear the boxer shorts and t-shirt.

Our conservatory gets quite hot, especially during the summer months. If I run naked I will stay cool *and* not have to bother trying to work that flaming washing machine, with all its strange dials and incomprehensible settings.

It's the perfect solution. Provided I shut the lounge curtains at the front of the house I will be able to run completely in the nuddy, without fear of discovery.

And so I embark on a new fun-filled regime of naked exercise— and before long I start to wonder why I ever did it with clothes on.

There's something tremendously *freeing* about running in the nude. There are no shorts or jogging bottoms to chafe you around the delicate parts, no t-shirts to get covered in sweat and hang off your frame like an uncomfortable second skin. The whole process takes on a new, liberated quality I find extremely agreeable.

Zoe's not so sure, though. 'You only do that when I'm out of the house. The last thing I need to look at while I'm watching "MasterChef" is your penis bouncing up and down in front of me.'

I don't know what she's complaining about. I take a great amount of joy in looking down and seeing the old fella swinging merrily back and forth as I pound my way to a slimmer figure.

All in all, naked running is where it's at, as far as I'm concerned.

With the end of the competition fast approaching, Zoe and I have really started to knuckle down on the exercise.

For instance, on Saturday morning she headed off down to the gym for a lengthy swim with Elise, so I decided that a good solid hour of naked running was in order.

At eleven o'clock I stick Metallica on the stereo at an absurd volume and bound onto the treadmill, ready to burn some calories. It's a lovely sunny day so I point the treadmill out into the garden to give myself a pleasant view.

With heavy guitar riffs and strident vocals as my accompaniment, I'm off . . . running like a man possessed.

After twenty solid minutes I've built up a healthy sweat. It's running down my back in rivulets.

My hair is stuck up at all angles thanks to the perspiration, while downstairs, my cock is slapping about to and fro on my thighs in perfect rhythm with the heavy metal sounds chugging from the stereo behind me. The heat of exercise and constant motion have made him agreeably large.

I'm feeling good.

I'm feeling strong.

I'm feeling fit.

. . . then I look round to my left and see Wilf the postman staring at me from next to the garden shed.

I wish I could say he's looking at my face.

'Oh fuck!' I screech and promptly lose my footing. I start to stumble and have to grab the treadmill's hand bar to stop myself from shooting off the back of the machine and doing myself a serious injury. I stab the control panel, bringing the treadmill to a halt. I also shut off the pounding heavy metal coming from the stereo.

Breathing heavily, and holding one hand over my genitals, I look up to see that Wilf has disappeared from sight.

Odd.

Maybe I imagined the whole thing.

Maybe all the running has starved my brain of oxygen and I just *thought* I saw our postman standing in the garden, looking at my naked, partially engorged penis. In reality, he might not have been there at all!

Ding dong goes our doorbell.

Oh, fuck it.

I'm going to have to answer it, aren't I? He knows I'm in the house, after all.

I run upstairs and grab my dressing gown from the back of the bedroom door. As I descend I try to think of something to say to the poor old bastard when I open the door.

Hi Wilf! How's your morning going? Say, did you think my cock was impressive or not? On a scale of one to ten, what would you give it?

No, I don't think so somehow.

In the end I elect to go with the good old-fashioned awkward British apology. 'Morning, Wilf. Sorry about that,' I say as he hands Zoe's latest purchase over to me.

'That's okay, Mr Milton. I should've rung the doorbell a few more times.'

Bless him. I'm the one who's just indecently exposed myself, and he's sorry for not being more proactive about announcing his presence.

A crushingly uncomfortable silence then comes between us, as is only natural when one man has accidentally seen the other man's cock.

'Yes, well, have a nice day,' I offer blandly.

'You too, Mister Milton. Enjoy the rest of your . . . er, exercising.'

He's saying *exercising*; you can tell he means *wanking*.

'Yes, thank you very much.'

Having little else to contribute, I shut the door slowly in Wilf's face and go back into the lounge. I then spend a good five minutes rocking back and forth on the couch.

Needless to say, I have been forced back into my clothes following that incident. My balls now chafe after half an hour of running and the sweat stains on my t-shirts are hell to shift in the wash, but at least I'm not risking a criminal prosecution every time I go for a jog.

I have also banned Zoe from ordering anything online until such time as Wilf the postman is dead.

Regardless of unwitting exposure to a divorcé in his early sixties, I have found the treadmill to be the best form of exercise for me. It's helped me to shift five stone of bulk already, and in the next few weeks until the final weigh-in I intend to drop another, no matter how many hours I have to spend pounding along on the never-ending path the machine creates.

I guess that's really the gist of what I've been trying to say here. You have to find what works for *you*. There are a thousand companies out there that will claim their product is the perfect weight loss tool for *everyone*, but it doesn't work like that. You can't just create a catch-all product that suits every Tom, Dick, and Harry. Especially Dick.

We all have different tolerances, strengths, and weaknesses, and it's only through trial and error that you arrive at the right method for you.

Hopefully you can learn a bit from my mistakes, though.

There is no shortcut when it comes to exercise. You have to commit yourself to it properly—and understand that you *do* have to put a lot of effort in. Don't be fooled by websites, infomercials, or magazine advertising claiming an easy way to a thinner body. They're lying to you, and taking a great deal of money from your pocket that could be used for something far more productive.

Keep it simple, that's my new motto.

Actually, my new motto is 'Don't exercise in the nude if you don't want an old man to see that you're not circumcised,' but that wouldn't look quite so good on a tea towel.

ZOE'S WEIGHT LOSS DIARY
Saturday, August 9th
10 stone, 3 pounds (4 stone, 4 pounds lost)

My relationship with Greg is by and large a non-competitive one. We're not the kind of couple that thrives on rivalry. We both appreciate that there are things the other can do better. I, for instance, am absolutely awful at ten-pin bowling. I am equally terrible at parallel parking, discerning between a good Merlot and a bad one, putting up shelves, and poaching an egg. Greg, on the other hand, cannot play table tennis to save his life, is dreadful at pub quizzes, wouldn't know how to knock up a stir-fry if you put a gun to his head, and defers to me in all matters involving holiday arrangements on the internet.

In our many years of marriage I have built up a mental list of all the things I handle myself, and all the things I let Greg take a lead on.

By and large, this has been a highly successful arrangement that has prevented no end of petty jealousies, night-time arguments, and slamming doors.

. . . and then I am disgusted to discover that there's every chance he's a better writer than I am.

Before the competition started back in March neither of us had ever kept a diary, and neither of us had ever spent so much time writing about our lives. At first the whole process was like pulling teeth, but as the weeks have gone by I think we've both discovered that it's actually rather a lot of fun. It's made us both better writers as well, given that practice generally does make perfect, if you give it half a chance.

Between us we must have written well over a hundred and fifty thousand words in the last six months, which is quite incredible when you think about it. When we're not exercising or dieting, we're hunched over the laptop *writing* about exercising and dieting.

The Stream FM audience will never get to read a majority of it, of course. Our lengthy essays are generally chopped down into far smaller bite-sized chunks; they probably have to cut half of what we write out just to make it palatable to a family audience, to be honest. We know how much effort we've put into the process, though, and how many hours have been spent slaving over a hot keyboard.

Unfortunately, Greg and I now find ourselves in a situation where we're both pretty good at something, which has inevitably led to comparison and the aforementioned competition.

I want to be better at writing than Greg—and I'm sure he feels the same way.

In fact I know he does, because I've caught him re-editing his diary entries on more than one occasion recently. Greg is not one of life's perfectionists, and tends to pull the stops out only when he's really invested in a project.

I'm just as bad. Where once I would dash off my entries, I now take my time to go back over them and make sure they're as witty as possible.

I also read every one of Greg's entries before he sends them off to Stream FM to be butchered. He does the same with mine. Quite often in the evenings the television is now switched off, and we sit in silence reading each other's work and sipping on small glasses of wine. It's a very pleasant way to pass the time.

I read Greg's most recent entry on Thursday night, about all the exercises he's tried. When I got to the bit about Wilf seeing his penis I nearly spat my wine out.

'You never told me that happened!' I said, making him look up from his iPad.

'Nope,' he replied with a broad grin. 'I wanted to save it so you could read about it.'

'Oh, so now you're keeping stuff from me to use as material, are you?'

'Don't be so silly. I just thought it would sound better on the page.'

I have to confess it does. Greg is not a good oral storyteller. I've never heard him get to the end of a joke without making at least one cock-up along the way.

When I'd finished reading the entry I felt just a little bit jealous of how my husband's writing has improved.

'This is really funny, baby,' I grudgingly admitted to him.

'Thanks. It was fun to write. Very cathartic, I'd say. I wasted a lot of money on all that crap, so it was good to have a moan about it.'

'I bet.'

'You should do the same about all those ridiculous diets you've tried. What was that one? The Chapstone diet?'

'Chatman.'

'Yeah. That was it. I reckon people would love to hear all about that.'

Bugger.

I hate it when he has a good idea I wish I'd thought of first.

So here we are, then.

I'm going to tell you all about my dieting experiences of the past few months—and I'd better do a good job of it or you'll think Greg is a better writer than I am. Which would be just *awful*.

Let's get one thing straight—most diets are idiotic. *Comprehensively* idiotic.

There really is only one diet that actually works, but I'll come on to that later.

For now, let's concentrate on all those weight loss programmes that sound like miracle cures in the short term, but are actually a complete waste of time in the long run.

I have to whole-heartedly agree with my husband on one thing: most diets—like the exercise equipment he talks about—trade on the idea that they can make you lose weight easily and quickly.

Why bother to put the effort in of eating a balanced, calorie-controlled diet, when you can just follow the simple three-step program you've just downloaded off the internet? The one that will see you three stone lighter and ten times more attractive within a fortnight?

Good gravy.

I've already talked about the cabbage soup diet, which made me fart like a cow and resulted in absolutely no long-term weight loss.

This is just one of a series of slimming regimes I like to call the 'object diets,' the ones that are based around the consumption of a single food type. They all trade on the idea that by restricting yourself to one food you will lose weight in no time at all. This is in direct contradiction of all evidence provided by nutritional science, but never mind: the internet says it works, so it must be true!

In all I tried three of these diets before common sense prevailed.

Yes, *three*. I am nothing if not a glutton for punishment.

After cabbage soup came the baby food diet.

Why not? Cheryl Cole and Jennifer Aniston swear by it, so why shouldn't I give it a go?

It's *disgusting*, that's why.

The idea is that you eat about a dozen small portions of baby food throughout the day, thus keeping your metabolism ticking over nicely. Yep, you heard that right . . . a *dozen*.

How can anyone—other than a millionaire celebrity—possibly hope to find time to fit in a dozen small meals of pureed awfulness a day?

Perhaps you're supposed to sneak a few mouthfuls of apple and pear while you're sitting in rush hour traffic waiting for the lights to turn green? Or maybe you should eat some pureed butternut squash when you nip to the loo? That way what goes in will look exactly the same as what's coming out.

I tried the baby food diet for a day. My taste buds still haven't forgiven me.

It doesn't sound too bad when you read about it. After all, what is pureed baby food other than a really thick smoothie, right?

Oh, *hell no*.

At least with a smoothie you can convince yourself that you're just having a nice refreshing drink as the mulched fruit slides down the back of your throat. With baby food there is actual effort involved. You have to pro-actively set your mouth to the task of shifting it down your gullet. If you're lucky this will involve just a bit of jaw movement and swallowing. If you're unlucky it will involve—oh, God in heaven—*chewing*.

If anyone has invented a worse thing to put in your mouth than boiled, pureed parsnip and swede, then I don't want to know about it.

Over the course of the day my gag reflex was put to the test more than that of a trainee sword swallower. If I wasn't nearly throwing up banana all over the breakfast bar at home, I was gamely trying to prevent the up-chuck of broccoli and spinach over my keyboard at work.

There's a reason why babies cry a lot when you're trying to feed them. It's because of the horrid concoction you're trying to force down their throats.

For me personally, being on the baby food diet just served to remind me of my inability to get pregnant. So not only was I force-feeding myself disgusting gunk, I was also being reminded of my failings as a woman. *Brilliant.* It's a wonder I lasted until six o'clock that evening.

With a muffled curse I spat the pureed potato and leek into the bin and put the whole sorry day behind me by making a lovely chicken and mayonnaise sandwich.

Don't worry, I used fat-free mayonnaise and the chicken was free range.

You'd think I'd have had my fill of the 'object diet' after that, but then I saw the grapefruit diet.

Grapefruit!

Grapefruits are healthy, right?

How can you bloody go wrong eating a diet that recommends you eat loads of fruit?

Even the science sounds plausible. There is apparently an enzyme in grapefruit that burns fat, meaning you can eat small quantities of tasty unhealthy food, providing you mainly consume grapefruit so that that enzyme gets in your body and takes care of all those nasty fat molecules.

You can eat *bacon*, for crying out loud. This is the best diet ever, people!

Or so it seemed on paper.

Have you ever noticed how good things always *seem* on paper?

Diets, package holidays, car insurance policies, fashion tips . . . the list goes on and on.

I often wonder how much better the world would be if none of us had developed the ability to write. Then we'd actually have to see something in action before agreeing to have any part of it. I can't help but feel this may have made our lives a whole lot easier. You can con me into wearing gold Roman sandals and a sequined poncho in the pages of a fashion magazine, but if I actually see some other poor bitch walking down the road towards me wearing such a hideous combination I'm going to avoid it like the bloody plague.

I started the grapefruit diet quite keenly. I dutifully ate my half grapefruit and drank my grapefruit juice with every meal. Okay, this did get a bit boring after a while, but I was happy to put up with it as it also meant I could eat bacon sandwiches.

This went on for five happy days until my stomach started to emit sharp, shooting pains at regular intervals.

Why?

Well, grapefruit may or may not have a fat-burning enzyme in it, but what I can guarantee you it does have is a high level of citric acid.

I may have been loving every minute of eating bacon and eggs for breakfast, but my stomach lining was not having such a good time with all that acid I was dumping into it.

After a week, the processes going on in my intestines probably resembled the day-to-day activities of a chemical factory—one that will be shut down very soon for its poisonous health and safety record.

I have never suffered so much bloody heartburn in my life. The amount of milk of magnesia I had to consume just to keep the fire at bay was frightening.

Greg may think that the Electromax 2000 is a great way of curing constipation, but it's nothing compared to swigging a bottle of milk of magnesia, I can assure you. It was a bloody good job we had two toilets in our house during that week.

Needless to say I stopped the grapefruit diet before the allotted ten days was up. I just didn't think my stomach lining could take it.

That was the last object diet I tried. I may be a glutton for punishment, but even I have my limits.

You simply can't hope to exist eating predominantly one food source for any length of time.

What's more, any weight loss you do achieve is likely to be wiped out the minute you return to a normal diet. Our bodies aren't meant to consume just one thing. We're omnivores and need a diet that's got a lot of variety in it. Forcing yourself to stick to one food because some stupid internet website tells you it will shift a stone in two weeks is nothing but an exercise in self-harm and disappointment.

To be honest, object diets are quite easy to dismiss if you just sit back and think about it for a while. They're just too simplistic to work.

The process of effective weight loss is a complex and time-consuming business. After all, the human body is quite difficult to wrestle under your control at the best of times, so effecting radical change is always going to be a tricky proposition.

By extension of that thought, any diet that sounds quite complicated and scientific should be far more likely to result in long-term weight loss . . . right?

Yeah.

Riiiiiight.

Let's start with the Chatman Diet.

Or should I say, let's start with the Professor Montague Chatman Approach to Effective Nutrition and Metabolic Health.

Sounds impressive, doesn't it?

Montague Chatman sounds like the kind of serious, bearded intellectual who has spent decades in a laboratory somewhere, coming up with new and interesting ways to help you lose enough weight to fit into that black party dress you saw in H&M last week.

What's more, his Approach to Effective Nutrition and Metabolic Health is contained within three hundred pages of hardback book—full of diagrams, pie charts, complicated formulas, and big long words like 'glucagon,' 'epinephrine,' and 'oxidization.'

The book has been a bestseller in thirty countries, further adding weight to its credence as a weight loss method.

. . . So thinks Zoe Milton anyway, as she purchases a copy of the book from WH Smith with the voucher her mum sent on her birthday.

What a magnificent-looking book it is, too!

It's got a *bright* red cover, with *bright* white and green writing. The excitement of all that potential weight loss fairly leaps out at you when you're just holding the damn thing. *'The multi-million bestseller!'* it informs you in a splash across the top of the book's jacket. *'The scientifically proven way to a slimmer waistline!'* another equally bold strapline screams at you from the bottom.

When you crack the book open you find that the actual content is written in a large, easy-to-read font . . . so they've even taken steps to prevent you suffering eye strain. This must be the reason for such big letters. It can't possibly be because they're having to stretch a small amount of spurious and badly researched information across enough pages to fill a whole book. *Oh no.*

I sit down in the living room early one dull Sunday afternoon with a glass of fruit juice (mango, not grapefruit) and begin to read this marvellous book.

Ten minutes later I'm more confused than a Tory politician in Lidl.

The tactic of Montague and his cronies is to baffle you with enough long words and pseudo-science that you just end up believing everything they say, so as not to come across as a thickie.

What I did manage to glean from the first fifty pages or so was that the Chatman diet is about controlling the amount of carbohydrates, fats, and acids that go into your body, which will in turn affect your metabolic rate—speeding it up to such an extent that cream cakes don't stand a chance against the cleansing fire burning from within every molecule of your body.

By following Chatman's method you avoid what he likes to call 'metabolic anti-stasis.' This sounds extremely nasty.

The book then goes on to discuss the best way to accomplish this. Again, a lot of long words are thrown around with gay abandon.

I thought a jam doughnut was just a jam doughnut, but it turns out that it is in fact a 'negative metabolic inducer' which can lead to a 'higher density of lifoproteinates.'

Now I don't know about you, but having a higher density of lifoproteinates sounds like a bad thing to me. I don't have a fucking clue what a lifoproteinate is, but I'm damn sure I want to keep my density of them low.

It's frankly amazing how many foods are bad for your metabolic rate according to Professor Chatman. Human evolution would seem to dictate that there are at least *some* food substances out there that are good for you—otherwise the human race would have died out millennia ago as soon as it took a bite out of the first banana it came across. But old Montague seems to completely disagree. According to him, the human body is not meant to eat all the food that's just lying around. That way lies madness—and an unhealthy amount of back fat.

Carbohydrates might as well be the work of the devil as far as he is concerned, and the way he rips into foods heavy with lactose gives me the impression that at some point in his youth he must have been molested by a milkman.

Monty (after two hundred pages I feel like we're on first-name terms) then starts to talk at length about amino acids. He has decided, in his infinite wisdom, that my metabolic rate is dependent on the level of amino acids I use. Why? Because of the enantiomers and stereoisomers, silly!

You know what enantiomers and stereoisomers are, don't you?

They're just by-products of the isoelectric process!

Still a bit confused?

You're not the only one.

I have the distinct feeling that any passing biochemists would look at Monty's theories and claw their own eyes out with the stupidity of the whole thing—but I'm no expert, am I?

Who am I to judge the veracity of Monty's claims? After all, his book has sold millions of copies, and there can't be *that* many people who would just blindly follow a load of hack scientific blather in their desperation to lose a few pounds, can there?

By page two hundred and fifty I have entered a state of near catalepsy. I've been bombarded with so much information I'm finding it hard to uncross my eyes. According to Monty, I am a methanogenic and carbonic life form low in selenocysteine and hydroxyproline.

But then . . . salvation!

Friendly, helpful Professor Montague Chatman is now ready to explain all of this nonsense in simple, easy-to-understand sentences that feature words of no more than three syllables.

It turns out that Chatman and his colleagues have done all the painstaking research so we don't have to! We don't need to know which foods are negative inducers or isoelectric inhibitors! Woo hoo! Just when I thought I'd have to take the entire biology section of the library with me every time I go to bloody Tesco, the good Professor has come along to save me all that time and inconvenience.

You see, his crack team of nutritionists have devised and created a whole smorgasbord of healthy foods and drinks, designed to speed up your metabolic rate and kick those evil lifoproteinates to the kerb.

The last thirty pages of the Chatman diet book is basically one long advertisement for their own brand of health shakes, health bars, health snacks, and health meals.

Now, I'm not normally the kind of person who pays that much attention to advertising if I can help it, but I have spent the past four hours reading about how the food I eat is effectively killing me in a slow, painful and lifoproteinate-rich way. Professor Monty has more or less convinced me that if I don't immediately start eating and drinking his products I will become so full of poisonous amino acids that my weight will balloon to elephantine proportions and I will die of metabolic anti-stasis within the month.

Helpfully, the book contains links to the Chatman website, where I can purchase all the healthy Chatman-approved food I need to dodge this grim fate.

The website recommends I buy the full weekly complement of products, which includes a snack for every morning, a shake for every lunch, and a meal for every dinner.

All of this costs . . .

. . . wait for it . . .

Seventy-five pounds!

Yes, for just seventy-five quid a week I can stave off the spectre of chubby thighs *and* metabolic cell death.

Having not been brought up in a small room with no access to the outside world, I instead order a box of ten lunchtime health shakes. This is still twenty-five quid's worth, mind you, so I obviously haven't seen enough of the outside world, regardless of where I was brought up.

Monty's book begrudgingly admits you can just supplement two meals a day with the health shake, provided you eat a meal of less than five hundred calories in the evening. Obviously someone down in marketing realised that not everyone can afford the complete package, so there must be an alternative that's slightly easier on the pockets of the poor. Better to fleece them of some money than none at all.

A couple of days later the shakes arrive and I embark on the carefully laid out programme that the book provides in a handy fold-out section.

So now I'm a fully grown adult drinking two thick shakes a day. The last time I consumed this kind of drink in such quantities I was eight years old and didn't give a shit about my weight.

Apparently, the shakes have all the necessary vitamins, minerals, and trace elements I need to keep me going through the day. This is all very well, but they don't appear to contain much actual taste. They are also a rather unpleasant shade of grey. I ordered the banana-flavoured ones as I love a nice banana, but I can only assume that the nearest this gloopy mess ever got to a real banana was having one waved over it for a couple of seconds before they put the lid on.

Keeping your lifoproteinate levels down may well be important to your metabolic rate, but it sure as hell doesn't do much for your taste buds.

Nevertheless, I stuck at the diet for a whole month. This is officially the longest I have managed to stick with one of these programs in the entire time I've been part of the Fat Chance competition.

Not because it was any *good*, of course—don't be so silly. The only reason I stuck with it is because Professor Montague Chatman had scared the crap out of me with all his talk of metabolics, lifo-bloody-proteinates, and isoelectric processes. He'd done enough to convince me that if I didn't stick to his program, I'd just keep getting fatter and fatter until my brain was consumed by my own body lard.

It has to be said that over the course of the month I did indeed lose weight from drinking just the shakes and eating a low-calorie meal for tea. After thirty days I actually began to believe that the diet was worth it—that Chatman's claims were valid. Maybe there was something to all this metabolic anti-stasis, enantiomer whodoyouwhatsit business after all.

Then Greg saw the credit card bill and we had a lively discussion about it.

'A hundred fucking quid on milkshakes!'

'They don't have milk in them.'

'I don't care if they're flavoured with pure gold and give you superpowers. It's a hundred fucking quid!'

'You wasted enough cash on all those stupid exercise machines!'

'I know! That's why I'm sure you're wasting your money on this Chatman shit.'

'No, I'm not!'

'Really? Go on Google and look him up,' Greg challenged me.

So I bloody well did!

Shit.

It didn't take me long to scroll down past the promotional Chatman website entries and get to the independent opinion sites.

It wasn't pleasant.

The science of the Professor Montague Chatman Approach to Effective Nutrition and Metabolic Health was as big a load of steaming horseshit as I'd first feared. I discovered reams of proper scientific study that showed how Chatman's methodologies were made up out of nothing but fresh air.

What's more, Professor Montague Chatman wasn't even a bloody Professor. Monty turned out to be a disgraced doctor from Middlesex who'd been struck off the register thirty years ago for giving out blank prescriptions to his old Eton buddies in exchange for cold, hard cash.

His name wasn't even Montague.

I'd spent over a hundred pounds of my hard-earned money on a weight loss program devised by Barry Chatman.

Barry. Is there a less dependable-sounding first name in the English language?

Oh, and Barry had popped his clogs in 1997 anyway. All that money had in fact gone to the company that now runs and owns the Chatman diet brand. It's called ACP Petrochemicals. They also own three sugar refining companies, a fast-food brand, and a mail order business. The same mail order business I'd received my shakes from during the previous month.

I would have felt crestfallen if I hadn't felt so bloody stupid.

'But the diet worked!' I pleaded with Greg once I'd got him to stop laughing.

'Did it?'

'Yes!'

The patronising tone he effected made my teeth itch. 'Now Zoe, don't you think you would have lost all that weight anyway? Even if you'd been drinking one-pound Asda smoothies? Or, you know, water?'

I wanted to argue. I really, really did. But the bastard was absolutely right.

I'd been well and truly suckered. In my desire to lose weight—and to make it seem like I hadn't been completely baffled by all those scientific terms—I'd become a gullible idiot.

Still, I'm not alone.

The diet industry is worth a purported *thirty billion quid* worldwide, I'm led to believe. Barry and his fellow shysters are slicing themselves a pretty big chunk of that cake.

I stopped the Chatman diet there and then. My body—which had dropped into fat storing, self-preservation mode thanks to Barry Chatman's bullshit—made sure I paid for my gullibility by piling six pounds back on in the following two weeks. It didn't matter how little I ate, or how much exercise I did, I simply could not prevent my metabolism snapping back like a rubber band after having been so artificially stretched for a month.

Needless to say I was despondent.

That was when I booked an appointment with a nutritionist on the NHS. A proper, bona fide nutritionist, with certificates from recognisable medical institutions. Her name was Claire. Her skin looked very healthy.

'Can you tell me which one of these diet programmes I should go on, Claire? I've tried so many now and none are working for me,' I pleaded from across her neat desk.

'You don't need to go on a diet programme, Zoe,' she replied. 'You just need to eat a balanced variety of foods, watch your calorie intake, and exercise regularly.'

This didn't make any sense, so I asked her to repeat it.

She did so.

It still didn't make any sense. It sounded *far* too simple. 'Just run that by me one more time?' I said doubtfully.

Claire the nutritionist sighed. 'I get this a lot. For some reason people think it's complicated when it really isn't.'

She went on to explain a few cold, hard facts to me.

Weight loss is about burning more calories than you take in. Our bodies are essentially engines. If you put in less fuel than you burn off, then your body turns to its fat reserves to compensate. That's how you lose weight.

That is the *only* way human beings lose weight.

From the *dawn of time* that has been the only way human beings have *ever* lost weight. Everything else is just gravy—if you'll pardon the rather on-the-nose expression.

Like Greg and his exercises, it just comes down to simple human biology, and understanding it properly.

Billions of pounds are wasted every year because people—including me up until this revelatory conversation—just don't realise this plain and simple truth. If you eat a balanced diet and exercise off more calories than you consume you *will* lose weight. It's a biological certainty.

Unfortunately it isn't a *quick* biological certainty. To burn off fat and keep it off permanently requires time, effort, and patience—three things the Western world doesn't have much of.

Hence that thirty billion quid.

All the weight loss programmes, books, websites, videos, packaged meals, snacks, health shakes, and pills in the world don't really make a blind bit of difference, if you don't understand and appreciate the effort it actually takes to get thin. Once you do, everything becomes a lot clearer, and a lot easier on your purse.

I walked out of Claire's office with a renewed sense of purpose.

She'd given me a pamphlet detailing all the do's and don'ts of proper dieting and I intended to stick to it religiously. I still felt a bit strange about following a diet that hadn't cost me a single penny, but tried my level best to ignore the feeling.

Since that day I have seen a more gradual—but *permanent*—loss of weight over the last three months. There has been no yo-yo effect whatsoever.

Neither have I suffered from bad breath, runny bowels, acid reflux, or extreme lethargy. In fact I've never felt better in my life.

I am highly fucking annoyed by the entire thing.

GREG'S WEIGHT LOSS DIARY

Sunday, August 31st

13 stone, 10 pounds (6 stone, 6 pounds lost)

I looked at myself in the mirror this morning.

Can you remember the last time you looked at yourself in the mirror?

I don't mean the quick glance in the morning to check that none of your breakfast is still between your teeth, or the thirty seconds you spend in the changing room at Primark deciding whether stone wash jeans are still a good idea in the twenty-first century.

I mean the act of just standing in front of your own mirror (preferably full length) and taking a long, hard look at yourself.

It's a surreal experience. Especially when it's the first time you've done it for about ten years.

I've never been one for much in the way of narcissism, even when I was young and thin and should have cared about that kind of thing. I could go days without looking in a mirror if my hair was short enough and I wasn't attending a job interview.

As I grew older and my waistline grew larger, the *last* thing I wanted to do was stand and see my flabby, naked body staring back at me. It wasn't a conscious decision, of course. I don't think anyone intentionally goes out of their way to avoid looking in a mirror because they're fat. It's just something that naturally happens when your sense of physical self-worth ebbs away as the pounds pile on.

Today, however, is a special day. And on special days you can find yourself doing things you never thought possible.

I woke up at six thirty in the morning feeling refreshed and well rested. I have *never* woken up at six thirty before feeling refreshed and well rested. If in the past I have been forced to awaken at such a god awful time it has been with sleep dust jamming my eyes together, a groan escaping my lips and a long, sonorous fart escaping my backside.

Not only am I refreshed and well rested this morning, I am also excited . . . and not a little nervous.

The reason is simple: today is the day of the grand final weigh-in. Fat Chance ends today, and there is every chance Zoe and I will be fifty thousand pounds better off this evening.

With this cheery prospect running through my head I leave Zoe dozing in bed and pad softly through into the bathroom for my customary early morning piss.

Look at the way I described that, would you?

I *padded softly* through to the bathroom.

I did not stumble, plod, or shamble through to the bathroom: I padded softly.

Six months ago I would have been incapable of padding softly anywhere, unless I was on a planet with a far lower gravitational pull than ours.

In the bathroom I have the decided pleasure of taking a piss butt naked. The opportunities to take an early morning whizz naked in Great Britain are few and far between. It's normally never warm enough. But we're experiencing a mini heat wave at the moment in these parts, which gives me the chance to walk around with *my* parts swinging free. I'm not going anywhere near the conservatory, though.

I finish the piss and turn to leave the bathroom. Then I stop in my tracks as I notice something fixed to the back of the bathroom door that I've not thought about in a long time.

No, not the ratty dressing gown I haven't worn in months, or the threadbare towel Zoe uses when she's dyed her hair. I'm referring to the thing hidden behind them both.

I unhook both dressing gown and towel and give the mirror a wipe. It's very dusty, and I have to stifle a sneeze so I don't wake Zoe up.

Having cleaned the reflective surface to a satisfactory degree, I drop the gown and towel and stand straight.

The man looking back at me is a complete stranger.

The kind of guy I'd probably be quite jealous of if I saw him in the changing rooms at the gym.

This man is lean and fit. He stands confidently, his shoulders squared and his head cocked to one side, a rather perplexed expression his face. Sure, there's a small spare tyre around his middle, but nothing too offensive for a man rapidly approaching his forties.

This is a bloke who looks like he can jog for miles without suffering much damage. There's at least thirty press-ups in those shoulders before they give out, and maybe even twenty sit-ups in those abdominals.

All in all, he seems pretty well put together. Someone with a lifestyle to be envied.

. . . and I have no idea who he is.

A sudden wave of emotion washes over me. Tears start to form at the corners of my eyes and I find myself having to take a deep breath.

I think back to an early spring barbecue, a Mister Benn suit, and a broken chair—and have to fight back a choked sob.

They hit me all at once. The feelings of inadequacy, the lack of self-worth, the sure and secure knowledge that for a decade I felt and acted like a fat, lazy failure. All those neuroses and doubts that you bury deep, deep down where you think you can safely ignore them.

But they are always there, you know. Always ready, willing, and able to climb from the recesses of your soul if you give them a decent leg up. All it can take is the decision to do something you haven't done in years—like taking a long, hard look at yourself in the mirror.

It takes me a few seconds to calm down, to remember that I have done so much to change the way I look and feel since March and that bloody barbecue.

When I look back into the mirror I do so not as the fat, inadequate man I once was, but as the fit, healthy, confident man I am *now*.

A fierce sensation of pride overwhelms me. It's a strange and alien emotion I don't quite know how to handle.

I have done this.

I have lost six stone, and in doing so changed the person I am forever.

Every step on the treadmill, every curl of the dumbbell, every pound spent on a useless piece of exercise equipment. It's all represented in the new and improved Greg Milton looking back at me with a smile on his face.

Hell, now I've lost all that fat around my thighs and waist even my penis looks bigger.

This man in the mirror is no stranger. He is *me*, and I am damn proud of that fact!

'Are you taking a shit in there, Greg? Only I really need to pee,' Zoe says from beyond the mirror's reflection.

I throw the door open and give my wife a massive hug. I am delighted to discover she is as naked as I am thanks to the early morning heat.

'Oh, get off, you lunatic,' she says, pushing me away. 'I can smell your B.O. from a mile away.'

'Come and look in the mirror with me, baby,' I say to her.

'What?'

'Look in the mirror with me.'

'I need a pee, Greg. Stop being weird and let me by.'

I take her hand. 'In a second. Just humour me.'

I drag my reluctant spouse into the bathroom, close the door, and position us both in front of the mirror.

Zoe rubs her eyes. 'What the hell are you doing?'

I stand behind her and drape my arms around her neck.

For the briefest of moments I flash back to the day I first met Zoe, and the pose we stood in for Lionel the Pervert's camera. 'Just look at us,' I say in a soft voice.

Zoe sighs and forces her eyes to focus on her own reflection in the mirror. In them I see the exact same emotional process I've just gone through. At first Zoe looks confused, as if she's never seen the gorgeous woman staring back at her before. Then comes the shame, the shame of knowing that this woman was underneath all that fat, screaming to get out for so many years. And finally, there is the mixture of pride and pleasure at a job well done, and a human being rediscovered.

'We did . . . we did it, didn't we?' she says to me, fighting back the tears.

I kiss her softly on the neck. 'Yeah, we did, baby. I'm so proud of you.'

Zoe kisses me with a fierceness and passion that takes my breath away. The tears stream from her eyes. 'Not half as proud as I am of you, my gorgeous man.'

I kiss her again, moving my hands down her back and squeezing her bottom. She breaks away, grabbing my rapidly hardening penis as she does. 'I still need the loo, Greg. Go back into the bedroom and make sure you keep this where I can see it.'

I've never been a big fan of morning sex before, but I now recommend it without reservation.

The final weigh-in is due to start at Fitness4All at 2 p.m., giving Zoe and me plenty of time to prepare. We eat unsweetened porridge for breakfast like the good little weight watchers we are and then take ourselves off for a nice walk around Langtree Lakes in the sun. I had planned on an hour of vigorous jogging on the treadmill, but Zoe convinced me otherwise.

'We've done everything we can, Greg. Let's just have some fun this morning, okay?'

This turns out to be a wise decision. The fluttery nervous sensation in my stomach goes away a few minutes into our walk. It's a little hard to be on edge when you're walking through the rich English countryside on a warm late summer's day.

Even though this morning wasn't supposed to be about the exercise, we still covered a good five miles by the time we return home for a light lunch at midday. That's the thing about regular exercise—the more you do it, the easier it is to find yourself falling into it even when you haven't planned to.

By the time we're driving to the gym, my butterflies have returned. Zoe is in much the same state. The next couple of hours are the culmination of six months of hard work. Will all the effort have paid off? Will we have lost enough combined weight to win the competition?

I bloody hope so, as I can hear the suspension knocking on my Focus as we turn into the car park, so will no doubt need some of that fifty grand when the MOT rolls around in a month.

Zoe gasps as we catch sight of the gym entrance. There's an enormous crowd outside. Ten times the size of the one we saw at the start of the fun run in June. The gym security is having to keep them from streaming into the lobby and trampling the art deco sofas.

There are Stream FM banners and posters everywhere, the largest of which is strung across the top of the entrance screaming that the finale of Fat Chance is here today at two o'clock. Not that anyone needs reminding—the station's been playing near constant adverts about it for the past week.

It dawns on me that we'll have to walk through the crowd to get into the gym.

'I don't think I can do this,' Zoe says as she slides down the seat to hide herself.

'We haven't got any choice love,' I tell her as I park the car and stare out of the window at the gathered masses.

'No, no. I can't.' She points a finger. 'Look. There's Angelica and Dominica trying to get in. They can barely get past them all!'

'They don't appear to have lost that much more weight,' I notice, a slight note of triumph in my voice.

'They gave up weeks ago,' Zoe reminds me. 'This thing is between us and the FrankieBen.'

It's a lot more fun to pit yourself mentally against the competition if you've given them a cool-sounding nickname.

I open the car door and grab our kit bags. 'Come on. Let's get this over with.'

Zoe slides down even further in her seat. 'No. No, I can't do it.' She folds her arms across her chest. 'I'm staying here.'

'Don't be so silly. It won't be that bad. They're just a group of fans.' I look over and study the crowd. 'Perfectly harmless.'

'You think so?'

'Absolutely. They look like a fun bunch of people to me, baby. One of them is even wearing a top hat.'

I manage to grab Zoe before she can run out of the car park. I'm sure the bite marks on my arm will fade in the coming weeks.

We approach the throng together on unsteady feet. 'Just keep your head down and muscle your way through,' I tell Zoe, putting my arms out to protect her. This must be what being a bodyguard to the stars is like.

I have a hairy moment when the woman in the top hat tries to thrust her breasts into my face and poke me in the eye with a marker pen, but other than that we manage to make it through into the gym lobby more or less unscathed.

'They still haven't taken that bloody stand down,' Zoe says with disgust, looking at the cardboard display featuring Photoshopped versions of us both that turn my stomach.

'Just ignore it. That isn't us any more.'

'When this thing is over I'm burning that fucker,' Zoe hisses.

'Hi guys!' It's Hayley, the Fitness4All meet and greeter, and all-round young man's wank fantasy. She's looking so enthusiastic it makes my soul ache. 'Glad to see you both! It's an exciting day!'

'Yes, I suppose it is.'

'You're the last to get here, guys.' Hayley does very well to keep any signs of irritation out of her voice. 'Go on through to the changing rooms. We'll let the crowd in once you're out of sight.'

'Thanks,' I tell her.

Zoe is still staring at fat cardboard Zoe with a glowing hatred you could toast marshmallows on. I grab her hand to pull her away and walk us both in the direction of the changing rooms. 'Come on, woman. Let's get these stupid tomato costumes on for the last time.'

She reluctantly follows, flashing Hayley a brief smile before we both hurry up the stairs and disappear around the corner.

We split up, making our way through the building, and I eventually find myself in the calm, relaxing environs of the men's changing room.

In here with me is Shane—who must have lost a good six stone, but still sadly looks pretty fat—and Benny, who looks like he's about to enter three marathons at once.

My heart sinks. He's obviously lost more weight than I have. Beating him and Frankie is going to be nigh on impossible.

We just have to hope that Zoe's lost more weight than the other half of the FrankieBen team.

'Hello, Greg,' Shane beams at me from where he's getting changed. The man-boobs he's sported all his life are definitely smaller, but Shane is still a man who looks like he's no stranger to a cream cake. I'm startled to realise that he looks about as big as I was when this competition started.

'Good morning, Greg,' Benny also says, as he drops into a warm-up lunge. This is clearly some kind of psychological warfare, but I'm not having any of it.

'Morning, Benny,' I say cheerfully. 'You want to watch you don't strain anything before the big show.' This is greeted with an arch of the eyebrow and a dismissive grunt.

I reluctantly drag out my hideous red Fitness4All kit and put it on. Thanks to all the weight loss, this is in fact the *fourth* kit I've been through in the past six months, and even this one is looking a little baggy these days.

'I will be very glad to never wear this idiotic outfit again,' I say to Shane and Benny.

'Agreed,' Benny says, managing a smile.

'Mum says I look like the number ten bus,' Shane adds, which indicates his mother has a sense of humour, if not a lot of compassion.

I heave a sigh and pluck at the front of my t-shirt in disgust. 'Well, let's go entertain the masses one more time, shall we?' I say to my fellow contestants.

And with that, Greg, Shane, and Benny—the three tomato-red gladiators—step through the changing room doors and out onto the gym floor.

Not that you can see much of the floor, thanks to the number of people crammed into the hall.

We're used to fairly large crowds at these events, but this one is at least twice the size and three times as vocal as any that has come before.

After all, this is the finale of the most popular local radio competition this area has ever seen. Elise even told Zoe last night on the phone that the *Daily Mail* and Sky News might be in attendance, provided no members of the royal family had been seen anywhere with their clothes off in the interim few hours.

It's no wonder they had to change the venue from the Stream FM offices to Adam Edgemont's gym. If they'd tried to cram this many people into that building, there would have been some serious health and safety issues. I wouldn't have been pleased to have lost all this weight, only to get crushed to death by a horde of marauding Stream FM listeners.

The set-up for the weigh-in has been brought over from Stream FM lock, stock, and barrel. There sits the dreaded metal scales, with the flashy LCD scoreboard hung above them. Off to the left is the desk from where the live radio broadcast will be made. I can pick out at least four video cameras that will broadcast the event on Stream FM's website.

Everything is set to give the baying crowd exactly what it wants to see—a bunch of people who are now less fat than they used to be, embarrassed for their delight and entertainment.

Just remember the fifty grand, Gregory, I say to myself, and follow Shane and Benny over to the row of chairs at the back of the hall.

I see Zoe coming towards me with Angela and Dominica. All three look like deer caught in the headlights. When they reach us and sit down, the full complement of performing monkeys is assembled.

The organ grinders arrive a few seconds later.

Will is dressed in a dapper grey suit, but no-one's really looking at him, as Elise appears to have turned into a movie star. Her hair's up, her make-up is thick, her black dress clings like a second skin, and her heels are pointy and high. It's completely inappropriate dress for wearing around a fitness centre, but who cares? She looks like a million dollars.

My threesome fantasy rears its ugly head again as I watch her wave to the crowd and make her way to the broadcast desk.

The sharp dig in the ribs from my left brings me out of my reverie.

'It's never happening, Gregory,' Zoe says in a flat voice. 'Never in a million years.'

Life is full of little disappointments.

The production assistant standing by the desk gives Will and Elise the ten second countdown to air. Elise adjusts her headphones and lifts the microphone to her mouth.

I take a deep breath.

Six months of effort are—hopefully—about to pay off.

'Good afternoon, everyone!' Elise cries into her microphone. The crowd goes fucking mental.

'Yeah, hi guys and welcome to the grand finale of Fat Chance!' Will bellows into his own microphone and waves his arm around to whip the crowd into an even bigger frenzy.

Love them or loathe them, Will and Elise know what they're doing in front of an audience. All that road show experience is obviously paying off.

'For a whole six months our couples have been losing a huge amount of weight,' Elise carries on. 'We've heard every week about how their diets are going. We've also read their weight loss diaries online, and got to know each and every one of them. I don't know about you, but I feel like every one of them is a friend of mine now.'

More cheers from the crowd. They obviously agree. I hear Zoe groan from beside me. 'I'm the only one who has to listen to her complaining about her love life, though,' she says.

'That's right, Elise,' Will takes over. 'We've watched these guys exercise and diet their way to a better life. We've seen them tackle two extreme challenges, and have marvelled at the way they've supported one another through thick and thin.'

Really? Supported through thick and thin? I barely know any of these buggers beyond being on first name terms, even after all this time.

'And now, after six months, thousands of miles run, hundreds of sit-ups, and countless low-calorie meals—' Elise is now strutting up and down in front of the crowd, her hand held high, '—we've come to the final weigh-in. One couple among our six will walk away today as Fat Chance champions, and will be fifty thousand pounds richer!'

Hoot. Holler. Cheer. Roar. Clap. Etc.

Will takes over again, crossing right in front of Elise's path as he does so. There's some not-so-subtle one-upmanship going on here. 'This has been Stream FM's most successful competition ever! And we couldn't have done any of it without you!' he says.

Technically, you couldn't have done any of it without us fat bastards over here, mate, but I'll let you off as you're obviously over-excited.

'Yes!' Elise agrees enthusiastically. 'And of course we also couldn't have done any of it without the help, support, and sponsorship of Adam Edgemont and his company, Fitness4All!'

. . . and his cock, Elise. Don't forget his cock.

Edgemont joins the two DJs to what I'm happy to hear is rather muted applause.

'So how about we stop talking and get on with the show?' Elise shouts to the crowd. The applause is a hell of a lot louder this time.

Good. Time to get this over with.

Sadly, I'll have to wait a while longer, as we now have to sit through an interminable twenty minutes of recap. This consists of a sizzle reel cut together from interviews, weigh-ins, and challenges across the six months of the competition—all with a load of asinine pop tunes of the past decade running behind it. There's some Boyzone in there, along with Lady Gaga, Chipmunk, that skinny woman whose name I can never remember, and Thirty Seconds to Mars. It's all uplifting, tub-thumping rubbish, but it's also perfect for a cheesy sum-up of all that we've been through.

I confidently expect the package to end with Queen's 'We Are the Champions.'

'I hate the sound of my own voice,' Zoe points out as we relive her talking to Elise about the cabbage soup diet. 'Especially when I'm talking about having the farts.'

I have to say I'm not that much happier about listening to myself moan about blisters, but I grit my teeth and bear it.

Eventually, the recap climaxes in an orgy of bombastic music and I breathe a sigh of relief as I hear Freddie Mercury start singing.

Time to get on with the weigh-in and see if we're mildly rich or not.

But first there are adverts.

Many, many, *many* adverts.

Stream FM is wringing every last brass farthing out of this little venture. I can't say I blame them much. All this must have cost them a fortune.

Finally though . . .

'Okay guys, it's time to start the weigh-in!' Elise shrieks, threatening to shatter everyone's eardrums.

The crowd goes mental as Will introduces couple number one—Valerie and George.

My heart rate increases.

There's every chance these two old codgers could pip us at the post. Both of them look like they've dropped a huge amount of weight.

To be honest, I don't really think they look better for it. Rosy-cheeked chubbiness suited them and this new trimmer look has eradicated much of their combined homely charm.

Val's up first on the scales. The numbers tumble into place, and we see she's lost an impressive three and a half stone. George has done much the same with the three stone and nine pounds he's managed to shift. The couple's weight loss percentage therefore comes in at sixteen percent.

I think Zoe and I are alright here, though. I'm sure our combined percentage is better.

Next up is Angela and Dominica. Their combined loss is a rather anaemic four stone one pound, or eleven percent of their total body mass. They look quite happy about it, though, as they hug and kiss each other in a way any nearby members of the Christian church probably wouldn't approve of.

Lea and Pete are the surprise package of the day so far. She's shifted four stone six pounds and he's dropped five stone five pounds. My heart starts to race again as we see that their efforts have given them a weight loss percentage of twenty-three.

'I think they've had us,' I say to Zoe.

'It's not over yet,' she tells me and squeezes my hand.

Shane and Theresa take the stage next. Shane's lost five stone eight pounds, but Theresa's not been so lucky with just two stone eleven pounds. This puts them in fourth place with nine percent total loss.

And here come the big guns. The FrankieBen.

Frankie is up first, to the roar of the crowd. They know that she and her husband are the favourites to win here today.

It doesn't surprise me in the slightest when Frankie registers five stone one pound of weight loss.

Zoe groans.

'Don't worry,' I tell her. 'She was bigger than you to start with. It's all about the percentages, remember.'

I sound quite convincing, but even I have to put my head in my hands when a triumphant Benny registers six stone five pounds. That's as much as me, if not more. He's easily lost the most weight of anyone so far.

This gives the Jamaican couple a combined percentage of thirty-two percent, and a very healthy lead.

I hold Zoe's hand, expecting to hear her name called next, but am surprised when Elise calls out mine. She's obviously decided that her friend is going to be the last one to take the stage today. The nails digging deep into the back of my hand tell me that Zoe is less than happy about this turn of events.

I stand on slightly watery legs and make my way over to the scales. From the crowd I can hear my name being chanted, over and over. I look for the source of the chant and see my friend Ali jumping up and down on the spot right in front of me. He's got his iPhone out and proceeds to take about eighty pictures of my stunned expression as he continues to scream my name at the top of his voice.

I stand up on the scales and steady myself. I know roughly how much weight I've lost, but the scales at home are old and deeply inaccurate. This is when I find out if Benny's beaten me or not.

The scales do their thing and I can hear a collective intake of breath from everyone in the room.

The electronic scoreboard digits settle down and come to a halt. It shows my weight as thirteen stone ten pounds, and my weight loss of six stone six pounds.

I've beaten Benny by a pound. I've lost the most weight out of everyone in the competition.

The crowd erupts. The noise is deafening. Ali has gone stark raving mad and has pulled off his t shirt to wave it around his head.

I thrust a fist into the air and cheer.

Waves of relief, triumph, and vindication wash through me.

Suddenly Zoe is by my side, tears in her eyes.

I lean over and give her the biggest hug I possibly can. I squeeze her so tight I can feel her heart pounding away at the same speed as mine.

This is truly a glorious moment. One I will not forget as long as I live.

Eventually, Elise comes over and breaks us up. 'Okay, guys. Sorry to split you up, but this thing isn't over yet. Zoe needs to be weighed.'

I look into my wife's eyes, hug her tightly one more time, and step off the scales.

ZOE'S WEIGHT LOSS DIARY
Monday, September 15th
9 stone, 8 pounds (4 stone, 13 pounds lost)

As Greg throws his arms into the air with triumph I feel a deep and overwhelming sense of pride.

Whatever happens to me, my husband will walk away from here today knowing that he lost the most weight, beating everyone else. I couldn't be happier for him.

With my vision blurring, I hurry to his side to share in his moment of glory.

The pure, happy smile he greets me with sends a huge rush of emotion through me and I can't help but cry. I'm just so proud of him.

Greg wraps me in his arms and for a split second the crowd, the competition and the fifty thousand pounds are completely forgotten. This is a moment for us, and nobody else.

Sadly, the moment doesn't last that long as Elise comes between us, telling me it's my turn to get on the scales.

I kiss Greg one more time and step up onto the cool metal platform. My heart is hammering so hard I feel it may burst out of my chest.

Here we go, then.

Last time pays for all.

I cross my fingers and stare out at the maddening crowd. I seek out Mum and Dad, finding them in the front row, off to the left.

Their excited smiles actually calm my nerves a bit. It's funny how just the sight of your loved ones can centre you.

The numbers on the scoreboard above me tumble. I can see most of the people in the crowd leaning forward as the numbers start to come to a rest.

And there suddenly, for all the world to see, is the net result of all the diets, all the exercise, and all the effort I've put in over the last six months.

Zoe Milton's weight is nine stone and eight pounds. That's four stone and thirteen pounds of fat shifted from my body in the most exhausting—and rewarding—half a year I've ever experienced.

What an amazing thing!

But.

Frankie has lost more weight, and we were of a similar size when we started this thing.

I crane my neck up as the scoreboard calculates the combined weight loss percentage that Greg and I have achieved.

There is now nobody in the crowd who isn't leaning forward expectantly. Mum and Dad are holding hands and staring up at the scoreboard. I can see Elise's fingers crossed and an anxious look on her face. Will is biting his knuckles. Even Adam Edgemont has his hands clasped together.

The only person who isn't staring intently at the scoreboard above our heads is Greg.

He is looking at me.

A half-smile plays across his lips and I can see his eyes have gone a bit glassy. It's such an open, honest look of love that it makes me forget about the scoreboard too, if only for a second. He mouths 'I love you' and smiles. I blow him a kiss. As the numbers on the scoreboard fall into place, and as everyone in the room gasps in surprise, my husband steps up onto the scales with me, and kisses me in such a way that I suddenly feel even lighter than nine stone eight.

We will spend a great deal of time in the near future recounting what happened on this day to friends and family, and every time we do it this will be the moment that we spend the most time talking about.

And no matter how many people want to hear the story, neither of us will ever get tired of telling it.

A vast sigh ripples through the crowd and I break away from Greg's soft, warm lips to look up at the scoreboard.

31%.

We've lost thirty-one percent of our body weight between us. And lost Fat Chance by a single percentage point.

Frankie and Benny start to jump around the stage, whooping like lunatics and punching their fists in the air. The crowd join them in their celebrations at a decibel level that won't do anyone's eardrums many favours.

Elise looks directly at me with her mouth downturned and her brow furrowed.

'Don't worry about it,' I mouth at her. Before she can reply, Will has grabbed her arm and is leading her over to what will no doubt be a joyous interview with the two winners of the competition.

'Fuck it,' Greg says, as his shoulder slump.

'It doesn't matter,' I tell him.

I think I actually believe my own words for once.

Of course, I do still feel a small lump of disappointment in my stomach. That money would have come in enormously handy. Right now, though, it's such a relief that the whole silly circus is coming to an end. I'm finding it hard to feel really disappointed, especially when we've lost by the smallest possible margin.

If nothing else, this is the last day I'll have to wear a bright red t-shirt proclaiming that I am fat but fabulous. An occasion to be celebrated in itself.

Most of the crowd have now surged down onto the stage area and are swarming round the victorious couple. In the centre of the scrum Elise and Will are trying their best to conduct an interview with Frankie and Benny, who look both giddy and overwhelmed.

The other five couples all have their own smaller crowds of friends and family surrounding them. There's a lot of back slapping, hugging, and crying going on. From the look of Lea and Pete's friends there might well be some theft of exercise equipment going on as well, but I turn a blind eye to it as I'm far too busy hugging and kissing my own well-wishers.

Mum and Dad are full of congratulations, of course, though Dad does keep looking at his watch every thirty seconds. These kinds of public events have always made him feel uncomfortable. I'm just delighted they both turned up at all. Along with my parents, the girls from the office are here . . . as are Greg's mates from the rugby club. Most of them are already drunk, which is to be expected, really.

Before long we are joined by my best friend Elise, the person responsible for bringing us all here in the first place. She now has a beaming smile on her face as she muscles her way through to Greg and me.

'Zoe! Greg! Huge commiserations on coming so close to winning! How are you both feeling?' she says and thrusts the microphone into our faces.

'Exhausted,' Greg says.

'Light-headed,' I add.

'I bet! You were just one percent away from taking the fifty thousand pounds. Are you disappointed?'

'Our mortgage advisor certainly will be,' Greg says, while fending off a few hard punches to the arm from Ali.

'Do you think you could have done anything differently?' Elise asks me.

'Well, I did eat half a Jaffa cake three weeks ago,' I tell her. 'That might have been a mistake.'

This makes her laugh. 'But you're not too disheartened, are you?'

'Elise, I'm the skinniest I've been for nearly twenty years. I'd have *paid* fifty thousand pounds for that.'

'Good point! And what are you planning on doing now?'

'Well, I thought I might take Zoe home,' Greg starts to say, a smile playing around his lips. He's also gone very wide-eyed. I know what's coming and can already feel the flush of embarrassment working its way across my cheeks, 'and give her a good hard shagging,' he finishes, patting Elise on the shoulder.

Greg's rugby club mates all roar with approval at this—which is just as well, as I'm sure the comment was intended for their benefit.

Elise's eyes bulge out of their sockets, not for the first time during an interview with my husband and me.

I'm sure she's absolutely *delighted* that she never has to speak to us live on air again after today. The radio station won't be able to afford to pay the fines for much longer.

She wraps up the interview in a rather strangled voice, and throws the attention back over to Will, who's now with Valerie and George.

Once the microphone is off, Elise glowers at the both of us. 'You know what? Sometimes I hate the pair of you!'

Greg gives her a big sweaty hug that makes her squeal. 'Aww, we know you're just saying that, Elise. You love us, really!'

'Get off, you smelly sod!' she cries, whacking him with her free hand.

I feel it's time to step in at this point.

I wrap both arms around her in a grateful embrace and kiss her cheek. 'Thank you for putting us forward for this, Elise,' I say to her rather shocked face. 'You've changed our lives.'

Her eyes fill with tears. 'It . . . it was my pleasure, sweetie. Thank you for doing it.'

'Coffee tomorrow?' I ask. This has been a very strange time in our friendship, and I'm eager to get it back to normal as soon as possible.

'Sure, that'd be great,' Elise replies, wiping away a tear.

She smiles, turns on a high heel, and races off after Adam Edgemont, no doubt in order to get his opinion on how the competition ended.

If it doesn't involve at least three plugs for Fitness4All I'll be amazed.

Over the course of the next half an hour we manage to speak briefly to all the other couples involved in Fat Chance. While we haven't made firm friends with any of them, these are the people we've been on a long journey with, so it only seems appropriate to mark its end with them before leaving.

Frankie and Benny are somewhat insufferable about their victory, but I let it slide. I can see Greg's eyes rolling a few times as well, but he also manages to keep the conversation cordial. Val and George just seem relieved the competition is over, Angela and Dominica look equally happy to see the back of it, and Lea and Pete can't wait to get out of the door with the electronic scoreboard and radio desk they've already loaded into their mate's van.

It's Shane and Theresa who take us by surprise.

'Thank you so much,' Shane tells Greg.

'What for?'

'The fun run,' Theresa says. 'What you did meant a lot.'

'I've never been cheered before,' Shane adds in such a small but proud voice. I have to blink away yet more tears.

'My pleasure, mate,' Greg replies in a voice cracking with emotion.

It's the small victories that count the most. They tend to add up to big ones if you give them half a chance.

During the time we spend with our fellow competitors, we're also signing autographs for members of the crowd who have stuck around after the show has ended.

This is a bizarre experience, as I'm only used to signing my name on legal documents. To scrawl your name across a piece of paper for no other reason than that someone has asked you to feels extremely strange.

And yes, I even end up signing Veronica's bloody tits. It was either that, I imagine, or have her pursue me to the ends of the Earth. I don't particularly want to be strolling around Sydney one day and see her running towards me from the Opera House, swinging her chest around and screaming my name.

Greg also signs her boobs. He seems a lot more happy to do it than I am.

'Thank you, thank you, thank you!' Veronica exclaims when we're done, and claps her hands together.

A sudden thought crosses my mind. 'Veronica?'

'Yes, Zoe?'

'Why me?'

'What do you mean?'

'There are twelve of us in this competition. Why did you want my autograph so much?'

She chews her lip nervously for a moment. 'Because you remind me of myself.' She pauses and looks away from me. 'Only . . . only better.'

My jaw drops.

What kind of thing is this to hear from another person? What am I supposed to do with it, exactly?

In lieu of a more poetic, erudite response I smile at her and ask, 'Can I wear your top hat for a bit? I really like it.'

Veronica's eyes light up and she laughs. The top hat is plucked from her head and plonked onto mine. The brim nearly drops down over my eyes and the plastic geranium waggles merrily as I adjust it.

'It suits you,' Greg lies, grinning.

Veronica stands looking at me for a second with a thoughtful expression on her face. 'You know, I think it might look better on me than it does on you,' she eventually says in a grave voice.

'I couldn't agree more,' I reply and give her back the hat.

By about half past four I'm starting to get hungry and pretty damn tired. It's time to leave. The crowd is thinning out now that the excitement is over. There will be other competitions to cheer—I'm sure Fat Chance will be back next year given the profit margins—but for now the fun is over, and everyone can go home to return to their normal lives.

This includes Zoe and Gregory Milton, who will quite happily drop back into the warm bosom of obscurity, thank you very much.

We say a last goodbye to friends and family, and wend our way back out of the gym and over to the car. It's hard to believe only three hours have passed since we got here. It feels like a month.

On the way home we stop at Dominos—because we figure fuck it, we've *earned* it.

It's a testament to how much our lives have changed that we spend five minutes looking in the window at the collection of grease- and meat-laden monstrosities on offer, before getting back in the car and driving to Marks & Sparks to pick up the ingredients for a home-cooked stir-fry.

Greg's predictions of after-show shenanigans do indeed come true, though it is by no means just a 'shag.' It is, in fact, some of the most romantic sex we've ever had. Not because we light candles or listen to Barry White—though that's always nice—but because it marks the end of a long journey that we've been on together. A journey that has brought us much closer as a couple . . . if for no other reason than there's a lot less of us getting in the way.

೧౨

Fast forward one week.

It's four thirty in the afternoon and I'm alone in the house.

Greg is out with Ali and the rest of his rugby cronies. He's just been picked for the first team, an accomplishment last achieved four years ago. This means, of course, that all foreseeable future Sunday afternoons will consist of him rolling around in a field on top of other men with an oddly shaped ball.

I have absolutely no problem with this, given that I've been feeling pretty sick for the past few days following the climax of Fat Chance, and am more than happy to spend some time on my own in a bath full to the brim with hot soapy water and the pile of *Hello!* magazines I haven't got round to reading yet. The feelings of nausea have been affecting me on and off all week, and this is the first time I've had the chance to just stop and give myself some much-needed pampering.

I can only put the sickness down to the end of the competition. They often say that things only catch up with you when you stop, and with all the excitement of the final weigh-in, it's no wonder I've felt a bit under the weather ever since. I guess I just need some rest.

The sickness has been particularly bad in the mornings and today was no exception. I figure a long hot soak will do me a world of good.

I'm absolutely right.

The hot water is *glorious*.

I never used to like taking a bath much. It would mean being alone, being naked, and being forced to look at that bloated, naked body. Showers are much kinder to the self-esteem when you're fat.

Now, though, with my new trim frame, baths have become a delight—especially the long, uninterrupted ones where you're immersed for so long that your skin goes wrinkly.

As I lie back and close my eyes, I think of my husband running around on that cold, muddy field and thank my lucky stars that I'm not a rugby player.

My eyes snap open.

You're not a rugby player . . . but you do have a rugby kit stashed somewhere safe, don't you?

My heart starts to beat faster in my chest as I recall the bet I laid with myself back in June. This is the first time I've thought about it.

Within seconds I'm out of the soapy water and towelling myself off.

I know exactly where the rugby kit is stored. I can still see the big brown cardboard box, tucked discreetly at the back of my wardrobe among other assorted debris, out of sight.

I find it quickly and lay the shorts, socks, and top out on the bed, standing back to contemplate what I'm about to do.

I find that I can't make my legs work.

I just stand naked in front of the rugby kit, unable to move myself into action.

This is it.

Never mind a silly radio competition, this rugby kit is Zoe Milton's *real* challenge.

It has been all along.

But can I do it? Can I bring myself to put the damn thing on again?

What if it doesn't fit? What if I've failed?

Wouldn't it be better to just fold it back up and put it away?

Wouldn't it be better to just forget about it? Be proud of what I've already accomplished and not push my luck?

Isn't Zoe Milton the kind of person to leave well enough alone? Isn't Zoe Milton the kind of girl who likes to play it safe?

Ha!

Fat chance.

The socks go on, the top goes over my head and slides down over my boobs with no difficulty, and I easily pull the shorts up over my hips, the fabric whispering against my skin as I do so. I fasten them at the waist and take a breath so deep it makes my head spin.

All of a sudden I'm eighteen again. Young, bold, in love with life, and blessed with a future, ever stretching ahead of me with the man I adore.

For a few moments I just stand still, letting the feeling of accomplishment wash over me.

I think about the scared fat girl staring down from all those billboards across town. I marvel at how she is gone forever, and how pleased I am to be rid of all the self-doubt she carried around in her heart for so long.

These thoughts result in a prolonged bout of crying that I have to staunch with the hem of the rugby top. I really don't know what's up with me lately; I seem to start crying, devoid of reason, at the drop of a hat. My hormones are all over the place.

Almost as soon as the tears cease, the urge to manically fling myself around the room overwhelms me.

I also think I need to wave my arms about. Yes . . . waving my arms about seems just about perfect.

I do this for about three minutes.

It's *wonderful*.

And I'm not even out of breath when I'm finished.

No one will ever see this victory dance.

No crowds will stand and cheer while I joyously parade around my bedroom like a show-pony. No radio stations will stream it live on the internet into thousands of homes across the local area.

No one will ever know, or indeed care, that Zoe Milton can fit into her size 10 rugby kit again.

And that suits me just fine.

There's only one person who needs to know, and he will be home in about an hour.

With any luck he'll still be wearing *his* rugby kit.

I know I'll be wearing mine.

ABOUT THE AUTHOR

photo: Gemma Waters, 2014

Nick Spalding is the bestselling author of six novels, two novellas, and two memoirs. Nick worked in media and marketing for most of his life before turning his energy to his genre-spanning humorous writing. He lives in the south of England with his fiancée.

20541757R00169

Printed in Great Britain
by Amazon